D1522342

Synopsis

A pregnant Laydii has just received some information that her sister Toni's killer was not who they suspected it was. On top of receiving this new revelation, Laydii is also hit with some more tragic news that her best friend Keya is missing. They say what don't kill you, can only make you stronger, but that may not be the case this time. Has Laydii finally been given more than she can handle, or will she fight through it all and still come out on top like always?

The search is on for a missing Keya. After she vanished into thin air, everybody has come together to search high and low for her. The police are not helping, as they feel that she has left on her own free will. Also, no one is aware that Keya had been in contact with Sam. Without the crew having that valuable piece of information, to guide them in the right direction, odds of finding Keya is almost the same as trying to find a needle in a haystack. Will Keya be found before it is too late, or will she become the next victim of a deranged, Sam?

Aaron is still in Jail, and is trying his best to deal with the fact that Keya betrayed him, by abandoning him when he needed her most. But as luck would have it, he receives some information from his lawyer that he will be released from Jail. When Aaron gets out, he is hit with devastating news that Keya is missing. Will Aaron put aside those hard feelings that he has for Keya, and help to bring her back home safely, or will he turn his back on her just as she had done him?

John is back, and is trying his best to be there for Laydii like a good boyfriend should. But when something from his past comes back to haunt him, he realizes that his own problems might be more important than being there for the woman in his life. Will John continue to be the shoulder that Laydii can lean on, or will he leave her to pick up the pieces of her own life, while he handles his own?

Jeremy is sick of being with Nancy, his nagging baby mama. She finds any and everything to complain about, and she may have finally pushed Jeremy away with her crazy ways. Because of her constant nagging, Jeremy finds himself in the comforts of another woman. Will Jeremy finally find happiness with his new beau, or will Nancy change her ways and get him to remain by her side?

Take another drama filled journey with these characters, as they continue to take you through the Dirty South City of Memphis.

N.L. Hudson

Love in the Deep South: A Memphis Tale 2

Natavia Presents

Acknowledgments

I would like to thank my publisher Natavia for giving me the opportunity to share my work with the world. She is one of the best authors, and it's such an honor to work for her. I would also like to thank Marqu'alla for all that she does for Natavia Presents. You guys are awesome, and I appreciate all that you do for us.

Dedications

First, I would like to give thanks to God, whose head of my life. Without him in my life, I don't know where I would be. Through his glory, I can say that I am truly blessed beyond measures! I thank him for the gift of life, and the opportunity he has given me to share my stories.

Now, to my family. I would first like to thank my mother, Janice Crayton-Williams. You have been one of the best inspirations that a child could have. Growing up, you sacrificed so much for us, and provided everything that we needed, and mostly wanted. Because of your love, and strong upbringing, I can say that it is attributed to the woman I am today. You encouraged me to go for what I believed in, no matter what it was. I am forever grateful for your love, and the values you instilled in me. I love you with all that I have, boo, and this is for you!

To my brother and sister, Jaylon and Jordan. I've watched you grow from tiny little kids that followed me around everywhere, to the young adults that you are today. We have our ups and downs, but you guys are the best siblings that anybody could have. I hope that you are proud of your big sis and the role that I have played in your lives, because that's the example that I wanted to set for you. I love you guys to the moon and back, and this is for you!

To my babies… my wonderful kids. Kaleb, DJ, and Brookelynne. You guys are my inspirations, and I never knew that I could love someone as much as I love you. Everything that I do, it's done with you in mind. I want to be the person that you guys look up to, and I pray that I am doing a good job in fulfilling that role. I love you guys to pieces, and this dedication is to you!

To my support system, my cousin/sister Tammy, and my best friend Nicole. You ladies have been there for me through it all. Thanks so much for believing in me and always encouraging me to go after my dreams. We have had our fair share of disagreements, but I wouldn't trade you for anything in the world. I love you guys so much, and this is to you!

To my husband. Wow, where do I begin? We have been rocking with each other since 2007, and through the good and the bad, we are still here holding each other down. I have learned so much from you over the years, and I thank God for letting you find me. We will be celebrating eight years of marriage this year, and I hope that we can make it 100 more years. (lol) You are a great provider, husband, father, brother, uncle, and son. I am so blessed to have you in my life, and I love you with all my being. Thank you for all your love and support, and this dedication is to you baby!

To the rest of my family and friends. Jeannetta, Henderson, Lovie, Mattie, Ebony, Mya, Macy, Marc, Jenny, Ne-Ne, JurLonda, Uncle Mike, Jacinda, Nettra, Leon, Shenika, Nae (a.k.a Diva), my grandmother Fannie Mae, (RIL), and my sister Brookelynne (RIL), I love all of you with all my heart and thanks for your support!

Finally, to my readers. I thank you all so much for your support. You took a chance on a new writer, and I am forever grateful for each of you. I am also thankful for the opportunity to share my stories with you, and I look forward to bringing you many more. Much Love to you all, N.L. Hudson

1

Laydii

"Wait, Mrs. Harris, what do you mean that Keya is missing, and why is Aniya there by herself?" I asked.

"I don't know, but I think that something has happened to my baby," Mrs. Harris boohooed into the phone.

I swallowed down the golf ball sized knot that was inside of my throat. "Okay, Mrs. Harris, when was the last time that you talked to her?" I asked.

"James was over yesterday evening helping Keya set up the rest of the items inside her apartment.
He said that when he left she was fine, but that it seemed like she was trying to rush him out. He thought that she was just trying to get rid of him because she wanted her privacy, but now we don't know what to think. That's why I was calling to see if you have talked to her," she said.

"No, I haven't talked to Keya in a while," I said, suddenly feeling guilty.

"Oh," Mrs. Harris said. "Well look, the police are here now. I will keep you posted," she said.

"Wait, Mrs. Harris. I'm about to come over there now," I said.

"Okay, sweetie, I will see you in a minute," she said just before ending the call.

"Laydii, what the hell is going on now?" My mama asked.

"That was Keya's mom, and she said that Keya is missing. I don't know the full details yet, but she said something about Aniya being left alone inside of her apartment," I said.

"What?" She screamed, and I nodded.

"Mama, I have to go. I need to go over to Keya's apartment and see what is going on." I said and stood up. I walked over and gave her a quick hug. After hugging my mom, I grabbed Laila in my arms and gave her a hug, too. I placed her down on her feet and briskly walked over to the door.

"I love you, Laydii, and keep me posted on everything," my mom called out to me.

I love you, too, ma, and I will definitely keep you posted," I told her and rushed out of the house.

When I got inside of the car, John was just getting off the phone. "Did everything go aight with ya moms?" he asked.

"Everything is okay with us, but she told me that Greg didn't shoot himself, because he was shot in the left side of his head, and he is right-handed," I told him.

"No shit! So, who the fuck killed him and Toni then?" He asked with a high-pitched tone.

"We don't know! Me and my mama didn't get a chance to finish talking about it, because Keya's mom contacted me with some more shocking news. John, she told me that Keya is missing, and that Aniya was left alone inside the apartment," I said with tears coming to my eyes.

"Da fuck! What do you mean that Keya is missing?" he asked.

"Just like I said. Her mama is with the police right now," I said becoming hysterical.

"Shh, Shh," John said, grabbing ahold of my hand while trying to calm me down. You want to go
over there and see what's going on?" he asked.

"Yes," I replied just above a whisper. So much shit was going through my head, and that same feeling that I had when Toni was killed had suddenly come back. I left my eyes closed the entire time that we rode over to Keya's apartment. When we finally pulled up, John hopped out, walked around the car, and opened my door. I noticed that there were two police cars parked in front of the apartment building.

"Come on, bae; it's going to be aight." John told me as we walked towards the door. When we got to the door, there was a policewoman standing guard; she tried to stop us from going inside.

"You can't go in there," she said.

"This is my friend's house, and her mom called me over here," I told her.

"All right, what's your name?" she asked.

"Laydii," I told her and rolled my eyes. She was standing here trying to keep us out when someone had already gotten inside to Keya.

"Please let her in," I heard Mrs. Harris say behind her. Shortly after, she came into view, and I noticed that her eyes were swollen from crying. "Come on in, Laydii," Mrs. Harris ushered us in.

The police lady moved out of the way and allowed me and John to walk inside of the apartment. When we got inside, I saw Keya's dad sitting in a chair, and he had Aniya on his lap. He wore a sad look on his face, and I knew that he was hurting, because Keya was his baby girl, and he really loved her. With John's assistance, I walked over to the couch and took a seat. I noticed a police walk from the back where Keya's room was, and he was writing something in a notepad. He walked over to Keya's dad, and I scooted to the edge of my seat so that I could hear what he had to say.

"Sir, I've looked all around the house, and it appears that there is no sign of broken entry. Now, you said that you last talked to her yesterday when you were over here, right?" he asked.

"Yes, I told you that already," Mr. Harris huffed.

"Okay, I'm just trying to get a good understanding of everything," the police said while looking at Mr. Harris. Now, did you see her phone, because I've looked all over, and I couldn't find it anywhere." he said.

"No, I didn't see her phone, or purse. And I done called her number a half dozen times, but all it does it go to voicemail," Mr. Harris stated.

"Well, I hate to say this, but with there being no signs of a break-in, and with her items missing, it looks like your daughter might have just walked away." The policeman said.

"Now, hold the hell on! You trying to say that my daughter walked out and left my grandchild behind?" Keya's dad shouted.

"Look sir, there is no reason to be hostile right now. I'm just trying to tell you that it doesn't appear that your daughter was in any harm, and it looks as if she walked out of here on her own free will. And since she's over the age of eighteen, there is nothing that we can do if she decided to leave," he said.

"What?" I screamed, and John grabbed my shoulder.

"Wow, you muthafuckas are a trip. My daughter would never just disappear like this and leave her child behind. Somebody has taken her, and you need to do your job to bring her back home to us." Mrs. Harris said while standing in the officer's face. Now in all that time that I had been knowing Keya's mother, I had never heard her raise her voice, or curse like that. I knew that the officer must have pissed her off, because she was definitely out of character. She had her hands in the policeman's face, and the other officer that was guarding the door was trying to move Mrs. Harris away from her partner.

"Ma'am, calm down." The policewoman said.

"Don't you tell me to calm down when my daughter is out there somewhere, and I got y'all bastards trying to tell me that she just up and left her daughter without so much as a second thought given." Mrs. Harris spewed.

"Waa. Waa. Waa." Aniya started crying from all the commotion.

I walked over to Mr. Harris and took her from his arms. I knew that she was missing her mama, and I had to do my best to calm her down. I turned to the police and stared at him. "Sir, I don't know what type of situations y'all are used to dealing with, but my friend would never do anything like you are suggesting. You see this beautiful little face right here? Just know that the mother of this child would have never walked out on her. She loves this little girl too much and would do anything in her power to protect her." I said.

After I had finished giving the officer a piece of my mind, I couldn't hold my tears back any longer. It was like everything had finally hit me, and I broke down. John rushed over to me and wrapped his arm around my shoulder. We walked back over to the couch, and I sat down with Aniya on my lap. Mr. Harris was now pacing the floor, and Mrs. Harris looked like she was on the verge of losing her mind. I rocked back and forth trying to soothe both Aniya and myself.

"I understand that you guys are really upset, but as I stated, there is nothing that we can do right now.
If she doesn't turn up in the next week or so, then give us a callback," the dickhead officer said.

"Get the hell out of here," Mr. Harris yelled, and both officers walked out of the door shaking their head. Mr. Harris immediately slammed it. "Fuck," he yelled out, and I jumped.

"Calm down James," Mrs. Harris said as she pulled him into the backroom.

"Bae, we gone find your girl," John was saying, but I couldn't even focus on him. I kept thinking about how Keya had just called me the night before, and I had ignored her call. I hoped that we were able to find her soon, because if not, I would never be able to forgive myself if something seriously had happened to her.

2
Keya

Later that day….

My eyes fluttered open, and I scanned the dark room. I knew that I was no longer inside of my apartment, because the room didn't look familiar. It was small and dark with a musty smell. I glanced to my right and noticed a dresser and one of those old-fashioned big back televisions on the wall. When I turned my head to the left, I saw Sam sitting in the corner in a chair, and I jumped. *Where the hell am I?* I wondered.

The last thing I remembered was Sam being at my house, and how I had this funny feeling about him, so I had asked him to leave. I checked on Aniya while she slept, and when I saw that she was okay, I left out of her room, and that's when I bumped into Sam. He had asked me to walk him, and as I walked towards the door, he-wait!

"Sam, you kidnapped me?" I yelled, as the memory of him placing something over my face suddenly came rushing back to me.

"Don't worry, Keya. You safe here with me," he said like everything was normal.

"Sam, listen to me. Where the fuck am I, and where the hell is my damn daughter?" I shouted.

He chuckled. "Nah, Keya, I want you to listen to me, and I want you to listen good. I tried to do shit your way, but since you wanted to play with my fuckin' feelings, we gon do shit my way from here on out. Now, I left your daughter back inside of your apartment, and hopefully, somebody will find her little ass in the next couple of days," he said, and I snapped. I jumped off the bed and ran over to him. Using my fist as a weapon, I tried to knock his head off. Obviously, my lick didn't faze him, because all he did was laugh. Sam grabbed a hold of my arm when I tried to hit him again. I jerked my body and tried to get loose from his hold, but it was too tight. Suddenly, he pulled a gun from behind his back and put it to my head.

"Shut the fuck up before I blow your head off," he bellowed.

"Okay, okay…please don't kill me, Sam," I pleaded.

"Don't worry, as long as you do what I say then we gone be good. But if you do anything that draws attention to us, I will kill you before the police even gets here," he said, and I bucked my eyes.

His ass is really crazy, I thought, as I stared up at him. Sam finally dropped my arms, and I had to rub them because they were sore.

"Sit down," he said pointing towards the bed with the gun.

"Sam, you don't have to do this. If it's money that you need, then I can ask my parents, and I know they will get it to you," I said. "But I really need for somebody to go and get my daughter."

"Don't worry, I'm gonna get what I want soon enough," he said with this demented look. It was like he had snapped. He was always a little crazy, but this here was a different type of crazy, like maybe psych ward crazy.

"Sam," I tried to say, but he held up his gun.

"Keya, please don't make me hurt you," he said through gritted teeth. He walked over to me and roughly grabbed hold of my face. My body trembled as he held my face in his hand and pointed the gun at my head.

"What are you about to do?" I asked, but he didn't reply. And after staring at me for what felt like forever, he leaned down and covered my mouth with his. I shook my head from side to side to stop him from kissing me, but he bit down on my lip.

"Stop fighting," he gritted.

"Sam, please don't do this," I cried.

"It's gonna happen, Keya, and it ain't nothing you can do to stop it," he said while gripping my breast roughly.

"No, no, no," I said, but he didn't listen to me as he put his lips back to mine. I pursed my lips tightly together, but he put the gun back to my head.

"I told you that you couldn't stop me," he said pushing the gun further into my head.

"Okay, Sam. Please don't kill me," I said, and he slowly removed the gun.

"Good girl," he said with a laugh. "Now go take a shower so that I can get me some of this pussy." He said while palming between my legs.

Hot tears leaked down my cheeks, but I didn't try to fight him. I figured, if I did, he would kill me. I stood up from the bed and slowly walked towards the bathroom, and when I got inside, I tried to close the door.

"Nah, leave it open," Sam yelled out to me.

Shit, what am I going to do now, I thought to myself. But as I looked around the bathroom, I realized that there wasn't a way for me to escape anyway. It wasn't no windows, and the only exit was in the room with Sam. I had to think of something quick, because I needed to get away from him and fast, or my ass was gone to wound up dead.

3

Aaron

One day later…

"Your honor, you just heard council say that my client's fingerprints were not found at the scene of the crimes, and since she doesn't have any other evidence to give, besides those pictures that they received from the anonymous tipster that has yet to come forward, I ask that you move this case to be dismissed." My lawyer Michael said to the judge.

They were having a preliminary hearing to see if the charges against me would be strong enough to take me to trial. After I had been arrested for killing Sam's mama and that nigga June Bug, they told me that I was also being charged with the murders of the other three people that were found dead in the house that night. The fucked up part about that was, I hadn't killed Sam's mama, or that nigga June Bug. I only had one body that night, but of course I couldn't tell them that, or snitch on my niggas. It's not like the prosecutor hadn't really been interested in my crew anyway. In fact, she had told me that she was more interested in me, and the drug business that I operated. She had wanted me to confess to killing those people, and say that it was because they owed me some money or something else drug-related.

The only good thing was that they didn't have any evidence on me selling drugs, so the only thing that they could do was charge me with those murders. When I first got locked up, I called up my lawyer that I had on payroll to see what he could do to get the charges dropped. But all his fraud ass had told me was that I should just confess, since they had evidence that I had done it. He didn't even attempt to look into my case, so I fired his ass and that's when I hired Michael.

Michael was one of the best defense attorneys in Memphis, and a lot of the hustlers had him on their payroll. So far, he was doing a good job in proving why his name spoke for itself.

"Your honor, we ask that you do not do that. We have good reason to believe that the defendant is responsible for those murders, and if you give us a little more time, we will give you more evidence," The prosecutor said. She was this white woman that looked to be in her mid-fifties. Her glasses were so big that they covered most of her face, and her face was so tight, that it looked like she was sucking on lemons. I couldn't even lie, the bitch looked like she didn't play any games, and I hoped that Michael was ready for her ass.

"Well, how much more time do you need, Council? It has been a couple of months, and besides those pictures, you haven't given me any more evidence that convinces me that he is the killer." The judge said, and I smirked. "Have you heard anything else from the tipster?" he asked.

"No, your honor, we haven't heard anything, but we do have reason to believe that the defendant is a drug dealer, and that is probably why the person that sent in the tip has not come forward. Mr. Thomas is known as a dangerous man around Memphis, and he doesn't need to be on the streets." The prosecutor said with a frazzled look on her face.

"I object," Michael said.

"Council, do I need to remind you that this is not a trial, and that no objections are needed here today." The judge told him.

"I understand your honor that this is not a trial, but I would like to point out that my client is not being held for drug charges. He is here for murders that he did not commit, and council over here is just grasping for straws," Michael said.

"But your honor," the prosecutor tried to say, but the judge cut her off.

"I agree, Council. The defendant is not here on drug charges. If you believe that he is distributing drugs, I suggest you find some evidence and bring charges against him for that. As for the murder charges, there is nothing here to prove that he was involved. You yourself said that his prints were not found at either crime scene, and besides that, you don't have any viable witnesses that can say that he was at those houses on the night of the crimes. Until you can give me some concrete evidence, I'm dismissing this case. Mr. Thomas, you are free to go." the judge said peering down at me. He banged his gavel and left the podium. I looked over at the prosecutor, and she was blowing steam. She was forcefully stuffing that bullshit evidence that she had back into her briefcase, and after grabbing her stuff, she stormed out of the courtroom.

"I'm going to go ahead and get the paperwork started for your release. It will probably take about an hour or two," Michael said while grabbing his briefcase.

"So, that's it?" I asked.

"Yes, that's it. But that doesn't mean that they can't bring more charges against you again, if they do find any more evidence. So, try to stay out of trouble, Mr. Thomas," Michael said. He didn't have to worry about that, because I would make sure that there was no evidence to give after I found Sam, and killed his bitch ass.

"I appreciate it Michael," I said.

"Not a problem. That's what you pay me for," he said before walking out of the courtroom. One of the guards came over and escorted me back to my cell. When I got back, I took a seat on my bunk.

"So, did you hear any news that mattered?" my cellmate, Chris, asked me. He was this middle age man that was convicted of killing two men that had robbed and killed his brother back in the day. He was now serving a life sentence for it.

"Yeah, the judge dismissed the case, because that bullshit evidence wasn't gonna hold up in court," I said.

That's wassup young blood," Chris said, then put his head back down in the book that he was reading. Chris was always reading something and had even tried to get me to read a few times. I wasn't against reading, but I had too much shit on my mind to focus on reading. All I could do to pass the time, was work out, think, and then before I laid down at night, I would work out again. I laid down in my bunk and put my hands behind my head. A couple more hours in this muthafucka, and I would walk out a free man.

A few hours later...

I walked up out of 201, relieved as hell. Being in that prison was not for me, and I had no plans of going back into that place anytime soon. When I looked around, I noticed that Jeremy was posted on his car waiting for me. I walked over to his Benz and opened the door. I slid inside and waited for him to finish his cigarette.

"What's good, my nigga?" Jeremy asked when he got inside of his car. We clasped hands, and Jeremy pulled away from the jail and got into traffic.

"Just happy to be up out that place," I said.

"Dig that! Aye, but what did they say in court?" he asked.

"They basically said the evidence against me was bullshit. There weren't any witnesses, besides the anonymous tip that they received, and we both know who that was. He also said those pictures that they received didn't prove that I killed them folks," I told Jeremy.

I still couldn't believe that Sam had sent those pictures of me in and claimed that I killed his mama.

To this day, I didn't know how he had even gotten the pictures, but whatever he had done to get them had been enough for the police to arrest me based off what he had told them. I also couldn't get over the fact that Keya had believed his ass. But I was gonna deal with her once I had Jeremy to drop me off at my house.

"I knew that shit wasn't gonna hold up in court. Them muthafuckas just wanted somebody to pin them charges on," Jeremy said.

"You already know, but they gone have to come better than that," I said with a slight chuckle. "But anyway, Ion really want to discuss that shit no more. What's been going on, on the outside? Is everything running straight," I asked in regards to my operation.

"You know everything gone always run smooth on that tip," Jeremy said and then paused.

"So why do I sense that you holding back on something?" I asked.

"Aye, mane, I need to tell you something, and I don't need you flipping the fuck out when I say it. Aight!" Jeremy said.

I stared at him, because if he had something to tell me, then he should have said it when I first got into the car. "You can go ahead and tell me, but I ain't promising shit. So, wassup?" I asked him.

Jeremy passed me a blunt that he had just taken out of a secret compartment that he kept inside of his car. I could tell that it was filled with some of the finest Kush, because I smelled it the minute he pulled it out. "Here, toke on this first," he said while handing me a lighter.

I took the lighter from his hand and fired up the blunt. Pulling in deeply, I let the smoke fill the inside of my lungs, and then hit it again. "Aight, so wassup," I asked him.

"Aight, so a couple of days ago, John called me on some shit about Keya being missing, and your daughter being left alone inside of her apartment." He said.

"What the fuck you mean that she is missing and my daughter was by herself?" I boomed.

"Yeah, he said that your girl's mama called Laydii and told her about it."

"Why the fuck is you just now saying something? I talked to you and John when I called and told you that I was getting out. Y'all should have been told me some shit like that." I said. I couldn't believe this shit; these niggas both knew that my girl was out here missing, and they had chosen to keep that important information away from me.

"Mane, we knew that you were gonna snap, and with you being released from jail soon, we didn't want to take those chances of telling you. That would have just given them fuckers what they needed to keep yo ass locked up," he said.

What he was saying was true. Everybody knew how I felt about my daughter and Keya, and had some shit like this been told to me while I was in jail, I probably would have killed every nigga up in there.

"Aight, I get that, but nigga you should have said something the minute that I stepped foot into this car," I told him.

"I know, Mane, but I ain't really know how to tell you," he said.

"Aye, turn this fuckin car around and take me to her folks' house. I need to find out what the fuck is going on and see my daughter." I told him and hit the blunt so hard that it made me choke. Jeremy knew exactly what he was doing when he gave me this blunt. Hell, I was so mad, that I didn't even pass it his way. I sat there thinking and smoke while he drove me to Keya's parents' house.

Once we got onto Shelby Drive, I instructed Jeremy on how to get to Keya's parent's house from there. We finally pulled up to the house after ten minutes of driving. Jeremy pulled up into the yard, and cut his car off.

"You need me to go in there with you, or you straight?" He asked.

"I'm good dawg! I don't want her pops thinking we trying to ambush them or som' like that. You already know that nigga hates my fuckin guts," I said. Jeremy nodded his head, but didn't say anything.

As I got out of the car, I kept asking myself where could Keya be? It was like so much shit was happening that once we got over one situation, we had to deal with yet another one.

I walked up to the door and rang the bell, then stood back and waited for somebody to answer. I knew that Keya folks were at home, because both vehicles were in the yard. Keya's dad finally opened the door, and when he saw that it was me, he frowned up his face.

"How you doing, Mr. Harris, is it alright if I come in and see Aniya and talk to you for a minute?" I asked.

"Nah, you ain't coming into my goddamn house for shit. You done dragged my daughter into your mess, and now we don't know where to find her," he barked. My jaw tensed, because this man was always giving me a hard time. I didn't put a gun to Keya's head for her to be with me, and I definitely didn't have nothing to do with her disappearing.

"Look sir, I understand that you're upset because Keya is missing, and trust me, I'm mad too, but I'm not gone keep dealing with the disrespect when I've done nothing but shown you the utmost respect." I told him. This nigga was really trying me right now, and if it wasn't for Keya, or the fact that this was Aniya's granddaddy, I would have been laid him on his ass. He thought because he was big as shit, that he could intimidate muthafuckas. That shit didn't faze me, and I wasn't about to let him chump me out like I was some boy.

"You disrespected me by dragging my daughter into your bullshit. You ain't coming into my house, and you ain't seeing my damn granddaughter," he said with his chest puffed out.

When he said that shit, I was getting ready to light into his ass. Nobody was finna keep me away from my daughter. She was my blood, and it didn't matter that her granddaddy thought I wasn't fit for her and her mother. At the end of the day, shit was what it was. And nothing he said or did would keep me away from them.

"James, who are you out here talking to?" Keya's mom asked while walking towards the door with my lil mama in her arms. When I saw my daughter, all that anger that was brewing inside of me, died quickly. Aniya was my world, and when I looked at her, all I could do was smile.

"Aaron, sweetie, I didn't know that you were out. Please come in," she said. I glanced at Keya's dad, and he looked pissed. I didn't give a fuck about that thought. I was tryna see my daughter and find out what was up with Keya. We could get back to that other shit at a later time.

He turned and walked off, and I grabbed the door and walked inside of the house. As soon as I stepped over the threshold, I immediately reached out my arms for my daughter. She was the exact replica of me, just in the girl form. As I continued to stare, all I could think about was how beautiful she was. And how I wished like hell that she could stay this size forever. For a split-second, I understood where Keya's dad was coming from. It was like when you had a daughter you just wanted to shield them from all the bad things in the world.

"You can take a seat sweetie," Mrs. Harris said. I walked over to the couch and when I sat down, I placed my daughter down beside me.

"So, Mrs. Harris, what's going on?" I asked her with urgency in my tone. Although I was happy to see her, it wasn't a social call for neither one of us. And I'm sure she felt the same way.

"The morning that we found Aniya, we had been trying to contact Keya because she was supposed to bring her over so that she could go to class. After calling her phone several times, and still not getting an answer, James went over to see if maybe she had overslept. When he got there, he said that she didn't answer the door, so he went ahead and used his key to get in. He said, that once he entered the apartment, he heard Aniya screaming at the top of her lungs, so he went into her room and got her. He looked around the apartment and didn't see any signs of Keya, and that's when he called me. Once I arrived, I told him that we needed to call the police because something had happened to my baby," she said with tears now rapidly falling from her eyes.

Damn, for Keya to just vanish like that didn't make any sense, and I needed to figure out what was going on. "So, what are the police saying?" I asked. Although I didn't fuck with the police, I needed to know what they had found out about Keya, so I would know where to go from there.

"They are trying to say that maybe Keya was tired of being a mother and just left my grandbaby alone because they didn't find her personal things, or any signs of a break in. But I know that something happened to my baby, and I need you to get to the bottom of this. I also know that you really love my daughter, and I have never doubted that. So, I'm begging you, Aaron, to please help me bring my baby back home," Mrs. Harris pleaded.

"You know that you don't even have to ask me that. Cause as soon as I leave here, I'm on it." I said.

Mrs. Harris nodded, and wiped away her tears. I looked back down at my daughter and then placed a kiss on her forehead. "I love you, and don't worry, we're going to bring mama home soon," I told her, as if she understood what I was saying. When I stood up, I handed Aniya back over to Mrs. Harris. Then, I bent down and gave her a gentle hug.

"Don't you worry, either, because I'm not stopping until I find Keya," I promised her. Mrs. Harris gave me a gentle smile.

"I'm out of here, Mrs. Harris," I said just before leaving out of the house.

Somebody had fucked with my family, and now this city was about to see the old Aaron, that I had been trying so hard to keep at bay, I thought as I jogged out to Jeremy's car.

4
John

"Say mane, we gonna find Keya soon," I told Aaron, who looked like he was about ready to set Memphis on fire. We were having a meeting with the camp at this little warehouse that we had. It was hidden in the woods, and nobody knew that it was back there. We only used it when we had meetings, or for instances like the one with Keya now being missing.

"Aaron, do you think that maybe Keya did get fed up with being a mama and left your daughter behind like they said?" Detrick asked.

I looked at Detrick like he was crazy. He knew better than to open his mouth and let some foul shit fall out like that. And I'm sure that if Aaron wasn't stressing over his girl then he would have put a bullet in his head.

"Why would yo stupid ass ask some shit like that muthafucka?" I asked.

"I'm saying, y'all said that the police couldn't find none of her stuff, and that her door wasn't broken or nothing like that, so what other explanation is there?" he asked while looking at me.

"Nigga, dismiss yourself," Jeremy told him with all seriousness in his tone. Detrick didn't say anything as he walked to a table that sat in the far corner of the room.

"Now, do anybody else feel like you got an opinion about this situation, cause we can put everything out on the table right now." Jeremy said. Everybody looked around the table at each other, but didn't say anything. We knew that whenever he spoke up about something, shit was serious. He was always so laid back, and it took a whole lot to get him out of his calm demeanor.

"Aight, since we got that taken care of, let's get down to business," he said. "John, I know the police said that nobody had seen anything, but if you got to, go around the neighbors one more time, and see if you can come up with some answers, aight!" I nodded my head at his instructions.

"Harold, I want you to go up to the school and talk to some of Keya's classmates. See if maybe they saw her around with anybody." Jeremy said, giving instructions to the newest member of our team. Harold
had only been with us for about two months now and was brought on as a recommendation from Detrick. Apparently, he was a real banger, and Jeremy figured that he could use somebody of his caliber on our team.

"I'm on it," Harold replied.

"Detrick, if you ready to come over here, and not be on that stupid shit then come on. But I better not ever hear you speak ill on my nigga's gal again," he told him with a straight face. Detrick stood up and returned to the table. I kept giving him the side-eye; he knew that he had fucked up by what he had said, because he didn't open his mouth not once. Detrick normally talked so much that we would have to tell him to shut up.

Jeremy continued to go over everything, and once he was done, everybody stood up to go handle their business. I hung behind, so that I could holler at my niggas.

"What you thinking Aaron?" I asked, because he appeared to be deep in thought.

"I'on really know what to think, but what I do know is that Keya would have never walked out on my daughter. Fuck what them police, or anybody else got to say. She got to be around this bitch somewhere, and I'm not gone stop looking until I find out where she is." Aaron said.

"I feel ya mane, and this shit ain't making no sense." I told him.

"Nah, it definitely ain't, but we gotta handle this shit. And another thing, whatever moves we bust from here on out we need to make sure that we are covering our tracks. When I was locked up, that bitch prosecutor mentioned something about me being a drug dealer. Now I'm not for sure, but I can almost bet it came from Sam. Good thing, she didn't have any evidence to back up that claim," Aaron said.

"Damn, that shit is fucked up," Jeremy said.

"Yeah, but I ain't gone let that shit stress me out. What I'mma do is change the location of the stash houses, and the only people that I want to know where we moving them to right now, is the three people in this room. And of course, whatever workers I put on em. But even with that, make sure that they are aware that nobody else should know of these new locations. If word gets out, then the person responsible for the leak will be handled accordingly," Aaron said.

"I'll holler at them, and make sure they understand the severity of the situation." Jeremy said.

"Preciate it, dawg. I'mma get up out of here, though. I need to run by and see Aniya before hitting the streets again," Aaron said, and stood up.

"Aight, we'll get up with you later, mane," I told him as he left out of the warehouse. After he was gone, me and Jeremy blew back a few trees before we finally called it a night.

5
Laydii

A day later….

Blargh, blargh. I threw up into the toilet for the third time today. This damn pregnancy was already starting to take a toll on my body, and I didn't know if I could deal with another seven months of feeling like this. I flushed the toilet, walked over to the sink, and washed my hands. After squirting some toothpaste onto my toothbrush, I began to brush my teeth. I had not been taking care of myself like I should, because I had been so stressed out. With Toni's death, Keya's disappearance, and the information about Greg, I was bound to have a mental breakdown at any minute.

I still hadn't told John about the pregnancy, and had been questioning myself as to if I even wanted to keep it or not. I was twelve weeks along, and there wasn't much time left if I wanted to get rid of it. I quickly dismissed that thought, though. John was already crushed the first time that I had an abortion, and I couldn't see myself doing that to him again.

After placing my toothbrush back into the holder, I walked into our bedroom and laid across the bed. Laying my head on the pillow, I let the tears that had started to fall soak it.

"Bae, you up?" John asked walking into the room, and I closed my eyes tight, so that he would think that I was still sleeping. I didn't want him to see me crying, because that was all that I had been doing lately, and I knew that I was starting to worry him.

"Come on, now, bae. Get up and talk to me." He said.

"Hmm," I groaned.

"Aye, yo ass ain't sleep, and I know that you been in here crying too," he said.

Damn, now how did he know that? I thought.

I sat up in the bed and pulled my legs to my chest. "You think you know me so well, don't you?" I asked.

"Damn right, I know you just like the back of my hand. Shit probably better than you know yourself," he said and leaned in and put a kiss on my lips. "What's up, though, bae? Talk to me!" He pulled my feet into his hands and started to massage them.

"John, I'm pregnant," I blurted out before I could stop myself. It was like I didn't want to hold it in any longer, and we needed some good news that would overshadow all the bad shit that we had been through lately.

With a huge smile on his face, he pulled me into his arms and hugged me tightly. "I had a feeling your ass was knocked up, but I didn't say anything." He said.

"Wait, so what gave it away?" I asked.

"It was just something about you that made me think you were pregnant. Maybe it was the glow that you had, or the sickness. But I didn't know for sure, because you hadn't been eating right, and it could have just been a result of that. So, that's why I chose not to speak up about it. But, when did you find out?" John asked, and finally let go of the hold that he had on me.

"Yesterday when I told you that I was going out. I actually had a doctor's appointment then." I replied, and John looked at me with a strange look on his face. "What?" I asked.

"Laydii, why were you just crying? Please tell me that you ain't thinking about killing my seed, again, are you?" he asked.

I huffed. "No, I'm not gonna do that John, and can you please not bring it up again," I said with a fresh set of tears coming back to my eyes. I hated whenever he brought the abortion that I had up, because it was a constant reminder of what I had done, and I didn't want to keep thinking about it.

He pulled me back into his arms and planted a kiss on my forehead. "I know that you wouldn't do that to me again, and I promise I'mma try my best not to bring it up," he said hugging me tightly. I nodded while wiping away my tears. And then I pulled away, and walked over to our closet. I pulled out a manila folder from our file cabinet. After taking out the sonogram that I had gotten yesterday, I handed it to him. He stared at it for a long time, and out of nowhere, he jumped up. "Yo this shit is crazy girl! I been wanting a little shorty for the longest, and now that my baby is giving me one, I'm just so fuckin' happy," he said. I smiled for the first time since confirming my pregnancy. I knew that John would be a great father, and I was happy with the decision that I had made to keep it.

"Thank you, Laydii," he said wrapping me in a bear hug. "I love you, girl, and I don't care what I have to do, I'mma make sure that I take care of you and our child. You don't have to worry about anything."

"I know, John, and I can't wait to have your baby." I said with a smile.

"Damn, girl! I still can't believe this shit," John continued to smile, but when he noticed that my attitude had changed, he became concerned.

"What's wrong baby?" He asked.

"What's going on with y'all finding Keya?" I asked. I know that we were supposed to be celebrating, but I just couldn't shake my thoughts of Keya. My girl was out there missing, and it just made me feel guilty to even be happy.

"Nothing yet, but I'm getting ready to head out in a minute to see if I can get some information from her neighbors. I know that a lot of them told the police that they didn't see or hear anything, but we all know that folks ain't really fuckin with them boys in blue. Maybe, I can get somebody to tell me something different, if I flash a little money in they face," John said.

"Well, I'm coming with you," I said, already walking back into our closet to retrieve my shoes.

"Fuck no, Laydii; you just told me that you were pregnant with my seed, and you think that I'm about to take you out there with me to put you into harm's way," he said.

"Look John, it couldn't be any worse than me sitting in that bed and crying myself to sleep at night. At least if I go with you, it will make me feel as if I am doing something to help get her back. Then, I can stop blaming myself for her disappearance," I told him.

"Damn, you blame yourself?" he asked.

"Yes, I do." I whispered.

"But why, you ain't have shit to do with it," he said.

"I know, but maybe if I had answered just one of her calls, I would have known what was going on with her. In fact, she had called me the night that she went missing, but I didn't answer because I thought that she was calling me like she always does."

"Damn, baby, you can't blame yourself for that shit. I'm sure Keya knows that you haven't been yourself lately. You done had a lot of shit to happen over the last couple of months, and she was more than likely just calling to check up on you," John said.

"I know, but do you see why I need to do this?" I asked.

John sighed, "Aight, Laydii, I'm gonna let you go, but you cannot get out of that damn car. Do you understand that, because if you do, we will have a problem?" He said.

"I promise that I won't baby."

"Aight, go ahead and put on your shoes then, and let's be out," he said.

John walked over to the wall and removed the picture that covered the safe that was hidden behind it. He punched in the code and opened the safe. After sifting through the safe, he took out some money that was wrapped in rubber bands and a big ass gun. After checking the safety on the gun, he tucked it in the waistband of his pants. I looked at him out the corner of my eyes, while silently putting on my shoes. I knew that he needed the gun for protection, but I hoped that he wouldn't have to use them.

After I had my shoes on, I picked up my phone and walked into the living room to wait for John. He finally emerged from the backroom and had a serious look on his face.

"Let's go," he told me. Normally, this was a side of John that I hated to see, but since the situation involved my best friend, I felt that it was necessary. I followed him out of the house, and we went in search for some answers that would lead us to Keya.

6

Keya

Two days later....

This couldn't be life, I thought. Sam had just raped me for the third time today. Between my legs was sore as hell, and my mouth was just as sore. It was a time when I enjoyed having sex with him, but now, just the thought of it alone made me sick to my damn stomach. My baby girl was also heavily on my mind, because I knew that she was probably starving and soaked. The only thing that kept me going at this point was knowing that I needed to survive for her.

"Sam, please let me go. I swear that I won't tell anybody about this," I told him. "Besides nobody even knows that I had been talking to you."

"Keya, don't ask me no muthafuckin more, cause you ain't going back there," he barked.

"Sam, my daughter is only ten months old, and she is at home by herself. What if something happens to her? If you won't let me go, at least will you allow me to call my folks to go and get her?" I begged him. He sat up on the bed and stared at me. I just knew that I had somehow reached the side of him that had a heart, but when he walked over and slapped me across the face, I knew that I had failed at trying to make him understand. The slap was so powerful that it made my ears ring. I stared at him through squinted eyes. *This muthafucka was becoming a little too comfortable with putting his hands on me, again,* I thought.

"Didn't I tell you that I didn't give a fuck about your daughter the last fifty fuckin times that you asked me? I don't want to hurt you, Keya, but you are really this close to making me go against my word," he threatened.

"You already have," I mumbled while gently rubbing my cheek.

"What the fuck did you just say?" He asked.

"Nothing Sam," I whispered.

"Come suck my dick, again, cause I see that you still ain't learned your lesson," he told me. Without protest, I got up and walked around the bed to his side. After dropping down to my knees, I pulled his dick from his boxers. I grabbed it tightly in my hand, and began to stroke him. I had half a mind to bite his shit off, but he had picked the gun up. "Aye, don't even think about biting me either," he said reading my thoughts.

I lowered my head to his semi-hard dick and took it into my mouth. While licking up and down his thing, I slurped all over it just like he had ordered. I had to force myself to think of something other than what I was doing. Just the thought that he was making me do this to him, had me wanting to slice his throat, but I knew that I would probably be the one that wound up dead if I moved too quickly. I was gonna slowly bait him in, and then I would make my move. I just hoped that I could keep it together, and not snap before then because I was so close to doing just that.

7

Aaron

"Y'all haven't found nothing out yet?" I asked Detrick and Harold.

"Nah, we even went up to the school and tried to holler at some of her classmates like J-Dawg said, but none of them muthafuckas had any answers." Harold said.

"Aight, so I want y'all to keep looking, and the minute you find out something, let me know," I said.

"We on it boss man," Detrick said, and he and Harold headed towards the door.

"Aye, Harold, before you leave, let me holler at you right quick," I said.

Harold walked back over and took a seat in the chair across from me. I didn't know much about him, besides the little info that Jeremy had given me. Jeremy had put him on the team while I was locked up and said that he was doing a good job. I didn't have a problem with Jeremy stepping in when I couldn't be there, but I wanted to feel Harold out for myself to see what type of nigga he was.

"So, I've been hearing good things about you. I heard that the little time you been with us you been about your business, and I can appreciate that." I said.

"Thanks, man. I appreciate you and J-Dawg for putting me on." Harold said.

"Don't thank me too soon, because this is still a preliminary period for you. I know that you came as a recommendation of

Detrick, but I don't know you personally. I need to see what you about for myself, before I decide that you worthy of being on my team." I said and paused for a second to allow my words to soak in. I needed him to understand that I didn't just let anybody around me without making sure that they were straight. No matter who knew them.

"I hear you," he said. "And I do want you to know that I'mma do everything in my power to prove to you that y'all made a good decision."

"I'mma hold you to that, but in the meantime, just know that I'mma keep my eyes on you," I said.

"I can respect that," Harold replied.

"Glad we got that understood. Now, I don't have to tell you how important this situation is to me. This is my baby's mama's life on the line, and I, not only need her back home, but I need her back home safely. Do what you have to do to ensure that is done." I told him.

"You don't even have to worry about that," he said.

"Good looking out," I told him and reached out my hand for a dap. We bumped fists, and I told him that he could leave. After he was gone, a thought came to me. I got onto the computer and typed in Verizon. When I had my account pulled up, I went to the call log on the second line. I looked at the calendar on the computer to get the date that Keya went missing and went back to my account. I fished through the call log, and when I came across a number that was on there several times, I wrote it down. I picked up my phone and hit *67 before punching in the rest of the numbers. The phone rang a few times, and a male's voice came onto the line.

"Hello," he said, but I remained quiet. I needed to hear him speak again, so that I could make sure that I was hearing his voice correctly. "Hello," he said once again. "Fucking playing on the phone and shit," I heard him mumble just before the call ended.

I laid my phone back down and reclined in my seat. All types of thoughts were swirling through my mind. Sam answering that phone had just thrown me for a loop, and now I wondered just what the fuck was going on.

8
Keya

One day later....

I had been holding my pee for so long that it felt like my bladder would burst open. I was willing to take that chance though, because I didn't want Sam to know that I was awake. Every time I opened my eyes, he was on me like white on rice. Sometimes I would still be sleeping when he would force himself onto me. I stayed curled up in the fetal position lightly rocking my body back in forth for as long as I could, but then I couldn't take it anymore and jumped out of bed to go to the bathroom.

"Ahhh," I screamed out when I noticed some guy sitting in a chair watching me. "W.h.h.o.o.o, are you?" I asked stammering over my words. I looked around and didn't notice Sam inside of the room.

Was he just sitting here watching me as I slept? I thought to myself.

"Look, don't ask no questions, shorty," he said with a blank expression on his face. "And where the fuck you think you going anyway?" he asked.

"Can I please use the bathroom," I asked him. I did my best to grip my legs together so that I wouldn't piss on myself.

"Go head, but don't take forever in there," he told me, and I quickly ran into the bathroom. After closing and locking the door, I hurried over to the toilet and sat down right before my pee came out. "Ahh," I let out while closing my eyes. It felt like I hadn't peed in forever, and it felt so good to relieve my bladder.

"Boom, boom, boom. The beating at the door caused me to jump, and my eyes popped open.

"I'm coming out in a minute," I managed to get out after I caught my breath.

"Aye, hurry up in that damn bathroom. It don't take that long to piss," the guy said. I hurried to wipe myself, and after I was done, I stood up and flushed the toilet. When I was done washing my hands, I walked over to the door and eased it open. The guy stood on the other side, with his arms over his chest.

"Get yo ass out here," he said grabbing me by my arms and pushing me over towards the bed.

Damn, he didn't have to be so rough. I would have walked out on my own, I thought.

I lifted my knees up to my chest and pulled the t-shirt that I was wearing down over them. When I looked up, the guy was staring me in the face. My eyes scanned his body, and I took him in. I could tell that he was young, maybe in his late teens, early twenties. He was rather tall, with big, dark eyes, and his hands were extremely huge. He was dressed like the typical corner boy in a long, white tee, Jordan's, and a pair of jeans that were like three sizes too big. The intent gaze that he had on me was making me feel uncomfortable, so I closed my eyes, and began to pray.

Please heavenly father, please don't let this man kill me, I said inside of my head. I also prayed that when I opened my eyes he wouldn't be staring at me. *Wishful thinking,* I thought. When I reopened my eyes, I realized his spooky ass was still looking at me. But I figured if he were going to kill me then he would have already done it by now. I was sure that he was somebody that Sam had put on me, so that I wouldn't try to escape. I decided to see if I could bargain with him.

"Look, I don't know who you are, or what Sam has told you, but this is kidnapping y'all are doing to me." I said.

"Didn't I tell you not to open your damn mouth," he said leaning forward in his chair.

"Please, just listen to me. My daughter is back at home in my apartment, and if you let me use the phone to call my parents, I swear I won't tell them anything about you. I just need to make sure that somebody can get to her before it's too late." I said. The guy looked as if he were thinking about it, and I anxiously bounced my leg, as I awaited his answer.

"Please, and I won't tell Sam either." I added.

He looked away, and after about a minute or so, his eyes made their way back over to me again. Suddenly, he stood up from the chair and walked over towards me. I had no idea what he was about to do, so I pulled my t-shirt further down on my knees. He could have been like Sam and thought that he could just take my stuff. If that were the case, I was gonna put up one helluva fight, because I didn't see that he had a gun. His six-foot frame towered over me as I sat on the bed. When he leaned in close to me and licked the side of my face, I cringed.

"Yeah, you scared ain't you? Well you should be" he said, and I stared at him. He ran his big hand up my leg, and I tried to push it back. My whole body trembled, as I felt his hot breath on the side of my neck. Suddenly, he stood back up and laughed.

"I'm not going to tell you again to shut the fuck up," he said.

I exhaled when he returned to his seat. It was like he was taunting me, and I could forget the idea of him helping me out. I covered my hands with my face so that he wouldn't see me cry, but even with me shielding my face, he could probably still hear my sniffles because there wasn't any sound in the room. Hell, the TV wasn't even on. But just then, I heard someone outside of the door, and my head shot up. A few seconds later, it popped open, and in walked Sam with bags of Waffle House food in his hands.

My stomach instantly started to growl. Sam had only been feeding me chips, and occasionally, he would give me water. The only other way for me to get something to drink, was when he allowed me to go to the bathroom. I would use my hand as a cup, and allow the water to run into it. Then, I would put my hands up to my mouth and drink whatever hadn't slipped back into the sink. It would have probably been easier to just place my mouth under the faucet, but the sink was old and dirty, and I didn't want to put my mouth anywhere near it.

Sam walked over to the little table that was attached to the wall and placed the bags down. He pulled a tray from one of the bags, and it was like my stomach was saying feed me; that's how loud it was growling. The guy that was watching over me, opened the second bag, and pulled a plate out as well. Sam took a seat in the chair, and they both dug into their food. My mouth hung wide open, and hot, angry tears spilled from my eyes and landed on my shirt. This was like torture, and I didn't know how much more of this shit that I could take. When Sam looked up, he had this shit eating grin on his face.

"What's wrong, baby? You hungry?" he asked stuffing some hash browns into his mouth. The strange ass guy thought that was the funniest shit ever, but I didn't see the humor in this situation.

"You want some?" Sam laughed while holding out his fork to me.

"Fuck you, nigga. I would rather die a thousand deaths than to beg you for anything," I spat. I knew that would piss him off, but at this point, I didn't care about the consequences. I was just so tired of him treating me like shit. But surprisingly, his demented ass just laughed. I shook my head, and rolled my eyes.

"You just made my dick hard. You know, that, right?" he said, motioning his head towards his pants.

"Whatever!" I said waving him off. I tucked my head back inside of my hands and tried my best to come up with a plan on how

I could get away from his crazy ass. While lost in my thoughts, I suddenly felt the bed dip in, and when I opened my eyes, Sam was sitting beside me. When I looked at his lap, I noticed the gun that he always had in plain sight. If he didn't have that damn gun, I would have jumped up and made a run for the door, but I couldn't chance him shooting me.

"You know what time it is," he said while staring at me.

I sighed. "Sam, not while he is in here," I said looking in the direction of the guy.

"Aye mane, take a walk," he said, and the guy looked at him with a frown on his face.

"Let me holler at you right quick," he told Sam.

Sam raised up from the bed, and they both walked over to the bathroom's door. Before Sam went inside, he held his gun up in front of him. "Keya, don't touch that damn phone, or you know what's going to happen if you do." He said. I rolled my eyes, and Sam walked inside of the bathroom. He left the door slightly ajar, so that he could keep a watch on me.

"How much longer you plan on keeping her here?" I heard the guy ask.

"I don't know, why?" Sam asked him.

"Cause I feel like you losing focus, and you need to stay on track with our plan," the guy said, and I wondered what plan he was talking about.

"Nigga, don't worry about what the fuck I'm doing. You just do your part, and everything gon' work out," Sam barked.

"Aight, mane, I'mma let you do this your way, but I ain't trying to get caught up," the guy said.

"You worry too much, nigga. I promise, once we have that money in our hands, we gonna kill that bitch and get the fuck out of town," Sam said and peeped out at me. It was like he wanted me to hear that part, and I had heard him loud and clear.

Oh, my god, I thought with my hand over my mouth. I needed to come up with something quick, before they executed on that plan. They both walked out of the bathroom, and the guy walked straight out of the room. Sam turned to me and smiled. I cringed, because just like he had said earlier, I knew what time it was.

9
Jeremy

Later that day....

"Oh Jeremy, this feels so good," Nancy screamed out, as she bounced up and down on top of me. "Tell me that you love me," she said, and I swear I wanted to knock her ass on the floor.

"I'm about to cuuummm," she said with her eyes closed, and her head hung back.

Thank God, I thought. I wanted to hurry up and get this shit over with, because I wasn't feeling it no more. The only reason I had given her the dick in the first place was because she had damn near swallowed me whole, and I felt obligated to fuck her after the head that she had blessed me with.

"Whew, that was good," she said, while smiling down at me. "Did you get yours?" she asked.

"I got it," I lied and moved her to the side of me. Planting my feet on the floor, I stood up and headed into the bathroom. I cut the shower on, and climbed inside. After I had washed her juices off, I climbed out and headed back into our bedroom. I walked straight pass Nancy, and headed into the closet to retrieve my clothes for the night.

"Are you leaving out again?" she asked, when she noticed that I was putting on my clothes.

"Yeah! I got something to do?" I replied.

"Jeremy, you have not been here for the last few days, and then you come in, fuck me, and leave right back out. What's up with that?" she asked.

"Fuck, I just told you that I had something to do. My man's girl is missing, and here you go with that nagging shit talking about us spending some time together. I'm getting real sick of it, and I'm this close to just saying fuck this whole relationship. I ain't got time to deal with this bullshit," I snapped.

"Look, I understand that Keya is missing, and I'm sure that Aaron is worried sick, but you cannot spend every day and night looking for her. We have a son, and do you know how that makes me feel to hear him always asking where you are?" Nancy asked.

"My son is good, and once we find Keya, then I will spend as much time with him as I can," I told her while going into the closet to grab my black hoodie.

"You know, I'm not going to keep begging you to spend time with us. If you're too busy, there is always someone else who will make the time. Plenty of guys have tried talking to me, but I always turned them down because of our relationship. Now I'm thinking that I just might give the next guy that asks to holler at me my number," she smirked.

I stopped what I was doing and stared at her. "Bitch, how about I do us both the favor and give the nigga your number myself. That way, you will become his problem, and I won't have to hear your fuckin' mouth no more," I spat.

Nancy's eyes bucked, and she placed her hand over her chest like she was having a heart attack. She thought by saying that it would get some type of reaction out of me, but the truth is, I been over this relationship with her ass. After she had snapped out of her shocked state, she ran over and tried to slap me, but I grabbed her hand and pushed her up against the wall. Wrapping my hands around her neck, I applied some pressure. Not enough to kill her, but just enough so that she would get my point.

"Bitch, don't put your fuckin hands on me again. And I don't know how many times I done told your crazy ass that," I said with my body weight pressed firmly against her.

"Let me go, Jeremy. You ain't shit!" she said, while kicking and screaming.

"Nancy, how many times I done told you that, that mouth of yours was gonna get your feelings hurt? I ain't want to put it to you like that, but you always pushing my fuckin buttons, trying to get some type of reaction out of me." I said, then forcefully let her go. I glared down at her for a minute, then finally went back to what I was doing. She ran up behind me and pounded on my back with both of her fists repeatedly. I turned around and pushed her off me, and her crazy ass fell to the floor.

"I hate you, Jeremy! I fuckin hate you! I'm taking my son and going back to Atlanta, and you will never see him again," she shouted.

I smirked. "You ain't crazy, and your ass ain't going nowhere with my fuckin son. You can try me if you want to, Nancy, but I put this on my life; you will not live to tell about it," I said through gritted teeth.

Once I had my hoodie on, I grabbed up my pistol, keys, and wallet, and headed out of the room. I made it downstairs and into the garage, then pushed the button for the door to lift. I slid into my Monte Carlo LS with the European front cap. This car was so bad, and it made me feel like I was on my Denzel from *Training Day* shit. I revved up the engine and let my girl come to life. It wasn't often that I brought her out, but when I did, it was always for good reasons. As I backed out of the garage, my phone rang. I glanced down at the caller ID and saw that it was Nancy, so I let it roll to voicemail. I didn't have time to deal with her bullshit. She wanted me to sit in the house and argue with her all day, and I wasn't about to do that. And if she thought for one second that I was about to let her take my son anywhere then she was sadly mistaken. I would kill her ass, before I ever let that happen.

10

Keya

The next day....

"Aye, let's go to the store, mane. I need to get some cigars," Sam told to the guy that was here with us. I don't know what it was about him, but he just spooked me the hell out. "Aight, what about her?" he said pointing to me.

"What you mean what about her? We take her with us," Sam said.

"You think that's a good idea, dawg. What if somebody notices her?" the guy asked.

"Mane, this little ass town, ain't nobody gonna notice her ass," Sam said while standing up.

"Come on, Keya, and if you do anything to draw attention to us, I'mma kill you," he said gripping me by the chin.
"I'm not going to do anything," I said, and pulled away from him. Sam smacked my butt, and I rolled my eyes.

"Aight, let's go," he said.

We walked outside of the motel room, and it was the first time in a week, since I had seen the outside world.
After forcing me into the backseat of his car, Sam and the other guy climbed in the front, and we drove off. Once we pulled up to the store, Sam told the guy to stay inside with me, while he went in to get whatever he needed.

My eyes scanned the parking lot, while looking to see if anybody was out, but I didn't see anyone around. Sam was right about one thing; this place was small. I didn't even know where he had us. I kept looking out the window to see if somebody would pull up.

"Fuck, I gotta piss," the guy said, and I rolled my eyes. "Come on, let's go inside, and you better not say or do nothing, or we're gonna kill yo ass," He said looking at me through the rearview mirror. He got out of the car and came around to my side. After opening the door for me, I climbed out, and we walked inside of the store. I looked around the store, and noticed Sam over by the snacks. He looked up, and when he realized it was us, he frowned.

"What the fuck is you doing?" Sam asked the guy when he walked over to us.

"I had to piss, mane," the guy replied.

"Yo ass stupid. Go ahead and handle your business so we can get the fuck up out of here," he said, and the guy walked off. I glanced towards the counter, and it was a skinny, white boy standing behind it. He kept looking at us, and I wondered if he had recognized me from the news or something. I didn't know for sure that there was even anything about me on the news, but I figured by now that my parents would have probably started looking for me.

"Keya, don't even think about it, or I will kill you and his silly looking ass!" Sam said and put his arm around my shoulder, and then pulled me close to his side. We walked over to the area were the chips were, and after grabbing a few bags of chips and soda, he walked us up to the counter and put the stuff down.

"How are y'all?" the kid asked while ringing up the items.

"Let me get two purple haze cigarillos," Sam ignored him.

After grabbing the cigars, the cashier finished ringing up the items, then placed them into a bag. "That'll be 12.38," he said, and Sam paid for the stuff. The whole time, I could feel the cashier's eyes on me, but I didn't want to look up for fear of what Sam might do. I couldn't have that boy's blood on my hands. Just as we were getting ready to leave out of the store, the crazy guy was coming out of the bathroom, and he caught up to us.

"Fuck took you so long nigga?" Sam asked the minute we were outside.

"Mane, I had to shit too," the guy said, and I frowned up my face.

"Dumb ass muthafucka," Sam mumbled.

When we made it back to the motel, we got out of the car and walked back inside. Sam handed me a bag of chips, and I scoffed them down like I hadn't eaten in a year. I was eating so fast that a chip got lodged inside of my throat, because I didn't chew it thoroughly. I started coughing and gagging, while Sam and the guy both stared at me.

"What's wrong? You want something to drink?" Sam asked with a grin on his face. I nodded my head while holding my throat.

"Yes," I managed to say with tears in my eyes.

"What you gonna give me?" he asked.

"Please, Sam, I need something to drink," I pleaded through a raspy voice.

"Open your mouth," he told me, and I opened my mouth. Sam held the soda over my head and allowed a small amount to fall into my mouth. I quickly swallowed it down, but it didn't do much to quench my thirst.

"Mane, yo ass crazy," the guy said shaking his head. He had nerve to talk. I felt that he was just as crazy, to sit here and witness the shit, and not do anything about it.

"Whatever, nigga, I don't give a fuck about her. She left me for some punk ass nigga. She lucky that I'm even letting her ass breath after the way that she played me," Sam said. I didn't say anything, as I stared at him. *Is this what all this was about?* I thought to myself. Was he really that mad over the fact that I had left him to be with Aaron?

When we were together, he did everything in his power to prove that he didn't love me like I loved him. Now he was sitting here screaming about how I left him. This shit didn't make any sense to me, and I knew that I had to get away from him quick, because he had just lost the last of his marbles.

11
Aaron

I took the bottle of Hen that sat on my desk and took a long swig from it. The warm, brown liquor burned my throat as it went down. I placed the bottle back on the desk, then took my hands and massaged my temples. My head was banging, and this shit with Keya wasn't making it no better. Until the other day, I had been relentless in my search for her. But when I found Sam's name repeatedly on our cell phone bill, it made me think that maybe he had her with him. I didn't know for sure, but the shit was suspicious, especially with her disappearing right after she talked to him.

"Damn, nigga, you must really be stressing, because I never see yo ass drink this much," Jeremy said, as he walked into the room.

"Mane, you don't know the half of it," I said.

Jeremy took a seat in front of me. "So, what's going on?" he asked while looking at me.

"Mane, you ain't gonna believe this shit, cause I still can't believe it," I said.

"Wassup dawg?" Jeremy said.

"Aight, so the other day, I'm having a meeting with Detrick and Harold, and I'm telling them to let me know if they find out any more information on Keya, because they said that they didn't get any answers when they went up to her school. After they had left, something clicked in my head, and I remembered that Keya's phone was on my plan. So immediately get onto Verizon and search through her call log. Then I go to the date that she went missing, and around that time, I see the same number on both her incoming and outgoing calls. I even looked through her text messages, and the same number was the last text received the night she went missing. You following me?" I asked Jeremy.

"Yeah, yeah…keep going," he nodded.

"Aight, so I hit *67 and dial the number. Tell me why that punk muthafucka Sam answers the phone." I said.

"C'mon, mane. You have to be kidding me," Jeremy said in disbelief.

"Nigga, I wish that I was," I replied.

"Aight, so what you do. I know you said something to the nigga," he said.

"Nah, cause I didn't want him to know that it was me on the line. If Keya is with him, then I need to find them, and if he knows that I'm onto him, he would probably just hide out somewhere else." I said.

"Mane, that's fucked up," he said, and we both became silent. My mind was full of thoughts that made me want to go out and murk somebody right then. But then a thought came to mind, and it made me realize that I needed to go about the situation in a different way.

"Aye, yo pops, he still got that connection with that guy that can do a trace on phones?" I asked.

"I believe so, but let me call him and see what's up," Jeremy said.

He pulled his phone from his pocket and dial his pops' number. After he had picked up, they talked for a few minutes before he placed the phone on speaker. "Aaron, my guy, what seems to be the problem?" Leroy asked.

Jeremy's pop was our connect and had been since we first stepped foot into the game. He had been talking about retiring soon and had mentioned to me and Jeremy that he wanted us to be the ones who took over his organization. I wasn't so sure yet if I wanted to take on such commitment, so I had been avoiding him whenever he called, and I knew that he wouldn't be too happy about that.

"What's good, Leroy?" I asked.

"Why is this the first time that I am hearing about your little problem? You know that you could have come to me, and I would have had somebody to get right on it," he said with a voice that held disappointment.

"I know, Leroy, and it really just crossed my mind," I said.

"Aaron, I know you just like I know my knuckleheaded son, and I know that you like to handle things by yourself. But we're family, and it should never come a time where you forget that I'm here for both of you all," he preached.

"You right, and that's my bad! But do you think that you can get your guy to trace a number?" I asked him.

"Shoot me the number really quick and give me about an hour, then I should have something for you," he replied.

"I'm on it," I told him and ended the call. I sent Leroy Sam's number once we hung up. Then grabbing the blunt that rested behind my ear, I lit it. I took a few tokes and passed it to Jeremy. We sat in silence and waited for his pops to hit us back with that info. I was getting anxious after we had been waiting for about forty-five minutes, but just then, Jeremy's phone finally rang back. He placed the call on speaker again.

"Aight, so this is what my guy found out. He said that the number was traced to a little area right outside of Nashville, called Franklin; maybe like twenty minutes or so from there. He doesn't know the exact location, but he knows that he is in that area. Do you want me to have somebody go down and check it out?" he asked.

"I appreciate that, Leroy, but this is personal, and I need to be the one to handle this." I said. I held the phone between my ear and my shoulder and stood up.

"I understand, but just let me know if you need any help. We don't need you getting into any more trouble," Leroy said.

"You don't have to worry about that, Leroy."

"Aight, well give the phone back to my son, and don't forget what I said." he told me, and I did what he asked and passed the phone back over to Jeremy. He wrapped the call up with his pops, and a few seconds later, I heard his footsteps following behind me.

"Hold up, mane. I ain't about to let you go out there by yourself. You don't know what you might be walking into," Jeremy said.

I thought about what he said, and although I would go up against an army to get to Keya, I did need to think more rationally about it. There wasn't any sense in going through all of this if I couldn't get her back home safely.

"Come on, dawg; let's be out!" I said, already heading for the door.

12
John
One day later….

"Aye man, how much longer Aaron gonna have us out here looking for this broad," Harold asked out of nowhere.

I turned the radio down, because I knew that I had heard him wrong. "Fuck you just say, nigga?" I asked.

"I was just saying, how long you think boss man gonna have us looking for her. I mean, it's been over a week since she went missing." He said trying to clean up his words.

"As long as it fuckin takes to get her back," I said.

"Aight, mane," he said holding up his hands.

"Man, you need to chill out with that shit," Detrick told him from the backseat.

I looked through my rearview mirror at him, and he was blowing the smoke from a blunt through his nose. He looked almost as mad as I was about what Harold had said. I cut the radio back up after seeing that Harold didn't have shit else to say. We had been riding all over Memphis trying to find something that would lead us in the direction on where Keya could've been. When we went down to Franklin where Jeremy's pops said that his guy had picked up Sam's phone, we hadn't been able to find him anywhere. There were only two motels in that area, and Sam's car wasn't at either of them, so after driving around for three hours straight, and not coming up with nothing, we finally gave up and drove back to Memphis.

I hadn't been to sleep not once, and as soon as Aaron dropped me back off to my car, I was right back out combing the streets to see what information I could come up with. Jeremy had gotten a tip on where Sam's baby mama Shauna was living with her grandma.

He gave me instructions to visit her and see what information I could get regarding Sam.

When I finally pulled up the address that Jeremy had given me, I cut the car off. I glanced up at the house, and there was an old lady sitting on the porch in a rocking chair. I assumed that had to be Shauna's grandma. I turned to Detrick, because I didn't have shit to say to Harold's ass right now.

"Come on, nigga. Let's go see what we can find out," I told him. It wasn't that I needed his assistance; I just wanted to holler at him about his boy.

"You want me to come, too?" Harold asked, and I frowned my face up.

"Nah, you sit right here and think about your actions," I told him like he was a child. He didn't say anything, but I could tell that he was pissed about what I had just said to him. I didn't give a damn, though. I jumped out of the car and waited for Detrick to get out.

"What's up with your boy?" I asked him as we walked away from my car.

"Mane, I don't know what that nigga was thinking with that shit he just said." he replied, while flicking the butt of the blunt to the ground.

"How good do you really know this nigga?" I asked him.

"Aight, so I would see him in passing, but we never really said anything but wassup to each other.
So, one day, me and a few of my homies was out hanging. You know, kicking the shit. Harold came to me and told me that he needed to holler at me, and I'm like cool. We walk off to the side, and he tells me that he had overheard a few jack boys talking about they were gonna rob me. I ask him who, and he says that they were some young niggas, and that he knew them if he saw their faces, but that he didn't know their names. I told him good looking out, and

after that, he was gone. From that day, I kept seeing him around, and we would stop and chop it up for a few, but that was about it. Then, one night I was out, and I watched him beat the brakes off some dude cause he said that the nigga had violated him by stealing something from him. I had to pull him back, because it looked like he was about to kill ole boy.

Once we walked off, we got to talking, and he was saying that shit had been hard for him, and that he took care of his baby mama and his son. He said that he hadn't been bringing in enough money to support them like he
normally would. I could understand that, because I gotta daughter and a baby mama, too, and I don't
know what I would do if I couldn't provide for them. After seeing how he looked out for me and didn't really know me, I went to Jeremy and asked if he could put him on." Detrick said.

After Detrick, had finished explaining how he knew Harold, I felt that I could dig it. It wasn't too many dudes out here that looked out for you, and when you ran across that type, it was good to keep them in your circle. Maybe Harold's ass just didn't know any better, but if he came out the mouth with some more slick shit, then I was going to murk his ass myself.

"Come on, mane. Let's go up here and see what we can find out." I told Detrick, as we walked across the street. We took the stairs that led up to the porch, and the little old lady that was sitting on the porch, stared at us.

"Can I help y'all with something?" she asked.

"Yes, ma'am, how are you doing today?" I asked, politely.

"I'm okay, but what can I do for you?" she said, and I laughed because this little old lady looked like she didn't play any games.

"Is Judy… I mean is Shauna here?" I said correcting myself. The old lady looked at us again, before wobbling up from the chair.

"Shauna, it's some little boys out here to see you," she said into the screen door, then slowly walked back over to the rocking chair and sat down.

"Thank you, ma'am," I said with a slight chuckle. She turned her head the other way and acted like she didn't hear me. A few minutes later, Shauna come to the door. She had on a pair of those women jogging pants that stopped right below the knees and a tight fitted t-shirt. I hadn't seen her in about a year. Her shape was still off the chain, but that face was still ugly as fuck.

"What's up, John? What you doing over here?" she said and opened the door. After stepping onto the porch, she stared up at me.

"Can you step off the porch, so I can holler at you?" I asked. Shauna took a couple of steps forward, and the old lady called out to her.

"Shauna, don't leave this house, because I ain't babysitting today. I'm supposed to be going to bingo," she said.

"Grandma, I ain't going nowhere," she said with a roll of her eyes. "Anyways, wassup?" she said, as we walked down the steps and off to the side of the house. "Hey, how are you?" Shauna said, cheesing in Detrick's face.

This bitch still thirsty, I thought to myself. Detrick threw her a head nod, but didn't say anything.

"Have you seen Sam lately?" I asked, and Shauna turned her lips up at me.

"You know that I don't fuck with that deadbeat," she said.

"He don't be coming to get y'all little boy?" I asked her.

"Nope. He ain't seen my son since he was first born. What, y'all must still be beefing? Is that why you looking for him?" she asked.

"Yeah, some like that," I replied.

"Good, somebody needs to beat his ass. That nigga ain't tried to see my damn son, or give me any money to help out. He told me that he hated me, so I guess it was fuck my son, too," she said with a sour look.

"Damn, that's fucked up. But aye, if you see him, let me know. Aye, and don't tell that nigga that we were out looking for him either." I warned her.

"Okay, but what do I get for doing you this favor?" she asked with a smirk.

"Same ole Shauna, huh," I said, while pulling a wad of cash out of my pocket.

"You know it," she said and held out her hand for me to place some money in it. I handed her two hundred dollar bills, and she held them up to the sky. After she saw that they were real, she stuffed them into her pockets. I turned to walk off, but she stopped me.

"Hey, how am I supposed to get in touch with you if I see him?" she asked.

I thought about her question. I didn't want her having my number, cause I didn't want no shit with Laydii.

"Detrick, give her your number," I said, before walking back over to my car. I knew that he would be mad about giving Shauna his number. You could see the thirsty look in her eyes that she had for him.

When I got back into the car, Harold was on the phone.

"I'mma hit you up later," he said just before hanging up. Aye, who is that thick ass broad?" he asked after he had ended his call.

"Just this little chick that I used to go to school with. Really she ain't nobody." I said.

"Well, that bitch thicker than a muthafucka," he said, and I laughed.

"I'm sure she will let you hit if the price is right," I told him.

Just then, Detrick jumped into the car, and he had a frown on his face.

"What's up, mane, everything good?" I asked with a slight chuckle. I knew why he was looking like that, and the shit was funny as hell.

"Mane, that bitch thirsty as hell. Then, her teeth dirty as shit," he said.

"Yo, that shit was like that when we were in school." I said still laughing.

"Dawg, you act like you got to kiss the bitch. I would put a pillow over her head and fuck her thick ass," Harold said, and I looked at him like he was crazy.

"Nigga, it's pussy all around this muthafucka, and just cause a broad thick don't mean she fuck worthy. If she ain't taking care of her mouth like she should, then you know between them legs ain't right. That shit probably foul as hell." I said.

"I'on discriminate," he said, and me and Detrick busted into a fit of laughter. That nigga was a lost cause, and ain't no telling who he would stick his dick into. I liked a broad that was thick, too, but that didn't mean I went around hitting every girl just because she was thick. We pulled off the block, and I headed to drop them off so that I could go home to Laydii.

13
Keya

Two days later....

Sam had moved us to another motel the night before. I'm not sure why, but after coming in from wherever he had been at, he told me and the guy that we were leaving. Maybe somebody had found out where we were, and if that were the case, I hoped that they would find me soon. When we got to this motel, I realized that it was the same as the other one. Small, rundown, and nobody here to help me. I still hadn't eaten anything, and my mouth was so fuckin dry that it felt like someone had poured a bucket of sand down my throat. The guy that was with us had left out a while ago, and I wasn't sure where he had gone to, but I was glad that he wasn't here. I didn't like the way that he looked at me whenever he thought that Sam wasn't looking.

"Why yo ass ain't take a shower yet? I already told you what time it was," Sam yelled bringing me out of my thoughts.

"Sam, please! My period is down, and it's gonna hurt if you try to have sex with me while it is on." I said with pleading eyes.

"I don't give a fuck about your period being on, or how it makes you feel!" He yelled again.

My body automatically jumped, because his violent rants had become more frequent, and I never knew when he would hit me. It was like the kind side of him that he had shown me had just been a plot to bait me in. Because all that niceness was long gone, and was replaced with this crazy, deranged person. He wasn't even this bad when we were together back in school.

A few tears slipped from my eyes, as I climbed off the bed. I kept looking towards the room door for the guy to come in, and I hoped that he would return before I got out of the shower. That was

Natavia Presents

the only time when Sam didn't make me have sex with him. Once I made it to the bathroom, I stripped out of my clothes. My period was super heavy, and when I peed, there were big blood clots falling out of me. Not to mention, my stomach was cramping something serious. I cried silent tears, and had to clutch my stomach because the pain was just that bad.

"Oh, my god," this shit hurts so bad, I thought while clutching my stomach.

"Keya, hurry the fuck up in there, before I come in and get yo ass!" Sam hollered to me.

I hurried to wipe myself, then flushed the toilet. After stepping into the shower, I allowed the steaming hot water to cascade over my entire body, including my hair. I felt so dirty, and was in so much pain that I just wanted to die, but I knew that I needed to keep it together. Call it intuition, but I felt like something was about to happen for me. I just didn't know what it was.

After I was done washing up, I climbed out and wrapped a towel around my body. When I looked down, blood was already saturating the white towel. As I walked back into the room, my head became real light and my vision became blurry. With each step that I took, I felt weaker and weaker. Before I knew what was happening, I fell to the ground and blacked out.

****

I rapidly blinked my eyes, while trying to adjust them to the light. I had to remember where I was. Then it came back to me that I was still in the motel room, when I heard Sam snoring next to me. When I looked down, I noticed that he was at least decent enough to put me into one of his t-shirts, which by the way was useless, since the blood from my cycle had seeped through it, too. I sighed, because I needed some tampons, pads, or something that would catch the heavy blood flow. The excruciating pain that I was experiencing brought tears to my eyes, and I needed some type of meds to cure my cramps.

I stared down at Sam with pure hate in my eyes. The fact that he could be sleeping so peacefully while I sat in torment had me seeing red. I suddenly looked around the room to see where his gun was. When I noticed it on the nightstand, my mind kicked into overdrive.

This was it. I was finally about to get my chance to get away from him, I thought.

As quietly as I could, I sat up on the side of the bed. When I looked at Sam, I could see that his chest was moving up and down at a rapid pace. He never slept, because he was always so busy watching over me. For a split second, I started to wonder to myself if this was some type of test, or if he was just that tired from being my damn watchdog. Or maybe it was all the drugs that he took. I didn't know, but it had me scared to make my move. But I pushed forward anyway, and decided to take my chances. I would rather die trying, than to just give up and let Sam kill me. I swung one leg over the side of the bed and looked back at him again. Then, I slid my other leg off the bed and prayed at the same time that the bed didn't make any type of noises. I eased up slowly and tip-toed over towards the door.

Oh, my god, I'm about to get away from this crazy ass nigga, I screamed inside of my head. My feet were in a sprinting position, while my hand rested on the doorknob. I twisted the handle gently and held my breath at the same time. The door slowly eased open, as I pulled it towards me.

"Where the fuck you think you going?" Sam's voice boomed out.

"Ahh!" I screamed.

He looked at me and smirked. "Keya, you ain't going nowhere so you might as well sit your ass back down before you make shit a lot worse than it already is," he said a little too calm for my liking.

With my hand still on the doorknob, I looked between him and the gun. Back at him, and then the gun again. I couldn't take any chances, so I snatched up the gun from the table and aimed it at him. At the same time, Sam leaped from the bed.

"Pow!" the gun fired off. Sam stumbled backwards and grabbed his shoulder where the bullet had pierced him. My hands were trembling so bad, that I dropped the gun just before running out of the room at full speed. Rocks, gravel, and glass embedded in my bare feet, but I didn't care. I sprinted across the motel's parking lot like I was running a marathon.

When I glanced up, there was a car just backing out of a parking space not too far from me. *Thank god,* I thought as I ran over to the car and beat on the window while looking back over my shoulder at the same time. I prayed that the driver would let me in, and that Sam wouldn't catch up to me. "Please help me sir!" I cried.

"Get in," the older gentleman demanded when he rolled down the window.

I heard the locks click, and I immediately climbed into the backseat of the car. I turned around and looked out the back window. When I didn't see Sam, I released my breath. The driver said something to me, but I couldn't focus on what he was saying.

"Young lady, are you okay? And can you tell me what is going on?" he asked in a gentle, but concerned voice.

I forced my head from side to side. "No, I waaas Kidnnnapped!" I managed to say. "Pleaseeeee, leave before he comes out and finds me!" I cried.

The man finally drove off, and it hit me that I had gotten into a car with a complete stranger and didn't know where he was going.

For all that I knew, this man could have been a killer, and then I would have just placed myself into a worse situation than what I was just in. As he drove off, I noticed that he kept glancing at me through the rearview mirror. He was probably wondering if he could trust me, just like I was wondering about him, or it could have been the fact that I looked like hell.

When I looked down at my body, I could see blood all over the t-shirt that I had on. A sharp pain suddenly shot up from my foot, and traveled up my leg. I lifted my leg to see what was causing the pain. Blood was pouring out of a cut that I had gotten from a big chunk of glass that was still stuck inside my foot.

"Argh," I cringed, as I pulled the glass out and laid it on the seat next to me. I noticed that my hands were still trembling, and all I could do was cry.

After about fifteen minutes of driving, the car came to a sudden stop. When I looked out of the window, I noticed that we were at a hospital. I closed my eyes briefly and thanked God for this man. He could have pulled off, but he didn't, and the fact that he had brought me to get help said a lot about him.

He climbed out of the front seat and walked around to my side of the car. After he had my door open, he reached in and grabbed my hand. When I looked in his face, I could tell that he was a kind person. He appeared to be in his mid-forties, with black hair, and I could see the grayish, silver that was trying to peek through. He was a little above average in height, and he had a medium build.

"Come on, sweetie. We're going to get you some help," he smiled. I weakly smiled back and allowed him to guide me out of the car. As we were walking in, a female hospital worker rushed over to us and asked what was the problem.

"This young lady told me that she was kidnapped, and as you can see, she's been beaten pretty badly. I saw her running out of the motel that I was staying in and brought her here. Please check on her, because she doesn't look too good," he said. I started to laugh like I was a maniac, and they both stared at me. I couldn't help it; my freedom was finally here, and I was beyond relieved.

The female nurse assessed my wounds. She rushed over to a male worker and whispered something into his ear. They both glanced my way, and the male nurse grabbed a wheelchair and rolled it over to me. "You can sit in here," he said giving me a sympathetic look. I don't even remember sitting down; all I could remember was the male worker placing my feet onto the footrest of the wheelchair.

"Sir, please hang here, and we're gonna call the police. They will probably want to get a statement from you, regarding the incident," the male nurse said to the guy that had saved me.

I looked up at the man as he scratched the side of his neck. "I really don't know anything. She ran out to my car, and I brought her here," he said shrugging. "Hopefully, that will be all that they need from me, because I really need to get to work," he added.

I felt so bad, because now I had gotten him involved in my drama.

"I'm sure that's all they will need from you, and I appreciate you cooperating," the male nurse stated.

"Alright, that will be fine," the man said and copped a seat in one of the emergency room chairs.

I glanced over at my guardian angel. "Thank you, I mouthed, and he smiled while giving me a head nod. Just when I was at the point of breaking down and giving up, this man had come along and saved my life, and for that, I would forever be grateful for him.

14
Keya

The next morning....

My eyes were closed, and I could hear machines beeping all around me. I didn't know how long I had been asleep, but it felt like it had been an eternity.

"Is she going to be all right?" I heard my mama say.

"Yes, she will be fine. She just needs to get plenty of rest, and we have an IV going to her for the severe dehydration that she has suffered from." The man said, and I assumed that was the doctor's voice.

"Good. Was there any other issues that she had?" I heard my dad say, and I wanted to cry.

My parents were here, and I felt so relieved that I was away from Sam. Only thing that had me worried, was that I didn't know if I had killed him or not. When I first came into the hospital, the police came to talk to me, and at the time, they weren't able to give me any information, because they still had police on the scene back at the motel. One detective had tried to talk to me, but I was so exhausted that I just kept falling asleep. He told me that he would be back to speak to me later once I had a chance to get some rest. One of the nurses, had asked if it was someone that they could call for me, and I had told her to call my parents. Shortly after, I drifted into a deep sleep, and I was just waking up.

"Oh, my god, James, she is awake," My mama said when she noticed that my eyes were open.

"Oh Good! Hi Keya, I'm Doctor Martin, and I'm the attending Physician on duty. "How are you feeling?" the tall, white doctor with a baby face asked me.

"I guess that I'm okay," I replied.

"Glad to hear that. As I was just telling your parents, you are suffering from severe dehydration, and we want to keep you so that we can get your fluid level up. Also, you might feel a little groggy, because we did give you some sedatives to calm you down, and to assist you with any pain that you might have been in. Now, as far as the rape, we didn't see any severe damages, and we did run several STD tests to make sure that you didn't contract anything. We should have those results back in the next twenty-four hours," the doctor said with a sympathetic look on his face.

I nodded, and when I looked at my dad, I could see the vein in his neck popping out. I hadn't wanted them to know about the rape, but it was too late, because the doctor had already told them.

"I'm going to go ahead and get out of here. I'm sure that you will like to spend some time with your parents. But if you need anything, please don't hesitate to call for assistance," the doctor said just before leaving out.

Immediately after he left, my mom came over and hugged me. She ran her hands through my brittle hair, while looking into my eyes.

"Keya, baby, are you okay?" she asked, and I gave her a weak smile. She quickly wiped a tear from her eye that had fallen.

My dad came into view, and he smiled at me. "Baby girl, I missed you so much," he said.

"Thanks, Dad, but did someone go over to get Aniya?" I asked while staring at my parents.

"Yes, we have Aniya, and she is okay. I left her with your aunt, and once you're feeling better, we will let you see her. Your dad actually got her the day that you went missing," my mama said, and I closed my eyes. I breathed a sigh of relief. My daughter was safe, and she hadn't suffered much, and that was what I had been praying for most.

Knock. Knock. Knock.

"Hi, Keya you're awake," the detective that visited me earlier said, as he walked inside of the room.

"Yeah, I'm up," I told him.

"Can I talk to you for a minute?" he asked, and I told him that he could.

"We went to the motel, and Sam wasn't there," he said with a dreadful look on his face.

"What?" I said with wide eyes.

"I'm sorry. When a unit got there, the room was already empty. There was a trail of blood leading outside, which lets me know that he walked out of there. Also, I remember you saying earlier that there was another guy with him. Did you ever get his name?" He asked.

"No, Sam never mentioned his name. All I remember about him was that he was tall, dark-skinned, and he had these real dark eyes that looked evil," I said.

"So, no distinctive tattoos or anything else that may have stood out about him?" he asked, and I shook my head no.

"Don't you worry, Keya. Since Sam has a gunshot wound, he will need to visit a hospital, and we'll get him then. There has been a warrant issued for his arrest, and once we find him, we'll see if he gives up the other guy that was with him." The detective stated, but I didn't reply. This was not good news to me, because that only meant that Sam was still roaming around somewhere. *What if he tried to come after me again*? That was the thought going through my mind.

"Here's my card. You can call me if you have any questions," the detective said handing me the card. I took it from his hand and laid it down on my chest.

"Oh, detective before you go. We would like to ask that you do not disclose Keya's name to the public in any way. Our daughter has been through enough, and we just want to handle this matter privately. We don't need the side looks," My dad said.

"I understand, and you have my word, that her name will be left anonymous when it comes to news releases, and things of that sort," the detective said.

"We appreciate it," my mom said while glancing at me.

"Not a problem ma'am. Keya, you take care of yourself, and I will be in touch," the detective said just before leaving. As soon as he was gone, my mama and daddy bombarded me with question after question, but I just couldn't face them right now. I rolled over onto my side, closed my eyes, and allowed my sleep to consume me once again.

15
Laydii

"Okay! We are getting up now," I said into the phone and hung up.

"John, John, you have to get up! They found Keya, and she is at the hospital," I said while shaking his shoulders.

"Wait, what did you just say?" he asked with a yawn.

"I said that they found Keya," I told him.

"Aw, damn, I'm getting up now!" he said.

John jumped out of bed, and we both scrambled around each other to put on our clothes. Since it wasn't the time to focus on my look, I put on a simple, black high-low dress and stuck my feet into a pair of Chuck Taylors. When I looked up, John had beat me getting dressed.

"Hand me my phone, baby. I need to call and let Aaron know," he said. I passed him his phone and walked over to the dresser where the mirror was. I had allowed my hair to grow back out, and now it was down to my shoulders. I grabbed a rubber band off the dresser and wrapped my hair into a bun on top of my head.

After handling our hygiene in the bathroom, we rushed out to his car. "Damn, I need to stop and get some gas," John said while we were driving down the street. He pulled up to a Shell station and cut the car off. Handing me a fifty-dollar bill that he had just taken from his wallet, John told me to go pay for the gas while he pumped. I snatched the money out of his hands and jumped out of the car.

　　　　Natavia Presents

When I walked into the store, there were a few people in line so I had to wait. I impatiently tapped my foot, because the person at the front of the line was taking too long.

"Damn, Laydii, I haven't seen you in a few months," a voice said behind me.

When I turned around, I came face to face with Big Dick Rick, or just Rick, if you were one of the guys. We had actually slept together a few times while me and John were broken up, but after I got back with John, I told Rick that we couldn't kick it anymore.

"Hey, Rick, long time no see," I said looking him over. Rick was average height for a guy, standing at only 5'10. He was dark brown, with a stocky build, and a cute smile. Normally, I preferred my men a little taller and slimmer, but it was something about Rick that made me find him attractive.

"What's going on with you, girl," he said, grabbing me into a big hug. I could smell the cologne that he had on, and it was the same kind that John wore; that damn Christian Clive cologne.

"Nothing much," I said pulling away from him.

"Dig that, but I wanted to tell you that I was sorry to hear about Toni. I remember how close y'all were," Rick said.

"Thanks Rick! I really appreciate it," I smiled.

"So how you and your mom holding up?" he asked, and at the same time, I realized it was my turn at the counter.

"Hold on," I told him, as I let the cashier know what I needed.

"Let me get fifty on six," I said handing him the money.

"Alright, fifty on six," the Arabian cashier repeated back to me, and I nodded. After he handed me my receipt, I turned around to resume my conversation with Rick.

"For the most part, I'm doing okay. I mean, I have those days where it is harder than others, but I'm doing my best to maintain," I said. I was giving him the less dramatic details of my life, because of course, I wasn't going to tell him what had really been going on with me.

"Well, I'm glad to hear that you holding up aight," he said. "Let me pay for these items, and I can walk you out."

"Um, that's okay. John is outside waiting on me, and we have somewhere that we really need to be," I said.

"Damn, I was hoping that, when I ran into you again, you wouldn't still be with him," Rick said, and his comment made me frown.

"Why would you say that?" I asked.

"C'mon, Laydii, you know that I always had a thing for you," he said with a smile.

"Well, I'm sorry, but I'm still with John, and in fact, we are expecting," I said, and his eyes immediately went to my stomach. He kept his eyes on my stomach, and finally, he drifted them back up to my face.

"Congratulations," he said, but I could hear it in his voice that he really didn't mean it.

"Thanks, but I really need to go," I said just before walking off towards the door. When I got outside, John was back in the car waiting for me. I hurried to rush over to the car, but Rick called my name.

"Laydii," he said, and I stopped walking.

His ass is trying to cause some drama, I thought to myself.

"It was good seeing you, and congratulations on the baby again," he said and walked off.

I slowly turned around and walked over to the car. John stared at me until I made it to the car and climbed inside.

"Fuck did he want?" John asked. He hadn't even allowed me to close the door good, before he went in.

"Nothing, really. He was just telling me that he was sorry to hear about Toni," I explained.

"That's it?" He asked.

"Yes, what else would it be?" I asked.

John ignored my question, and got out of the car to put the gas nozzle back up. Then as soon as he got back inside the car, he sped off.

"What's wrong with you?" I asked.

"Nothing. I just didn't like the way that nigga was looking at you," John said.

"And how was he looking at me?"

"I'on know; it was a look like maybe he wanted you or something," he replied.

"Wow, and you were able to determine that from just that little time we were talking," I asked. That I knew of, John didn't know that I had slept with Rick. So, his line of questions was throwing me off.

"Nah, I been knowing that he wanted you," John said.

"I don't think so," I said, and he laughed.

"What is so funny?" I asked him.

"What hospital is Keya at?" he asked, and I knew that was his way of saying that he was done discussing it. This was one time that I was going to let it go, because I didn't want to talk about Rick.

"She's at Vanderbilt University Medical Center in Nashville," I said, but John didn't reply. He cut the radio up, and I looked out of the window. I had no idea where his attitude had come from, but at the moment, I couldn't worry myself with something so trivial, especially since I was worried about the state of my friend.

Two hours later....

"Ma'am, can you please tell me what room Keya Harris is in?" I asked the receptionist with urgency. We had just arrived at the hospital, and I wasted no time in trying to locate her. The receptionist punched something into her computer, and it seemed like forever before she looked back at us.

"Ma'am, what is your name?" she finally asked.

"Laydii Mitchell, and this is my boyfriend John Jackson?" I stated. She gave a slight head nod and looked back at the screen.

"Can you show me some identification?" she asked with a blank expression on her face. I reached inside of my purse and snatched my wallet out. Once I had retrieved my license, I handed it over to her. "Is there a problem or something?" I asked.

"It is just a precautionary measure we are taking," she said with a smile and handed me back my license. After looking over John's license, the receptionist gave us both visiting passes and directed us to Keya's room. We had to get on the elevator and take it up to the third floor. Once we arrived on the third floor, I stepped out and looked around. There were people over in the waiting area, probably there for their loved ones, so I headed in that direction so see if I spotted Keya's parents. Mrs. Harris hadn't answered her phone when I called her. Just as I was getting ready to walk the hall, I spotted Keya's sister, Tina. When she saw me, she waved her hand for me to come over to her. John and I briskly walked in that direction, and once we made it over, Tina and I embraced.

"Oh, my god! Is she okay, Tina?" I asked.

"For the most part, she is. But she does have a lot of bruises from where that muthafucka beat her," Tina said, and I gasped.

"What?" I asked with tears in my eyes, and Tina nodded.

"Calm down, girl. She is going to be okay," she told me. "Oh, I'm sorry, John, how are you?"

"I'm doing aight." he replied.

"Well, where's Aaron and Jeremy? I thought that y'all were all riding together?" Tina asked.

"Nah, but I did call Aaron, and let 'em know what was up. He said that he was gonna go by and scoop up Jeremy, and that they will be on their way." John replied.

"Okay, I will wait out here for them," Tina said. "Oh yeah, and Mama and Daddy are both back there in the room with Keya. I had to come out and get some fresh air, because I felt like I was suffocating inside of that room. I believe that they are only allowing three people at a time, so why don't you go back there first, Laydii," she said to me.

"Are you going to be okay out here?" I asked John.

"I'mma be straight," he said, while looking everywhere, but at me. I guess that he was still mad about the Rick situation, and I didn't know why. But to be honest, I really didn't care, and he could stay mad.

I walked in the direction of Keya's room, and when I got to the door, I knocked twice and went inside. Keya's parents were in chairs on both sides of her bed. I looked at her mom and could tell that she had been crying. Her mascara had smeared, and her eyes were bloodshot red. When I looked over at Keya's dad, I noticed that he was wearing the same sad look from the last time that I saw him.

"How is she?" I asked, as I walked around and gave Keya's mom a hug. She hugged me back, but her body felt tensed.

"Right now, the doctors are saying that she needs as much rest as she can get. When they admitted her, she was severely dehydrated and traumatized," she replied with a sigh.

I looked down at Keya, and she was fast asleep. There was several IV's running from her arms that were hooked to a machine. I had to close my eyes for a minute, because it was so hard seeing my friend like that. When I reopened them, I grabbed Keya's hand and stared down at her. It looked as though she had lost some weight. Her skin was also blotchy, and her lips were severely dry and cracked. Then, of course, there were all the bruises on her face.

"Mrs. Harris, do you mind if we talk out in the hall?" I asked with my eyes still on Keya.

"Sure honey, I was just gonna suggest the same thing," she said. I looked down at Keya once again, and placed a gentle kiss on her cheek. Mrs. Harris walked into the hall, and I followed behind her.

Where's Sam?" I asked the moment we made it out in the hall. Mrs. Harris had briefly touched on the fact that Sam was the one that had kidnapped Keya when she called to inform me that she was in the hospital. I mean, I sort of had my suspicions it was him, when John had broken everything down on how Aaron had found Sam's number on their phone bill. I didn't know why Keya had still been talking to Sam, but I guess all that didn't matter now. Mrs. Harris looked at me with a regretful look on her face, and replied.

"We don't know, Laydii." Mrs. Harris sighed.

"What? You mean to tell me that he is not in jail?" I screeched. Mrs. Harris shook her head no, and I instantly became weak. Tears were rapidly falling down my face as I did my best to keep my legs steady.

"Calm down, Laydii. You got that baby that you have to think of," she told me, soothingly, and I nodded. "The police said that, when they made it over to the room that Sam was nowhere to be found. They did see the blood from where Keya had shot him," Mrs. Harris stated.

"Keya shot him?" I asked with wide eyes.

"Yes, she shot him, and that's how she was able to get away. It was a man that was staying in the hotel room, and he was leaving out for work when Keya ran up to his window. She told him that she had been kidnapped, and luckily, the guy had a good heart and brought her here to the hospital," Mrs. Harris explained.

"Wow. This is like the *Twilight Zone*," I said.

"Laydii, this is worse than the *Twilight Zone*." she said and stepped closer to me. "That sick bastard raped my daughter repeatedly," she finally whispered.

"Oh, my god!" I placed my hand over my mouth to muffle my sobs. "Please tell me that he didn't do that to her?" I asked. Mrs. Harris nodded, and her eyes became misty. I grabbed her into a hug and ran my hand up and down her back. For a few minutes, we stayed locked in each other's arms as we cried for my best friend. When we finally pulled apart, Mrs. Harris suggested that we go to the bathroom to get ourselves together before we returned to the room, and I agreed. I hoped for Sam's sake that he was somewhere dead in a ditch, because I knew that once Aaron got wind of this, he was going to kill him.

16
John

We were now back at home after being at the hospital for two days straight. Keya was still being held for observation, and the doctors were saying that she should be able to go home within the next week. The only reason we had come home was because I had forced Laydii to leave so that she could get some rest. I understood that was her best friend and all, but I needed her to remember that she was pregnant. And she needed to start taking better care of herself.

Plus, I was still a little mad about her and that nigga Rick. I know Laydii thought that I didn't know anything about them sleeping together, but I knew. I had just never mentioned anything to her, because it happened while we were broken up. He needed to steer clear of my gal, though, or I was gonna put som'n hot in ass. And the next time that I run into him, I was gonna be sure to let him know that too.

"Baby, do you think that you can take me down to the hospital to see Keya today?" Laydii asked.

I stared at her, because we had just gotten back home this morning, and she was already trying to leave back out. "Laydii, you know that you need to get some rest. I'mma fuck you up if you do something to hurt my seed," I told her.

"John, I'm not doing anything physical, so why are you trying to make me stay cooped inside of this house," she whined.

"You heard what I said. This shit is not up for debate!"

"Whatever!" she said and turned her back to me. I laughed to myself because she was so fuckin stubborn and spoiled. But damn what she was talking about, because I was serious about her needing to chill out. Just then, my phone rang, and when I looked at the screen, I saw that it was an unfamiliar number. I didn't know who the number belonged to, but I answered anyway.

"Hello," I said, but no one said anything. "Hello," I said, again, and there was still silence. I pulled the phone away from my ear and looked at the screen. Whoever it was hadn't hung up, so I put the phone back to my ear.

"Aye, who is this?" I asked, and the caller hung up.

I placed my phone back down on the nightstand and wrapped my arms around Laydii's waist. She bucked her body back and tried to get me to remove my arm. I ignored her tantrum and kept the tight grip I had on her. With all that had been going on, I hadn't been inside of Laydii in a good lil minute, and I needed to feel her insides.

"John stop, I'm mad," she told me and rolled her body over so that she was now facing me. I lifted her shirt and positioned my head close to her stomach. Then, I placed sweet kisses on it. Laydii tried to push my head back, but I took her arms and pinned them to her sides.

"I don't feel like doing this," Laydii whined, but I didn't pay her whining any attention. We both needed to release some of our pent-up frustrations, and what better way to do it than exchanging fuck faces?

I separated Laydii's legs with my knee and sucked on her neck.

"Mmm," she moaned.

I knew that would get her. Laydii's spot was her neck, and she loved whenever I kissed on it. Feverishly, I continued to suck on her, while dry humping her. She broke her hands-free of my grasp and stroked up and down my back. With her legs, wide open, I leaned down, removed her panties, then took off my boxers. I could feel the heat radiating from her pussy, and I anticipated climbing inside. Grabbing my mans, I guided it towards her soaking wet center, and with one push, I was inside of her hot box.

"Fuck." I groaned.

The pussy was sloppy wet, and it was extremely tight. I had to stop for a minute, because I knew that, if I kept going, I was gonna nut. Laydii raised her middle section up, and her walls gripped tightly around me. Fuck it, I had to go ahead and hit it. If I came prematurely, then I would just have to go for another round. Placing her legs in the crook of my arms, I stroked nice and slow.

"Yesssssss, baby," she cried out.

I closed my eyes and began to stroke a little deeper. I picked up my pace and started to hit her with those long, deep strokes. Laydii clawed at my back, as I lifted her legs onto my shoulder and dug deep inside of her guts. She was raising her hips to fuck me back, and the shit felt great.

"Ffff-ucccck" I yelled, as I dumped all my seeds inside of her.

If her ass wasn't already pregnant, then she would have been after the nut that I had just released. With my chest heaving up and down, I rolled over onto my back and pulled her into my arms. I placed a kiss on her forehead, then she snuggled her head into my chest. A few minutes after, we both drifted into a deep sleep.

17

Aaron

A week later….

Today was the day that the doctors were allowing Keya to finally come home. I had asked her parents if It would be okay for me to pick her up instead of them, and they both agreed since they were planning something special for Keya. So here I was to get her, along with our daughter. Aniya was getting bigger by the day, and I knew that Keya would be happy to finally see her.

Reaching into the backseat of my car, I unstrapped the seatbelt from over my daughter and picked her up. I smiled at Aniya and tickled underneath her neck.

"Wassup, Daddy's baby," I said to her. She grinned big, and her smile revealed the two front teeth that she had recently grown in.

After getting her out of the car, I walked into the hospital, headed straight for the elevator, and pushed the up button. As I waited for it to open, I played with my Aniya. Once the elevator came, I stepped inside, and it took us up to the 3rd floor where Keya's room was. After we had gotten off, I walked down the hallway until we made it to her room and stepped inside. Keya was sitting on the bed already dressed, and when she looked up and saw me and Aniya, she ran over to us.

"My babbbby," she screeched and took Aniya from my hands. She placed kisses all over our daughter's face, and Aniya just cracked up with laughter.

"Well, hello to you, too, Keya," I said.

Keya stopped playing with Aniya and stared up at me.

"Hello, Aaron," she said shyly. I ain't gone lie; that kind of messed me up, because we were now back at that place in our life where she couldn't face me. I walked over to Keya and grabbed her in my arms.

"So, do you have all your stuff together," I asked. She nodded her head and continued to play with Aniya.

I sighed and looked around the room. Walking over to where her bags were stacked together, I picked them up. "Is this all of your stuff?" I asked.

"Umm, I believe that's everything," she said while looking around the room.

"Aight, well let's be out!" I told her. She already had her discharge papers, so we didn't need to wait for those. She had just been waiting for me to pick her up. We walked down the hall, and then got onto the elevator. I stared at her the whole ride down, but I could tell that she was avoiding eye contact with me.

"Aniya is big, huh?" I asked trying to make small talk.

"Yes, she is," Keya replied softly.

When we reached the bottom floor, Keya stepped off first. I followed behind her, and when we got outside, I told her to stay by the door, and that I would go get the car. Once I had the car, I pulled back up to the entrance where she and my daughter stood, and climbed out. After grabbing Aniya from her, I sat her down in her car seat and made sure that I had her securely locked down. Keya had already gotten inside of the car, so I walked around to my side and got in too. I pulled off and headed back to Memphis.

The car was quiet, and I didn't really know what to say to her. I could see her out the corner of my eye picking her nails. She was trying to avoid me, and I had a feeling I knew why, but I didn't say anything.

"So, your folks want me to bring you over there," I told her. She nodded, but still didn't open her mouth, so I cut the radio on, because the silence was killing me. It took us about two hours to make it back to Memphis, and when I pulled up to Keya's folk's house, she jumped out of the car and walked inside. Once I grabbed my daughter from the backseat, I walked up to the front door and went in too. On the inside of the house, I saw that Keya's folks had balloons, streamers, and a sign that read Welcome Home on it. Keya's sister Tina had Keya wrapped in her arms, and I noticed the tears in Keya's eyes. I placed Aniya down in her walker and took a seat in one of the chairs that was at the table.

One by one, everybody took turns hugging Keya, and it put a smile on my face to see that she was now back at home safe and sound. Her father walked over to me and asked if he could talk to me outside for a minute. I nodded my head yes and followed him outside. Once we were outside, I turned and looked at him.

"Look, I know that I haven't always been the nicest person to you, and I'm man enough to recognize my faults. It's not that I feel you are this bad person; I just feel like you live a lifestyle that I never wanted either of my daughters to be a part of. But Keya is a grown woman now, and I can't stop her from making her own decisions. You have a daughter now, and when she gets older, you will see just how I feel," He said.

"Sir, I already feel that way about Aniya," I chuckled. "And even though you feel that I'm not good enough for your daughter, I love that girl. Since day one, I have always treated her with respect, and when I found out she was missing, I ain't gone lie, I wanted to kill somebody," I admitted.

"Exactly, so you see where I'm coming from?" he asked.

"Yeah, I get where you're coming from, and I can't do nothing but respect it." I said.

"Good. I'm glad we got that understood. I need you to make sure that you protect my daughter and granddaughter at all costs," he said, while reaching his hand out for me to shake it.

I shook his hand but still was a little hesitant. Keya's dad had never accepted me, and I didn't know if this was a plot or something.

We were silent for a few minutes, just looking out at the cars that passed by. I was in my thoughts, and I guess he had a few of his own.

"That nigga, Sam. I want that muthafucka dead!" he said out of nowhere, then walked off before I could say anything.

I stayed rooted in that same spot just thinking about what he had said to me. Nobody had to tell me to get rid of Sam, because it was already a done deal. The shit just took me by surprise to hear it come from Keya's pop's mouth. I don't know how long I had been standing there, but suddenly, I heard John talking.

"Say mane, you aight?" he asked.

"I'm good, but when did y'all get here?" I asked him, as we walked inside of the house. John was saying something, but I kept thinking about Keya's pops. It was like I now had this newfound respect for him.

18

Sam

A week later....

I couldn't believe that bitch Keya had shot me and escaped. Then, she shot me in the shoulder, and I swear that was the worse pain that I had ever experienced. After it happened, I rushed out to my car and got away from the motel before the police showed up. I called up one of my homies, Tank, that I had grown up with, and he told me about this doctor that just so happen to live in the Nashville area, who did work for street niggas on the side.

When I made it to the doctor, he told me that, if I had waited another thirty minutes, I would have been dead behind the wheel of my car from bleeding out. After telling me to get rid of my phone, so that I wouldn't be traced to him, the doctor finally took a look at my shoulder. Come to find out, the bullet had gone straight through, and he was able to fix me up with the equipment that he kept inside of his house. I stayed with him for a few days until I recovered a little. When it was time for me to go, I used the doctor's phone to call up my nigga, Tank, and told him that I was coming to hide out at his house. I had been hiding here ever since.

"What you gonna do now, mane? You know they had you on the news the other night?" Tank asked.

"I ain't worried about that. By the time they come looking for me, I'll be long gone," I replied.

"I hope so, because I ain't trying to have the jakes beating down my door looking for yo ass," he laughed.

"Nah, I just need to make sure that our friend sticks with the plan, and everything should go good," I said.

"Aye, he better," Tank said while firing up a Newport. "But to get your mind right, I got some girls coming through in a little bit," he said, and I looked at him like he was crazy.

"Nigga is you crazy. I'm wanted, and you telling broads to come through. What if they go running they mouths and tell somebody that I'm here?" I snapped at Tank. This nigga was dumb.

"Mane, them hoes ain't gone say shit. Cause both of them from the hood and ratchet as fuck. I'm sure they used to fuckin with street niggas, and know how that shit go." Tank said.

"I'on know mane," I said while looking at him.

"Yo, I'm telling you, dawg. Just throw they ass a few dollars, they gone get us straight, and then we send they ass packing." he said.

"Aight, dawg, I'mma trust you on this one," I said, and then there was a knock at the door.

Tank walked over and answered. When he opened it, two chicks walked in. One was tall and had a slim build. She had a cute face, but I could tell that she was ratchet from the black and pink hair that she had in her head and all the tattoos that were on her chest and arms. She had piercings all over her face. The other one was average height, and she was sort of on the thicker side. Her thighs and ass were fat, and she had a small pudge in her stomach. I could tell that she was a little ratchet too from the long, different color nails that she had, and the eyelashes that were so long and heavy that she could barely hold her eyes open. She didn't look as ratchet as her friend, though.

"Hey," they both said as they took a seat on the couch.

"Wassup," I said throwing them a head nod.

"Dawg, this is Peaches," Tank said pointing to the thicker one. "And this is Kasha," he said, pointing to the slimmer one.

"How y'all doing?" I asked, and the Peaches chick squinted her eyes, and stared at me.

"Hey, you that guy from the news that's wanted for kidnapping. Is it true that you really kidnapped somebody?" the girl Peaches asked, and I looked at Tank. *I knew this shit was gonna happen,* I thought to myself.

"Aye, Peaches, don't believe everything that you hear. My nigga didn't do what the news is saying, and y'all better not go running your mouth either. Just handle him like we agreed, and he gone throw you a few dollars," Tank said.

"Oh, I ain't gone say nothing. I just realized that it was you," she said, and I smirked.

"Good, now that we got that understood, I'mma holler at y'all in a few," Tank said, grabbing Kasha's hand, and they went into his room. After they were gone, Peaches stood up and walked over to me. She sat down, and I got a whiff of the fruity smelling perfume that she had on. While we sat in silence, I got a better look at her and realized that she wasn't all that cute, but I guess, since I wasn't trying to be with the broad, it didn't really matter how she looked.

"So, what's up? You trying to do this or what?" she asked, when she noticed me staring at her.

I laughed. "I see you about your business," I said, and she pursed her lips together.

"Always," she finally replied.

"Aight, I can dig it. How bout you give me some head first," I said.

Peaches didn't say anything as she slid off the couch and crawled between my legs. She unzipped my jeans and pulled my dick out of my boxers. After stroking me gently in her hands, she took me into her mouth, while staring into my eyes. Her mouth was wet and warm, and it felt like I was inside of some pussy instead of somebody's mouth. She slurped all over it and played with my balls.

"Damn, take care of that," I said, and she went to work like her life depended on it. After she domed me up, I threw on a rubber and told her to bend over the back of the couch. Spreading her fat ass cheeks with my hands, I dug into her guts from the back.

"Oh, yes," she screamed out, and I pounded a little harder.

She took her hand, placed it in between her legs, and played with her own clit. I ain't gone lie… that shit sort of turned me on, and it made me give her the dick harder. After fucking her for about twenty minutes, I let loose inside of the condom. Peaches put her clothes back on, and shortly after, Tank and Kasha came back into the room with us. Peaches kept looking over at me, but I tried not to pay her ass any attention. I hoped that she didn't think that I was about to ask her for her number, cause I wasn't digging her like that.

"Aight, well we gonna get up with y'all later," Tank said dismissing them.

"Um excuse me, but where is my money?" Peaches said, and I realized that's why she had been staring at me.

"Ah, damn, my bad shorty," I said, as I dug inside of my pocket and pulled out a few twenties. I gave her ass sixty dollars, and she was happy as hell to get that little money. She probably was finna go splurge it on some weed and liquor. She just seemed like that type of broad.

After they had finally left, me and Tank sat back, and tried to think of what our next move would be.

19
Keya

I had been back at home for two weeks now, and I was trying my best to adjust. As far as my physical appearance, I was healing on that aspect, but it was my mental that was still fucked up. I kept having these bad nightmares that felt so real that, by the time I awoke, my pillow would be soaked from my tears. One of the dreams was that Sam still had me, and I couldn't get away. The other dream was, I was the one that had been shot, and Sam would be standing over me laughing like a maniac. It was so crazy, and I hoped that they would go away soon.

I was staying with my parents, because I didn't want to go back to my apartment. Sam knew where I lived, and just because he was wanted, it didn't mean that would keep him away from me. I didn't put anything past him after what he had done to me.

Suddenly, there was a knock at the front door, and I got up to answer it. When I opened it up, I saw that it was Aaron, and he had Aniya in his hands. He had picked her up the day before, and she spent the night with him. Every time that he came around, I tried my best to avoid him, because I was so ashamed of what I had done.

"Hey," I said, as I opened the door and allowed him to come in.

"Wassup," Aaron said. He walked inside, and he and Aniya sat down on the couch. He removed the little jacket that Aniya had on and laid it down beside him. "So, I already fed her, and she's been changed. Her little butt was asleep in the car, so if you go ahead and lay her down, she might go back to sleep," he said.

"Okay, can you stay here until I lay her down? I need to talk to you for a minute," I said, and he nodded. I took Aniya from him and took her back to my room. After laying her down, I walked back to the front, and Aaron was looking through his phone. When he saw me, he tucked it inside of his pocket.

"You said that you needed to holler at me, right?" he asked.

I was so nervous, but I needed to get this off his chest. "I'm sorry, Aaron!" I said.

"Keya, it's cool," he tried to say, but I stopped him.

"No wait, let me finish while I still have the courage," I said, and Aaron tipped his head to me. "I should have believed you when you told me that you had nothing to do with killing Sam's mother, but It was like he was in my ear, and then the police said that they had all this evidence. I just didn't know what to do. It was stupid of me to not think that everything had been a set-up. Can you find it in your heart to forgive me and allow us to move past this?" I asked.

Aaron smiled, and when those dimples sunk in, it let me know that everything would be okay. "You know we good, and just so you know, I was never mad at you." He said, and I felt a little relieved.

"Thank you, Aaron," I said with tears in my eyes. I had really needed to hear those words from him, and when he spoke them, they were like music to my ears. Aaron stood up, pulled me into a hug, and kissed the top of my head.

"Keya, you are a good girl, and I hope that I haven't tainted you for the next man." He said, while staring down at me. My mouth dropped open, and I looked up at him with wide eyes.

"What are you talking about for the next man?" I asked in a panic.

"Keya, I will always love you, and if you ever need anything, I'm there for you and my daughter, but me and you being in a relationship will never work." He said.

"Wait, you just said that you weren't mad at me," I said to him. I was trying to search Aaron's face for some sign of this being a joke, but I didn't see any.

"I'm not mad at you, but I do realize that you can't handle my lifestyle. And that would be selfish if I tried to force you to," he said.

"How are you going to tell me what I can't handle. You are not me," I yelled.

Aaron shook his head and stared into my eyes. "Keya, I don't have to speak on the obvious. But listen, I don't want to argue with you. All I ask is that you don't keep my daughter away from me, and I hope that one day we can at least be friends," he said.

I felt pressure in my chest, and my throat felt as if it had a huge ball inside of it. The tears that were brimming my eyes felt as if they were going to drop at any minute, but I did my best to hold them back. He hoped that we could be friends. What kind of shit was that? I didn't want to be his friend, because I loved him too much to ever just be his friend. Aaron didn't understand that I needed him so much right now, and for him to turn his back on me at a time like this, it really broke my heart. I pulled myself from his embrace and turned my back to him.

"Keya!" Aaron said, while trying to place his arms around me.

"Just go! Please, just go right now," I said while pushing him off me. I walked out of the living room and back to my room. A few minutes later, I heard the front door open and close, and I assumed that Aaron was gone. This was like one of the worst feelings in the world, and my heart couldn't take it. I laid across my bed and cried the hardest that I had cried in a long time.

20
John

Two months later....

I drove around and smoked a blunt while trying to get my mind right. Laydii's ass had been stressing me out about who could have killed Toni. It wasn't that I didn't care about her death, because Toni had been cool people. It was just that Laydii talked about the shit so much that it was stressing me out, and until we found out who had actually done it, we couldn't do nothing about it. Laydii barely wanted to have sex with me anymore, and she complained when I didn't want to sit in the house and listen to her go on and on about Toni and Keya. I loved my girl, but it was beginning to be a little too much on my shoulders.

My phone rang, and I thought it was Laydii, because whenever I wasn't at home, she would blow my phone up asking when I would be home. When I looked at the screen, it was an unknown number. I hit the accept button and placed the phone to my ear.

"Wassup?" I said into the phone.

"Hey, John; I'm glad that you answered for me," the caller stated.

"Who is this?" I asked.

"So, you don't remember my voice?" she said.

"Nah, and I really ain't got time to play on the phone, so tell me who you are or I'm hanging up."

"Wow, you're still the same mean John, but this is Kim," she finally revealed her identity.

"Oh, what's good with you Kim?" I asked.

"Well, um, I called you a few times, but I always got nervous when you answered." She said.

"Oh, that was you playing on the phone, huh?"

"No, I wasn't trying to play on the phone. But look, I just need to tell you something. And I'm not sure how you're going to take it, but I feel that I need to tell you," she said.

"Okay, so go ahead and say it then," I said with irritation in my tone. I was already getting tired of her talking in circles.

"Alright, here it is. I'm pregnant, John, and you are the father," Kim said, and I damn near drove off the road.

"Fuck you mean that you pregnant and I'm the father?" I asked.

"Well, that time we had sex, I got pregnant. At first, I just thought that my period was late, but after going two months without seeing it, I finally took a test, and it came back positive," she said. "After that, I went to the, doctor and they were able to confirm it."

This shit could not be happening to me. Kim was the broad that I was kicking it with when me and Laydii were broken up last year. At that time, me and Kim weren't even doing nothing; I would just let her dome me up here and there. But one night, I got mad at Laydii, and I ended up over at Kim's house. I was drunk, and when she let me hit, I made the mistake of running up in her raw. Kim had told me not to worry because she was on the pill. Then, once me and Laydii got back together, I told Kim that we needed to cool out, because I was back with my girl. She told me that she understood, and we hadn't talked since. Now she telling me that she carrying my seed, and I didn't know if it was true or not.

"Kim, please tell me that you just fuckin with a nigga, and that you ain't really pregnant," I said.

"I'm sorry, but I would be lying if I said that I wasn't pregnant. Look, how about you meet me
somewhere, and we can discuss everything face to face," she said.

Damn, her ass is telling the truth. But then I thought about it and realized that, just because she was pregnant, it didn't mean that I was the father. I knew plenty of broads that had gotten a guy by saying that he was the father. Had them paying child support and everything, and then years later, it turns out not to be the dude's child.

"I'll meet up with you, Kim," I said calling her bluff. It was still a possibility that she wasn't pregnant, and I wanted to see for myself if she was lying or not.

"Okay. Where do you want to meet?" she asked.

"I'mma call you back and let you know, but don't call this phone again," I said and hung up. Fuck," I said hitting the steering wheel. If Kim is pregnant by me, I might as well prepare for my funeral. Cause once Laydii found out, she was going to kill my ass.

The next day…

I was sitting inside of my car in the gas station's parking lot. My patience was wearing thin, because I had been waiting for over thirty minutes. When I looked at my watch, I saw that another five minutes had gone by. I was about to burn out if Kim didn't show up soon.

I glanced out the window for the hundredth time, but this time, I noticed Kim and the round belly that she was toting coming my way. "Damn," I said aloud. *She really is pregnant,* I thought.

Kim pulled the doorknob of my car and climbed inside. I examined her body, and when my eyes landed on her round belly, I stared at it.

"So, wassup," I finally asked her.

"I'm sure that you can see what's up!" she said with a smirk on her face.

"Look, Kim, I don't have time for these games. How far along are you anyway?" I asked, pointing towards her stomach.

"I'm six months pregnant, John. You can do the math, and see that that was around the time when we were together," she said.

I thought about it, and she was right. If the baby that Kim was carrying turned out to be mine, then I would have two kids born a month after the other. Laydii had just turned five months pregnant with the child we were having, and Kim was saying that she was six months pregnant. Just when I thought that me and Laydii were finally getting our shit together, this comes back to bite me in the ass. I didn't know what the fuck I was gonna do, but I knew telling Laydii right now was not an option. She was still stressing over Toni's death, and something like this would probably send her ass barreling over the edge.

"I understand that you have a girlfriend, John, but this is your son that I'm carrying, and I really want you to be in his life," she said.

"Well, I hope you know that we gone get a DNA," I said.

"I have no problems with that. We can even do it at the hospital; that way, you can start bonding with your son right away," she said. I shook my head and glanced out of the window. I had hoped like hell when I mentioned a DNA test that Kim would tell me that she didn't want to give me one, and I would've known then that it wasn't my baby. But she had agreed to my demands, and I figured that it might just be my baby after all.

"For right now, Kim, let's just keep this shit between me and you," I said finally looking in her face.

Kim frowned. "What type of shit are you on? Me and my baby will not be a secret," she spat.

"Either you do shit my way, or we can just wait until that baby is here and get that swab. It's your choice," I told her, dead ass. I wasn't about to let her fuck up what I had going on with Laydii.

"John, you know you ain't right." She looked at me in disbelief.

"Aye, it is what it is. You already knew about my situation from the jump, so I don't have to explain that my girl comes first. She pregnant, too, and I ain't trying to hurt her, Kim," I said.

"Whatever, John! You should have thought about that before you slept with me without a condom. Will you at least come to my doctors' appointments?" she asked.

"I will be there, but don't call my phone unless it's got something to do with the baby," I said, and she nodded.

"For now, I won't say anything, but when my baby gets here, you won't be able to hide him," she said.

Kim leaned over and wrapped her arms around my neck. I allowed her to hug me, but then she turned her head, and placed a kiss on my cheek. When she trailed her lips along my jawline and tried to kiss my lips, I pushed her back.

"Don't do that shit," I snapped, while staring into her eyes.

"C'mon, John. Baby mamas and daddies do this all the time," she said and giggled.

"Fuck you think I am, Kim? I ain't pressed for no pussy, and you ain't about to start trying to manipulate me with that baby mama, baby daddy shit. If this is my baby, then I will be there for them, but don't come to me on no sneaky shit cause I ain't fuckin off on my girl," I said staring into her eyes. I needed her to hear me loud and clear.

"Okay. If you want to play hard, I will let you have that for now," she smirked.

"I ain't fuckin playing. I'm not messing up my home for you or nobody else. Aight!" I said.

Kim nodded again and pulled the handle on the door to get out. While climbing out, she looked back at me. "See you around, baby daddy," she said with a smile just before closing the door and walking off.

Fuck, now how in the hell was I gonna explain to Laydii that I had another damn baby on the way, and that it would be born before the one that we had coming. I would just have to come up with a plan to keep this shit with Kim concealed, until I found a way to break the news to her.

21
Jeremy

A week later....

I picked up my cell phone to dial a number that I had become real accustomed to. The phone rang a few times before a voice finally came on the line.

"Hello!" the voice said.

"Damn, what took you so long to answer the phone?" I asked her.

"I was just getting out of the shower," she replied.

"Aight, well are you still meeting me at the spot, later?" I asked.

"I will be there, but I need to make sure he is gone first. He's supposed to be going out with his brother tonight, so it shouldn't be that long," she said.

I sighed, because I was 'bout over this creeping shit. "Aight, mane, just hit me when you can come out," I said.

"What's with the attitude, Jeremy? You knew that I had a man when we first started this thing. Just like I knew you had a woman," she said. "Now that y'all are probably beefing, you want me to just up and disrespect my man, when he doesn't even deserve that," she spoke loudly.

"First off, lower your damn voice when you talk to me. Now, I ain't said shit about me wanting you to disrespect your man. Hell, you do that all on your own, every time you climb yo freaky ass in the bed with me and hop on my dick." I said, and she giggled.

"Whatever! I will be there. Just don't have me waiting, Jeremy," she said and hung up.

Crazy ass women, I thought. I don't know why, but I had always been drawn to that type. It's just when a female got too out of hand with that shit, it started to become a turnoff. That's why I was over Nancy, and her bi-polar ass. The other night when I woke up, she was just standing above me. I ain't no punk by a long shot, but I had to admit that shit spooked me the fuck out. When I asked her what she was doing, she told me that she always like to watch me sleep. I immediately hauled ass out of there, and went down to one of the guestrooms that we had. I locked door, and even took an extra step and slid a chair under the doorknob. I couldn't deal with her crazy ass no more, and that's why I had been slowly plotting my exit.

I picked up the blunt that I had in my ashtray and fired it up. With my music, loud, I rode around the city and thought about what my next move would be. I had started to feel like I was ready to head back to down Atlanta and get back to my own operation. Over the last few months, I had made a couple of trips down there and peeped how everything was running. My main lieutenant was still doing a good job at holding everything down, but I was missing my city. Memphis was cool, but a lot had changed since I was a teenager. Niggas out here were grimy, and there wasn't any loyalty with them. The shit was to be expected when you were getting money, but it was like the cats in Memphis were just on a different level than the ones back at home. Everybody was going against each other just to get to the top of the game, and I wasn't with that. Not to mention, my pops wanted me and Aaron to take over his operation. I didn't know how Aaron felt about it, but if my pops were finally stepping down, it was only right that I took his spot. For now, I would just stick around until we got rid of Sam, and then I would go from there.

I finally pulled up to the hotel room that I was meeting shorty at. I made sure to park sideways so that nobody would park beside me. I made my way into the lobby of the hotel, and over to the front desk. After getting the extra keycard that had been left for me, I took the elevator to the second floor. I found the room that she was in and pulled out the key card. Once I opened the door and stepped inside, I could smell the fresh scent of candles and could see the flicker of the flame illuminating off the wall.

When I turned the corner, shorty was laid out on the table wearing nothing but her birthday suit and a smile. A devious grin instantly covered my face. This was one of the reasons why I loved to fuck with her. She was always down for whatever and didn't give me the grief that I received from dealing with Nancy. I walked over to the table, while rubbing my hands together, and pulled up a seat. With her fat, pink, bald pussy in my face, I lowered my head and teased her pearl. I twirled my tongue around and spread her legs wider as I stuck my head in deeper.

"Yessssssss, Jeremy! Just like that," she moaned and took hold of my dreads. Her legs shook violently as she smashed her pussy into my face. I stuck a finger into her hole and worked it in and out. When I pulled my finger out, I stuck it into her mouth, and she sucked on it. That shit turned me on, and it was something about seeing a woman that could taste her own juices. I lowered my head back down to her pussy and licked from the top of it down to her ass. Her body tasted so good, and I anticipated her cum on my tongue.

"Cum for me, baby," I whispered, then I took my tongue and darted it in and out of her.

"Fuck babbbbbbbby!" She screamed out. A few seconds later, her juices rained down onto my tongue. After licking up her slit one last time, I stood to my feet and wiped my mouth off.

"Damn boy, you trying to kill me," she giggled, while breathing heavily.

"Fuck that, I'm trying to make you mine," I said with a smirk.

She pursed her lips together and stared at me. "Jeremy, I told you that I want us to be together, but we gotta do this the right way.

"Tina, what can we do to make this shit right, when we done already fucked each other more ways than one," I said eyeing her.

I had been messing with Keya's older sister Tina for a little minute now. We had met a couple of months after me being back in Memphis. She was over to Aaron's and Keya's one night, when I had stopped through. Seeing her sitting there with some tight ass legging pants on, along with the crop top and the fuck me heels, had my ass mesmerized. Even with her sitting down, I could see that she was thick. Her hips were protruding on the sides of her, her thighs were firm, and her breasts were nice and perky. She had a dimple in her left cheek and some dark brown eyes. When I trailed my eyes up to her hair, I noticed that she had it cut in some spunky little do. It was kind of crazy, and when I thought back to how everything played out, it made me laugh.

"Damn, can I help you with something?" she said with a frown on her face, when she noticed me staring at her. Aaron and Keya started giggling hard as hell.

"Nah, you can't help me with nothing, but you might want to help yourself to some lotion for them ashy ass feet," I said, looking down at her feet, and then laughing.

"Boy, please, ain't shit ashy over here. Maybe you need to grab you a glass of water, since you so fuckin thirsty!" she countered back. By now, Keya and Aaron were rolling over with laughter as they watched me and lil mama go at it.

"Whatever! You wouldn't have known that I was looking at you, if you hadn't been staring me down since I first came into the house," I told her.

"Boy, bye; wasn't nobody staring at you," she said waving me off. I shook my head, walked over to the other end of the couch, and took a seat.

"Anyways, mane, who is this broad that you got in your house that can't seem to mind her manners," I asked Aaron while looking at ole girl.

"Um, my name is Tina, and all you had to do was ask if you wanted to know," she said and flashed this Colgate smile.

"Alright, y'all, chill out," Keya finally spoke up. "Yes, that is my older sister Tina. Tina, that is Aaron's friend, Jeremy," she said giving a formal introduction.

I looked back at Tina and winked at her. I couldn't even lie; she was finer than a muthafucka, and the fact that she could hang with me on the joking tip was a plus. Most girls I knew would have probably started crying the minute I fired their ass up.

"Aye, dawg, you ready to go handle that business?" Aaron asked, as I continued to look at shorty. I looked up at him and nodded. I stood up from the couch and turned back around to Tina.

"I apologize for the way that I came at you earlier. I should have waited until we were alone before I told you about your ashy feet," I smirked then walked off with Aaron.

"Whatever! Next time I will give you my ashy ass to kiss," Tina yelled behind me. I laughed while I followed Aaron down to his man cave. "Aye, you wild, mane," Aaron chuckled.

"Dawg, I'm just fucking with her, but is she single though?" I inquired.

"Fuck nah, you ain't about to mess with nobody that Keya knows. I already have to hear her complaining when John fucks up with Laydii. Tina is off limits," Aaron said, while looking at me with a serious look on his face.

"Whatever, mane, I ain't checking for that broad. I just think she sexy," I said with a sly grin. Aaron laughed, and we got down to

business. *After we had finished wrapping everything up, I headed for the front door. As I got to the door, I made a quick detour to the bathroom cause I had to piss badly.*

As I was walking down the hall, I bumped into Tina coming out of the bathroom. When she saw me, she rolled her eyes. We stared at each other until I disappeared behind the bathroom's door. Once I was done taking a leak, I washed my hands and headed out. As I passed the living room, I saw Tina sitting on the couch by herself.

"Aye, where Aaron at?" I asked her while sweeping my eyes over the living room.

"Him and Keya doing what they do best," she said fake gagging.

I laughed. "Them muthafuckas are freaky as hell," I said. Tina nodded her head but didn't say anything else while she stared down at her phone. "Aight, well tell him that I'll get up with him later," I said turning to leave.

"Wait, do you mind walking me out, cause I ain't about to wait until they finish. Hell, they might be up there the rest of the night," she chuckled.

"C'mon. Daddy will make sure that baby is good," I teased.

Tina stood up and smirked. When she walked towards me, her hips swayed, and my dick instantly got hard. She was even thicker than what I had thought. I bit down on my lip, walked over to the front door, and held it open for her.

As she passed by, I got a good glimpse of that ass and had to fight myself from reaching out and grabbing it.

Damn, that muthafucka perfect, I thought to myself.

I locked the door and pulled it up behind me. After I had walked Tina over to her car, I opened the door while she climbed inside. We stared at each other for a minute, then I finally asked for her number. Surprisingly, she gave it to me without all that smart-ass mouth that she had. I closed the door to her car, and she rolled the window down.

"Oh, and I do have a man so just make sure when you call it's during the daytime," she said.

I smirked, because that shit sounded like something a nigga would spit. Looking down at my phone, I went to the number that she had just given me and pressed send. When I heard her phone ring, I hung up.

"Nah, how about you call me when you can get free from your man," I told her, then swaggered off to my car.

Tina ended up calling me the very next day, and me and her had been kicking it with each other ever since.

22
Laydii

I was at the grocery store picking up a few items for dinner. John had thought it would be a good idea for us to have a little gathering at our house, and I agreed since we hadn't hung out with our friends in a while. I was five months along in my pregnancy, and I was slowly starting to get back to my old self. I was still dealing with Toni's death, but it wasn't as bad as it had been.

Okay, I got the steaks, onions, and bread, I thought as I ran over the shopping list that I had. I only had a few more items to get, and then I could take my pregnant ass home. My feet were killing me, and I couldn't wait to get off them.

"Excuse me!" I heard somebody say behind.

"Yeah!" I answered. When I turned around, it was an average height guy, with medium brown skin, a stocky build, and a low haircut. He had a kind smile, and he looked a little familiar.

"Ain't you Laydii?" he asked me. I gave the man a questioning look.

"Um, do you know me or something?" I asked with a raise of my brow. I was trying to place his face, but for the life of me, it just wouldn't register.

"Nah, not really, but I used to work with your sister, Toni?" he said. "My name is Tim, and me and Toni were actually pretty close."

"Oh yea, now I remember you. I kept wondering where I had seen you before. How are you," I asked?

"I'm aight," he replied. "I wanted to tell you that I was sorry to hear about Toni. She was a cool girl, and she didn't deserve to go out like that," he offered sympathetically.

I nodded my head and fought to hold back the tears that were now coming to my eyes. "No, she didn't!" I told him. I was so full of emotions, and I wondered if it would ever get any easier to talk about her without shedding tears.

"So, you said that you and Toni were close huh?" I asked.

"Yeah, we were. I actually had a little thing for her," he said with a slight chuckle.

"Hmm, I'm sure she would have been happy to know that if she were still alive," I said. "You seem like you're a nice guy."

"Nah, Toni was too stuck on her baby daddy, to give me a try," he said, and I looked at him in confusion.

"I don't think that's the case, because Toni and her baby daddy weren't even talking when she died," I said.

Tim furrowed his brows like he didn't understand what I had just said to him. " Oh, she was still talking to him," he said. "Matter fact, the night that she was killed, I had worked with her and was supposed to take her home, but she ended up getting a ride with him instead."

"Sam?" I asked in shock.

"I believe that's what she told me his name was." Tim said.

"What?" I said with a frown on my face. As far as I knew, Toni hadn't talked to Sam in a long time before she had passed away.

"He even squared up with me and everything, but Toni came to his defense. I remember being mad at her, because she had told me all about how he wasn't in her daughter's life, so I couldn't understand why she even wanted to be around him at all." Tim stated.

My mind started to wonder a mile a minute. The police never did check out anybody else, because we all had thought that Greg killed Toni. And the last thing that I heard from my mama regarding the case, was that they didn't have any leads yet.

"So, you're saying that Toni was with Sam the night she was killed?" I asked him for clarification.

"Like I said, she told me that she was gonna get a ride with him, and that she didn't need me to take her home." He said.

Oh, my god, it had to be him, I thought.

"Tim, can I ask you why you never went to the police with this?" I asked.

"Because the news said that y'all mama's boyfriend killed her, and then killed himself. I figured that was the end of it." he replied, and I shook my head in disbelief, because now the shit was starting to add up.

"Tim, thank you for telling me." I said and got ready to walk away.

"Laydii, is it something else to Toni's death?" he asked.

"No, I just didn't know that she had been in contact with him is all." I lied. I wasn't about to tell him that Greg wasn't the one that had killed Toni. If he were to find out, then it would be from the police when they restarted their investigation.

"Oh, okay. Well take care of yourself," he said.

I half smiled at him and pushed my cart over to the next aisle. When I didn't see him anymore, I left my cart where it was and ran out of the door as fast as I could. I needed to get home quick, so that

I could tell John what was up. I could bet my last dollar that Sam had killed my sister. Why he had killed her and Greg, I didn't know, but from the information that Tim had just given me, I knew that he was responsible.

23

Aaron

Later that night….

"So, what you want to eat?" I asked Ohani.

Ohani was a chick that I had met about three weeks back. I had needed something to distract me from thinking of Keya, and I figured fuckin with somebody else would do the trick. I wasn't planning to get into a relationship with her or anybody else, but it didn't hurt to kick it here and there.

"How about a big, fat cheeseburger!" she smiled.

"You pretty easy to please, huh?" I briefly glanced over at her. I could appreciate a lady that didn't try to dig all in a man's pocket. Not that I didn't have it to give, but if you asked most broads what they wanted to eat, they would have just said lobster, or something else that they couldn't even pronounce just so they could run back to their friends and brag by saying a nigga tricked off them.

"I am! It doesn't take a whole lot a frills and thrills to keep me happy," she said licking her red-stained lips.

I couldn't even lie; shorty was the truth. Ohani was about 5'5 with dark brown skin, chinky eyes and a nice body. Her hair was in some of those *Poetic Justice*-style braids, and they were this auburn color. Normally, I preferred for my women to wore their natural hair, but the braids actually looked good on her.

When we first met, I had stopped by the liquor store to get another bottle of Hen. She was bent over looking at the bottles of wines, and me and every other guy in the store were staring at that ass. When she stood up, I caught a glimpse of her face, and I thought she was sexy as hell to me. We ended up exchanging numbers, and tonight was the first time that I was taking her out.

"Well, I know that you just got back to the area, but have you had the chance to eat at this place called Memphis BBQ," I asked.

She had told me that she was born in Memphis, but had grown up in Florida. She moved there with her dad when she was just ten years old. She said that she didn't have a good relationship with her mom, because they had never really bonded. Ohani admitted, that she had only moved back here, because the last relationship that she was in, didn't work out, and she just needed a different atmosphere.

"Hell, yeah! They got some of the best burgers in town," she said. "Me and one of my girlfriends went there when I first moved back."

"Yo, you my type of chick. I love eating at that place." I told her, and then I felt my phone vibrating in my pocket. I pulled it out, and when I saw that it was John, I answered it. "What's good, boy?" I said into the phone.

"Aye, dawg where you at?" he asked me.

I glanced over at Ohani, who was looking in her phone. "Just getting ready to grab a bite to eat. Why, wassup? I asked.

"Mane, I need you to stop by the crib. Some new shit just came up that I think you might want to hear," he said, and I sensed the urgency in his tone.

"Aight, I'm headed that way," I told him and hung up. I pulled my car into an empty lot and turned around. When I was back on the street, I drove a little while and jumped on interstate 240. I glanced back over to Ohani, and she was still looking at her phone. I didn't have time to drop her off, so I figured I would just take her with me. That way, once I left, we could continue with our plans.

"I hope you don't mind, but I need to stop by my boy's house for just a minute, and as soon as I'm done, I promise I'mma get you that burger," I told Ohani with a smile.

"Good! Cause I can just taste it," she looked at me seductively. I smirked, because I knew what she was insinuating. We hadn't gone there yet, because things were still so new, and I had been trying to respect her, but if she kept trying to entice me, I might be forced to give her ass what she was asking for.

I exited the interstate and drove down White Street for about five minutes. When I got to the condos that John lived in, I made a right and pulled up alongside Jeremy's Benz. I cut the car off and turned to Ohani. "You gone stay in here, or you want to come inside?" I asked.

"I'll come inside," she said.

"Aight, it shouldn't take that long," I told her, as we walked up to the door. I knocked a few times and waited for somebody to answer. After about a minute or so, Laydii opened the door for me, and when she saw Ohani by my side, she frowned her face up like she had smelled something bad.

Laydii abruptly walked off without saying anything to either of us. Me and Ohani walked inside, and I thought about how dumb it was for me to bring this girl to Keya's best friend house.

"John, you better get your damn friend before I cuss his ass out," I heard Laydii say, as I walked towards the living room. I sighed and stopped walking.

"Look, I didn't even think about how bringing you to Keya's best friend house would cause drama. If you feel uncomfortable with the situation, you can go wait in the car, and I should be right out." I told her. I was trying to make it easy on her, because I knew that shit was not gonna turn out good if she stuck around.

"It's okay, I would probably feel the same way if we had been dating and you brought a girl to my people's house," she said.

"You sure?" I asked her.

Ohani gave me a reassuring smile, and we walked into the living room. The minute we stepped inside the room, all eyes were on us. Jeremy, Laydii, and John were all occupying one couch, and when my eyes drifted over to the loveseat, I saw Keya and my daughter sitting there. Keya had a frown on her face, and it immediately made me feel like shit for taking Ohani there.

"Wassup, y'all!" I spoke, while making eye contact with Keya. She still had that look on her face.

"Hello, everyone!" Ohani waved. My niggas spoke back, but Laydii and Keya just stared at her.

"Aye, this Ohani. Ohani, these my people," I said. "And that little woman right there is my daughter." I pointed at Aniya.

"Awe, Aaron, she is too cute, and she looks just like you with those cute little dimples," Ohani smiled, and I saw Keya roll her eyes.

I told Ohani to take a seat in one of the chairs, and I walked over to my daughter and picked her up.
"What's up, Daddy's baby?" I asked tickling her side. Normally, Aniya would laugh when I did that, but this time, she just covered her face with her tiny hands. She was squirming inside of my arms for me to let her down, and it kind of fucked me up to see my daughter react to me in that way. "What's wrong with, Daddy's baby? I can't get no love?" I asked.

"She tends to act like that when strangers are around?" Keya said with an attitude.

I placed my daughter back into her arms and ignored the hateful daggers that she was throwing my way. "So, wassup? Y'all said that you needed to talk, right?" I said. John glanced behind me and looked over at Ohani. He was trying to let me know that what he had to say, couldn't be discussed in front of her. I walked over to Ohani and told her that we were going to step to another room and that I would be right back out. She slowly nodded her head, and I could tell that she was uncomfortable. Hell, it wasn't anything that I could do about it at this point. I tried to offer her a way out when we first got there, but she said that she could handle it. The way I looked at it, was the damage was already done.

"Let's go talk," I told them, and everybody got up, including Keya. She placed my daughter on her hip and walked ahead of me. I couldn't help but notice the tight ass jeans that she was wearing. It was almost as if they were painted on. Keya knew that I would have never gone for her wearing some shit like that, but since I was probably on her shit list right now, I was going to give her ass a pass.

"Wassup?" I asked after we were all inside of Laydii and John's spare bedroom. I was curious to know just what they had to tell me, since normally we wouldn't even discuss business in front of the women. I figured it had something to do with them, since they were in here too.

Nobody said anything, but finally, John told Laydii to give me the news. She stared at him with an evil look, but slowly turned her head back towards me.

"Okay, when I was at the store earlier, I ran into one of Toni's old coworkers, Tim, and he was telling me how the night that Toni was killed, he was supposed to take her home." She said.

"Okay," I said, not getting where she was going with this.

"Well, Tim told me that the reason he didn't take Toni home was because, when he went outside, Toni was out there with Sam." Laydii said, and I raised both of my eyebrows. Now, she was finally getting somewhere with this, but I needed to let her finish before I jumped to conclusions.

"He said that Sam was talking shit, saying that he was gonna be the one to take Toni home, and that when he left, Toni was still with him.

I allowed her words to sink in, and what it all boiled down to, was that Sam was probably responsible for killing Laydii's sister, too. When I was in jail, I had heard about Toni's death, and at the time, I remember thinking how that shit about their mama's boyfriend killing Toni and then himself didn't make any sense to me. Then the situation further confused me, when John told me that the boyfriend hadn't killed himself. Now with this information, it starting to sound more and more like it was a set-up on Sam's part. Just like he had done me.

"Laydii, I didn't know your little sister like that, but I'mma make sure that muthafucka pay for what he did to her, and that's my word," I said. She didn't reply, and I knew that she was still a little pissed about me bringing Ohani to her house. I could understand, and that's why I wanted to speak to Keya alone so that we could clear the air.

"Aye, can y'all give me and Keya a little minute?" I asked. Of course, my niggas got up without a problem, but Laydii looked at me like I had shit on my face.

"Laydii, I promise that I just want to talk to her for a minute, and that's it," I said, but she still wouldn't budge.

"Mane, get your ass up," John said. He walked over to her and tried to grab her by the arm, but Laydii snatched it back.

"Don't put your hands on me, John!" she snapped. "Now, I guess since nobody else is going to address this shit, I will. Aaron, you are dead ass wrong. How you gon' bring another bitch over to my house knowing how I would feel about it? Regardless if you and Keya are together or not, I don't like that shit. Then not only that, you tell her that you ain't messing with her, not even a week after she gets released from the hospital. Like wow, you couldn't even make sure she was straight first?" Laydii asked why hunching her shoulder at the same time.

"Aye mane, chill out. That's yo fucking problem; always getting into other folk's business, and this ain't got shit to do with you," John said.

"It's cool, bro. I deserved that shit! I had no right bringing her here knowing that you are cool with Keya. That's my bad, but your girl already knows why I ain't trying to go there with her no more, and she definitely played a part in me making that decision," I said.

"What! Aaron, are you fucking kidding me right now?" Keya said. She placed Aniya down on the bed, and stood with her hands on her hips. "So, I believed Sam, and yes I was wrong for that. But the minute I make a one mistake, you're ready to just say fuck me? Well, let's not talk about the fact that you fucked my best friend, and I forgave your ass." Keya said almost like she was foaming at the mouth.

"Don't try to hit me with that shit, cause you know that happened before me and you even got together," I said pissed about the fact that she would bring that up.

"It doesn't matter, you still hid." Keya was immediately cut off by Jeremy.

"Whoa, whoa, whoa" he said, like he was our daddy or some shit. He had a pissed off look on his face, and he had his eyes casted on all of us. Had this been any other time, I would have laughed at how he was trying to take control, but now wasn't the time for jokes.

"This shit is going way too far. We done already moved passed all of that other bullshit, so ain't no reason to bring it back up." He said, and I was with him on that. I still couldn't believe Keya.

When I looked at John, he was shooting daggers at me, and when he finally walked out of the room, he bumped my shoulder as he passed by. I wasn't going to trip on that though, because he had a right to be pissed off.

"Look, I'm sorry, Laydii. I should have never said that, but he got me fucked up. Can you run me home please, because I'm gonna end up slapping the shit out of him!" Keya said while glowering at me.

"Okay!" Laydii whispered softly, and I could tell that she was just as shocked as I was that Keya had brought up our old dirt. Especially since moments before, she had just been chewing my ass out on Keya's behalf. I looked over at Keya and she rolled her eyes at me. After grabbing up our daughter, she stormed out of the room and Laydii followed behind her.

"And you might want to come get your little girlfriend, because she looks a little lonely in here by herself," Keya yelled from the living room.

"Damn, this shit is bad," I said to Jeremy. I had forgot just that fast that Ohani was still in the next room.

"Yeah, I don't know what was going through your mind when you made that decision. But why don't you go drop shorty off right now, and we can all link up to discuss that little situation. We can deal with that other shit at a later time," Jeremy said.

"You right. I'mma go drop her off and meet you at the spot. Hopefully, John ain't too pissed to meet us there," I said. I stood up and walked out of the room to where Ohani was. When she saw me, she had this blank expression on her face.

"You ready?" I asked.

"I am," she replied, and quickly stood up.

I lead her out of the house, and when we got into my car, Ohani stared out of the window. I felt bad, and it was like I was pissing folks off left and right.

"Aye, I apologize for putting you in that situation. I really wasn't thinking when I came over here with you, and I definitely didn't know that she would be here." I said. Even though I had made Ohani aware of Keya and my daughter, I'm sure she wasn't expecting to meet her under such circumstances. My life was so complicated, and maybe I had made the mistake of even talking to Ohani in the first place.

Ohani finally turned her head towards me and looked into my eyes. "Yes, that was very awkward, and I know that we won't be having family dinners together anytime soon," she said while cracking a small smile. Her response sort of threw me for a loop.

"Damn, so you saying that shit ain't make you want to run the other way?" I asked curiously.

"Nope! Cause if all it takes is for one situation to pop off, and I'm gone, then that should make you question my motive for being here in the first place," she said.

This shit was crazy how Ohani hadn't known me for all that long, yet she had told me that she wanted to stick around. Me and Keya had been down with each other for a few years, and every time a situation has popped off with us, she was quick to leave me behind it. Ohani words played in my head again, and it definitely gave me something to think about.

Out of nowhere, Ohani leaned over the console and grabbed my face with both her hands. Pulling me closer to her, she placed a wet kiss on my lips. I bit down on her bottom lip, and then pulled it into my mouth while sucking on it. Her lips were even softer than they looked, and the kiss made a nigga rock up some. After we had been kissing for a little minute, she pulled back with a smile on her face. With the tip of her thumb, Ohani rubbed any traces of lipstick off my lips.

"Go ahead, and take me home before I do something that I might regret," she winked.

I smirked, then put my car into drive. As I drove off, my hand traveled over to hers, and I gently caressed it. Ohani had me intrigued, and it was taking me to a place that I had only gone with Keya. I didn't know what the future held for us, but for the time being, I would let shit flow how it flowed.

24
John

A few hours later….

When Keya said something about Aaron and Laydii fuckin, I had to get up out there, and quick. That shit still bothered me to this day. I know it was supposed to be in the past, but every time it was brought up, it made me think about it like it had just happened recently. I wasn't really mad at Aaron; it was Laydii who had me pissed. Call it a double standard or whatever, but a woman was never supposed to fuck off no matter how much her nigga cheated. She could leave him, and maybe try to teach him a lesson that way, but fucking with somebody else to get revenge; that shit was no go.

After I had been driving for about an hour without a destination, I found myself pulling into the apartment complex that Kim lived in. I wasn't sure why I had chosen her house for my escape, but it was like my car had just put me in that spot. *Fuck it,* I said with my door open. Since I was already here, I figured that I might as well get out and see what she was up to. I had been to a few of Kim's doctor visits, and I had to admit that I was kind of getting use to the idea of having a son. I was still gonna make sure to get a DNA test, but it was like I was starting to form a bond, and the little nigga wasn't even here yet. Don't get me wrong, I was happy as hell that Laydii was having my daughter, because I wanted to be that man that she could always depend on. But it was just something different when a man had a son.

When I made it up to the door, I told myself that I still had time to get my ass back into that car, and leave. I was going back and forth with myself when Kim's door suddenly swung open.

"Ahh," she screamed, and swung the trash bag that was in her hand.

"Aye, chill out with that shit, girl," I said taking a step back.

"John, what the hell! Boy what are you doing just standing at my door? You almost gave me a damn heart attack," she said dramatically, and I laughed.

"Yo ass so dramatic," I said as my eyes slowly roamed her body. She had on some little ass shorts that looked more like panties. I couldn't front, even in Kim's pregnant state, I could still see her figure, and it was right. The only thing that had gotten big was her round belly.

"Whatever! But what are you doing here?" Kim asked again.

"I really don't know. Matter fact I'mma get my ass up out of here," I said and started to walk off, but Kim grabbed my arm.

"Don't go," she said with a firm grip on my arm. I stared at her, and then looked out at my car. Against my better judgment, my feet started to make their way into her apartment.

"Wait, toss this in the garbage for me," Kim said holding up the bag that was in her hands. I took it from her and walked over to the dumpster that was right across from her apartment. When I got back, Kim had left the door slightly ajar so I stepped inside. Her place was really clean, and it smelled good. Kim was sitting on the couch watching TV, so I walked over and sat down beside her.

"You having problems with your girl, ain't you?" Kim asked out of nowhere.

"We good. What would make you say that?" I asked.

"Because that's the only time a man comes around another woman when he already has a woman at home," Kim stated.

"What you an expert on men, or some shit?" I asked, and she giggled.

"No, but I can tell when there is trouble in paradise," she said, but I didn't say anything. Kim must have realized that I didn't want to talk about my relationship, because she changed the subject. "So, I got some snacks, if you're hungry," she offered. She was starting to know a nigga well, because every time we were around each other, I was looking for the snacks. It was like I had picked up Laydii's pregnancy symptoms. Hell, maybe even Kim's too.

"What kind of snacks?" I asked and bent down to take my shoes off. For some reason, I just felt comfortable inside of her place. I didn't plan to fuck her or nothing like that, but a little time away from Laydii, would do me some good. After Kim ran down a long list of shit that she had, I told her to bring me a couple bags of chips, some cookies, and a drink. Kim stood up from the couch, and when she walked away, I stared at her ass. It was jiggling as she walked, and I had to tell myself to calm the fuck down.

After a few minutes, Kim finally returned with some snacks for me and her. For a couple of hours, we chilled out and watched a few movies. Then just as the last movie went ended, I felt my phone vibrating inside of my pocket. When I saw that it was Laydii calling, I knew that I had to get my ass home. I had been gone for hours, and was surprised that she hadn't called before now.

"Aye, I'mma get up with you later. Preciate you opening your home to me," I told Kim as I got ready to make my way home.

"Yeah, sure," she said and looked away.

"What's wrong with you?" I asked. I had a feeling on why her mood had suddenly changed, and that let me know right then that I couldn't hang at her house anymore. She was already starting to get in her feelings.

"Nothing, I will see you later," she said as she held the door open for me.

"Aight, just hit me up if you need something. But only if it's important," I said, and Kim slammed the door in my face. I guess she was mad, but I didn't care about that. My position was still the same, and she didn't have any other choice, but to deal with it, if she wanted me around.

25
Keya

I was so fucking pissed that I couldn't even play with my baby like she wanted me to. Aniya was splashing her little hands in the water, and usually that would make me laugh when she did that, but now I was just too consumed with thoughts of Aaron and that woman to enjoy our time. She appeared to be older than him, but I must admit she was actually pretty. I tried my best to find something wrong with her, but I couldn't find a thing. That made me even madder, and even though he and I weren't together, it still pissed me off that he was talking to somebody else. I knew that they had probably had sex, because she seemed like the type that would give up easily. "Oooh," I said aloud. How could Aaron do that to me? Aniya looked up at me as if I were crazy.

"Are you ready to get out of here my little chocolate drop?" I asked her. Aniya ignored me as she continued to splash around in the water. My baby was getting so big, and was just a couple of months shy of her 1st birthday. I had been racking my brain over the type of party I wanted to throw for her. We didn't have many kids around her age, so I knew whatever I decided wouldn't be very big. I leaned down and lifted the stopper in the bathtub for the water to drain out.

"Okay, baby girl; bath's time over," I said, while wrapping the towel around her little body. I stood up and walked with her to my bedroom. After laying her down on the bed, I took the pamper that I already had laid out and put it on her. Aniya kicked and squirmed, and I had to tussle with her just to get the sleeper over her head. I finished plaiting Aniya's long, curly hair and placed her on the bed beside me. She loved for me to read to her, so I picked up a book from off the nightstand and began to read it. I heard my phone beep with a text, and I picked it up. When I looked at it the screen, there was a text message from Aaron, so I read it.

Aaron: Aye, I apologize about what happened, but did you have to bring that other shit up?

Me: You left me with no other choice.

Aaron: How is that?

Me: because you conveniently forgot that you hurt me, and I forgave your ass. Look, just leave me alone and tend to your new bitch!

Aaron: you something else, but what my daughter doing?

I didn't even bother to reply to Aaron's last text, because he was playing games. How could he just go out and get somebody so soon. I understood that he was mad that I had left him while he was still in jail, but he needed to understand that, at the time, I felt I had a good reason. Him bringing another woman around to throw in my face was not the way to handle things. Suddenly my phone started to ring, and I snatched it up. *This nigga,* I thought as I looked at the caller id.

"What Aaron?" I snapped into the phone.

"Aye, you need to chill with that damn attitude," he said.

"Yeah whatever! Why are you calling me, when you know that I'm not feeling you right now? Didn't you get the memo when I didn't reply to your text?" I said.

"Keya, shit ain't even that deep with me and her, so I don't even know why you trippin." Aaron said, and I had to pull the phone away from my ear, because I just knew that I hadn't heard him correctly.

"Aaron, I don't care how serious you are with her. You should have never brought her around period us period. You introducing her to our daughter without talking it over with me first. What if I had brought a guy to John and Laydii's house, and had him all in our friends faces. Or better yet, in Aniya's face? What would you have done?" I asked.

"Keya, don't get fucked up," he said.

"You are so fuckin selfish and completely missing the point that I am trying to make. I'm not thinking about another man right now. My only point was to say that, if I had done something like that, you would be mad, and would have felt that I was purposely trying to hurt you. You're dead wrong, and you know it." I said.

"I admit that I was wrong, but what was your reason for talking back to Sam? Our shit was good, so I'm still trying to figure out how you believed him enough to turn your back on me." Aaron said.

I didn't have any words for that, and I could hear the hurt in his voice. "I'm sorry, Aaron," I whispered. "But when are you going to forgive me and stop throwing that in my face. If I could go back and change what I did, I promise you that I would, but you are not the only one who was affected by this situation," I said.

After I said that, the line became silent, and I had to look at my phone to see if Aaron was still there. When I saw that he was, I put my phone back to my ear. "Hello, are you gonna say something?" I asked.

"Look, we need to sit down and talk this shit out. How about I scoop you and Aniya tomorrow, and we can go out for lunch?" he said.

"I don't know, Aaron. Maybe we should just keep everything between us about Aniya. You're still mad at me, and I'm still pissed about how you disrespected me. Maybe we shouldn't be around each other right now," I said.

"Regardless if we never get together again, Keya, we still need to be able to hold a conversation for the sake of our daughter. Besides that, I don't want to fight with you anymore," he said.

I didn't want to go back and forth about this anymore, so I just decided to give him what he wanted.

"Okay, you can come pick us up." I finally said.

"What time you want me to come through?" he asked.

"You can come tomorrow afternoon. That way, I can go up to the school and see about re-enrolling for the next semester," I told him.

"Aight, I will see y'all then," he said, and we ended the call.

The next day...

"Do you want to order some mashed potatoes for her?" Aaron asked me. We were having lunch at the Texas Roadhouse. I normally loved coming here, because their steaks were so good, but this time, I really didn't have an appetite.

"No, it will be fine. She can just eat off my plate since I don't plan to eat much anyway," I replied.

Things were sort of awkward between us, and besides the small talk that Aaron made, I didn't have much to say to him.

"Did you get everything settled with school?" he asked.

"I got everything handled," I said, while looking down at my phone.

"Keya, I don't want to feel like we can't even hold a normal conversation. I know that shit ain't that bad between us, is it?"

"Well, what do you want me to do?" I asked.

"First, you can start with putting your phone down, and then we can go from there." Aaron said.

I put my phone down onto the table and gave Aaron my undivided attention. "Happy!" I said with a fake smile.

"Actually, I am. Now, I been meaning to ask you something, but I could never think of a way to ask you," he said and paused. Fuck it, here it is. Beside those bruises that Sam put on your face, did he touch you in any other way?"

A lump formed in my throat, and I did my best to swallow it back down without him noticing. That would have been a dead give away. Aaron stared at me while waiting for an answer, but I didn't know what to do. "What are you talking about, did he touch me. In what way?" I asked.

"You know what I mean," he said.

"No," I lied easily. I know that it was wrong, but I just couldn't bring myself to tell him.

Aaron stroked his goatee as he continued to stare at me. "Are you sure, Keya? Cause I don't think that I believe you." He finally said.

"You have no choice but to believe it, because it's the truth." I hated lying to him about this, but he would never understand. I still felt this dirtiness about myself, so I'm sure he would be disgusted with me, too.

"Aight, if you say that's your word, then I guess I have to accept it."

"I guess you do?" I said. So, where's your little girlfriend?" I asked to change the subject.

"Come on, now; she ain't my girlfriend! I done already told you that shit ain't that deep with us." Aaron said.

"Okay!" I replied.

"Okay, what?"

"That you say she's not your girlfriend," I said shrugging.

He was just about to say something else, but the waitress brought our food out. We sat and ate our food in silence, and I was glad because it gave me time to think. When we were done, Aaron paid the bill while I gathered Aniya up. As we left the restaurant, Aaron got a call on his phone.

"Hello," he said with a smile on his face, and I rolled my eyes. I figured I knew who it was and thought that he was so disrespectful to answer while I was still with him.

"Well, I'mma be that way soon," he told the caller and ended the call.

When we got in the car, I played with my phone as a distraction. Aaron cut the radio down and tried to hold a conversation with me, but I was mad and didn't want him saying shit to me.

"What's wrong with you?" He asked.

"Nothing," was all that I offered. Aaron smirked and cut the radio back up. After a few minutes of driving, I noticed that we weren't going in the direction of my house. "Where are, we going? You know my house is the other way," I said.

"Keya, I know where your house is?"

"So why aren't you going that way?" I asked.

He didn't say anything, and he had this mischievous grin on his face. I dropped the subject, because clearly, he was up to something. We finally pulled up to a car lot, that held some of the most exotic, and expensive cars.

I know damn well he ain't about to shop for a car and me and my baby is with him, I thought.

As soon as we came to a stop, a salesman immediately walked up to Aaron's side of the car. "What's up, mane? You got her ready?" Aaron asked.

"Yes, she's right in the back," the salesman responded.

"Cool! Come on, Keya. Get out, and I'll grab Aniya," he said.

"Really, you couldn't have waited until you dropped us off before you did this?" I asked in disbelief.

"Nah, I need to handle this right now. So, come on get your ass out," he said, already grabbing Aniya out of her car seat.

I sighed, but reluctantly did as he asked. After taking a short walk to the back of the dealership, we came upon another lot of cars. The salesman led us over to a row filled with newer model Lexus trucks.

"Here she is right here," the guy said pointing to a beautiful, black, Lexus GX SUV. I stared at the truck, while secretly admiring it. One thing I could say about Aaron was that, when it came to his cars, he spared no expenses.

"What you think about this truck, Keya?" Aaron asked.

"I mean, it's nice and all, but don't you think you got enough vehicles already?"

"A man can never have too many vehicles," he said, peering into the window of the truck. Aaron opened the door of the truck, and told me to look inside as well. As I looked around on the inside of the truck, I realized that it was even more beautiful than I had thought. It had leather seats with memory seating, a navigational system, sunroof, and a whole lot of other features. *This truck is the shit,* I thought.

"So, you really like it?" Aaron asked, as I continued to stare at the truck.

"Yes. I mean, it's nice as hell," I replied.

"What about you baby? You like it too?" Aaron asked Aniya, and she cracked a smile.

"Aight, well I guess that settles it. Keya, let's go get the paperwork to your new truck," he smiled.

I swung my head around so quick that I almost gave myself whiplash. "Quit playing, Aaron! You are not getting me this truck?" I said excitedly.

"Ain't nobody playing games with you, girl. All you gotta do is sign the paperwork, and it's yours." He said.

I looked at the sales guy, because I still thought that Aaron was playing some type of game with me.

"It's yours," he said. "He's been calling me all week to make sure that I had it ready for you guys. You are really lucky to have a husband that loves you so much," he said.

Husband? I thought. I looked at Aaron, and he winked at me.

"Anyways," I said. "But are you seriously getting me this truck?" I asked again.

"Yes girl. Damn! I need to make sure that you and my daughter have a reliable vehicle to get around in. And no offense, but that little car that your daddy got you riding in ain't gone cut it." He said, referring to the old Ford Taurus that my dad had given me.

"Wait, you're saying that my car isn't good enough?" I asked placing my hands on my hips.

"Exactly!" he replied, and he and the sales guy both laughed. "Now, let's go take care of this paperwork so we can get out of this

man's hair. I'm sure he has other customers that he needs to get to."
Aaron said.

He handed me Aniya, and we all walked into the dealership. The sales guy led us to his office, and once we got in there, I signed all the paperwork needed to obtain the truck. When it was time to pay, Aaron took out a wad of money and paid cash for my truck. That made me wonder to myself how much money was my baby daddy really sitting on. And then once we had the paperwork squared away, the salesman had someone to bring my truck around to the front of the dealership. Aaron got Aniya's car seat out of his truck and placed it into mine. I thanked him a million times for my truck, but all he told me was that it was his obligation to always make sure that me and his daughter was straight. When he saw that we we're good to leave, Aaron told me that he would see us later. He kissed Aniya goodbye, and then he was on his way. As I watched him leave, I fought to blink back the tears that were swelling in my eyes. Although he had gotten me such a nice truck, I would have passed on it, if I could have had him instead.

26
Aaron

One week later....

I looked over the shipment that I had just gotten and ran my hand down my face. My street soldiers needed re-ups like yesterday, but it was like I couldn't even focus long enough to get my work out. On top of all that, I still needed to find Sam, and it was fucking with my head that I couldn't find this one nigga. I ain't never been off my square like I had been over the last few months, and if I was being honest with myself, all this shit came about when I started messing with Keya. She had my head clouded and was causing my pockets to take some hits. Granted, she wasn't responsible for her punk ass ex coming at us first, but I couldn't help but to think how things would be for me had I not started messing around with her in the first place.

But then I wouldn't have my daughter, and honestly, I couldn't think of a life without Keya in it either. Things weren't always bad between us; it's just that I didn't know if we could get back to our happy place. My phone vibrated on the table bringing me out of my thoughts, and I looked at the caller ID. When I saw that it was Ohani calling, I placed the call on speaker, and reclined in my seat.

"Wassup, Ohani? You missing a nigga already?" I asked, because I had just spoken to her a few hours prior.

"You know I am! And that's why I wanted to know if I'll be able to see you today?" she said.

"Probably not, because I got some things to handle. Maybe I can take a rain check, though," I said.

"That's too bad," she whined into the phone.

"Why is that?" I asked with my interest piqued.

"Because, I had this new lingerie set, and I needed to get a second opinion on it. I mean, it looks nice
to me, but you never know," she purred into the phone.

I chuckled lightly and thought about how her ass was big business. Ohani was thirty-one, which made her like four-and-a-half years older than me. I had a birthday coming up the next month and would be turning twenty-seven. So, in my eyes, it was sort of like I was messing with an older woman. Which by the way wasn't a bad thing. It just meant that she was more experienced at what she did, and I could definitely learn to appreciate that.

"Well, maybe I can wrap those plans up a little early," I told her.

"That would be good. Just call and let me know what time you're coming through so that I can be ready for you," she said.

"Aight, I got you," I told her, and we ended the call.

Just as I ended the call with Ohani, my phone vibrated again, and this time when I looked at the caller ID, I saw that it was Keya calling.

"Wassup, baby mama," I teased her. She hated when I called her that, but I still did it.

"Aaron, can you come and get me? I locked my keys inside of my truck," she said sounding a little exasperated.

I immediately sat up in my seat. "Aight, where you at?" I asked.

"I'm at the Shell station on Poplar. I was about to get into my truck when I noticed that I had locked them inside."

"Fuck you doing out there?" I asked.

"Can you just come on, please?" she said, and I could hear the frustration in her tone.

"I'm already heading that way, but you still didn't answer my question?" I told her, while jogging out to my car. Climbing inside, I cranked it up and sped off.

"Well, if you must know, I had a job interview today." She answered.

"You had a job interview?" I repeated.

"Yes, did you forget that I had bills that needed to be paid. Besides, those funky muthafuckas at the distribution center let me go when all... when that stuff went down with Sam," she said in a low voice.

That shit infuriated me, how much that nigga had affected our lives. Keya had been out here working some part-time job at a warehouse company while trying to take care of my daughter and go to school. Now she was trying to find another damn job when all she should be focusing on is her education and making sure that my daughter was straight.

"Keya, I hope you don't think that you're going back to that apartment?" I asked.

"No, I'm not going back to that specific apartment, but am gonna find me another one. I can't live with my parents forever. And besides, me and Aniya like having our own space," she said.

"C'mon, now, Keya. It wouldn't take but a couple of knocks on somebody's door, and he could find out where you and my daughter are resting at," I said. This was the shit that made me mad with her. It was like she acted so green when it came to this street shit. Her pops had definitely sheltered her ass a little too much.

"So where am I supposed to go then, Aaron? I already told you that I don't want to be back at home with my parents. I mean I love them and all, but they are smothering me," she said.

I pulled my car into the lot of the gas station where Keya stood with her back to the road. She had on this black, two-piece pants suit with some high heels, and she was looking good as fuck. The pants were hugging her thighs and ass, and the short haircut that she had just gotten was looking good on her.

"Hello!" Keya said into the phone when she realized that I had gotten quiet.

"Turn around," I told her while easing out of my car.

Keya spun around on her heels, and when she realized that I was there, she ended the call, and put her phone away. Folding her hands over her breast, she stared at me.

"Why didn't you tell me that you were pulling up?" she asked.

"Because I wanted to look at you for a minute," I said and winked.

Keya blushed but quickly looked off. I walked closer to her truck and placed my hand on the doorknob. I pressed the little button and the lights flashed, indicating the doors were now unlocked. When I did that, Keya looked at me strangely.

"Um, how did you do that?" she asked.

"This truck is a keyless entry. If you push the button right here, and your keys are nearby, then it will open," I told her. Since I had the spare key to her truck, she was able to open the door.

"Oh, I knew that," she said.

I laughed, because her ass knew that she was lying. Keya never did take the time to figure shit out; she just went with what she knew. With her door still opened, I invaded her personal space. I placed my hand on the top of the truck and leaned in. She slid back in her seat and fiddled with her keys that were lying inside of the cup holder.

"What? Why are you looking at me like that?" she finally asked.

"I'm still trying to figure out why you didn't come to me for money if you needed some," I said to her.

"Because, the only time that I should come to you is when it involves Aniya. Other than that, I can handle things on my own," she said.

"Aye, don't insult me like that again. If it concerns you, then it concerns my daughter. Look, how about we do this then, since you feel that you can't take my money. You and Aniya come stay with m-." I tried to say, but she cut me off.

"Oh no!" she said waving her hands.

"Wait, let me finish what I got to say first, before you starting yelling no," I said.

"Okay, what you gotta say?" she asked.

"Now, you say that you don't want to be at your folk's house, and you know that I have all those rooms. You and Aniya could just come and stay with me. Aniya can be comfortable in her room, and you can take one of the guest rooms, until we figure this shit out. I need to focus while I'm out here, and I can't do that if I don't know that you and my daughter are safe."

As she stared into my eyes, I could tell that she was thinking about my proposition. I placed my hand on her beautiful face and gently stroked it. "Let us just handle this shit with that nigga, and when everything is good again, you can move anywhere you want to. If it's in the city of Memphis anyway," I told her with a slight chuckle.

"Alright, but what about your girlfriend?" she asked.

"Aye, what I tell you about that shit? She ain't my girlfriend, so you don't need to worry about her," I said.

"But you're still messing with her, right?" she asked.

"I'm not messing with her like that." I lied. I didn't want to admit that I still dealt with Ohani, because I didn't need Keya getting all in her feelings.

"Hmm. Yeah, aight!" she said.

"Yo ass a trip. But check it, follow me to the crib, and we can go pick Aniya up from daycare and then go get y'all stuff." I told her. Oh, and it's something else that I needed to run by you too."

"What's that?" she asked.

"Tomorrow, we're gonna go to the gun range and get you some practice with shooting. I know you think that you can handle a gun, because you shot somebody, but that was just luck, and we need to make sure you know how to handle a gun properly," I said.

"Wait, wait. You are doing way too much now." Keya said.

"Nah, you can never be too cautious. If somebody come for you and Aniya, you need to be able to protect yourself. And another thing, don't be out here riding around like everything is good. You already know that we haven't found this nigga, and I don't need you busting any moves without telling me first. More than likely, I'll probably put Detrick on tailing you around anyway. But until, I figure out what I'mma do, make sure you check in with me first. And I'm not saying that to keep tabs, is more so for your protection," I partially told the truth.

"Okay, that'll be cool. And you're right, I'll make sure to be more careful, and let you know when I go out" she said, and I thought that was pretty easy. Keya's ass was normally stubborn, and would do the exact opposite of what you told her.

Once I saw that she was secure in her truck, I headed over to my car and hopped inside. I waited for her to drive out of the parking lot and then I pulled out behind her. *I guess I'mma have to get up with Ohani some other day,* I thought.

27

Keya

Two days later....

"See this is how you hold the gun, Keya," Aaron said as he got behind me and positioned my hands around the gun. His touch felt so good, and it made my vagina pulsate a little. Besides the occasional hugs that Aaron would give me, we hadn't been this close to each other in a long time, and I didn't realize how good it would feel to be back inside of his arms again.

"You listening, Keya?" He asked bringing me back from my thoughts.

"Um, yes I'm listening." I said and focused on the target in front of me.

"Aight, now the kickback may be a little strong, but you have to remember that you control the gun; don't let it control you. And try your best to get as close to the target as possible," he said.

Aaron stepped back, and I did my best to tune out the other guns that were going off around me. I closed one of my eyes, like I had seen done in the movies, and gently squeezed down on the trigger.

Pow, Pow, Pow!

I let off three shots back to back, and with each shot that I took, I got closer to the target. I was proud of myself but still didn't like that I had to deal with guns. But I guess it was better to know how to use one, than not to. Like Aaron had said, I just never knew if I needed to use one to protect me and Aniya. After we were done with target practice, Aaron had gotten me a small, semi-automatic pistol. It was silver and black, and he told me to keep it with me at all times. After we had left the gun range, he took me to get my gun permit so that I could be registered to carry my new gun.

When we left from getting my gun permit, we stopped by the daycare and got Aniya. I told Aaron to stop by the Walmart so that we could get her some pampers. When we walked into Walmart, Aaron grabbed a basket and placed Aniya inside of it. I went ahead of them to the baby aisle, because I wanted to be in and out. After grabbing a case of pampers, I walked over and grabbed some baby wipes. Aaron came up behind me with the basket, and I put what I had in my hands inside of it.

"That's all she needs?" he asked.

I believe so," I said, while trying to think if it was anything else that I needed to grab while we were there. When I couldn't think of anything, I told Aaron that we could checkout. We walked over to the register, and Aaron loaded the items onto the belt. After the cashier had us rung up, he paid for the items, and we headed out of the store.

"Oh, I just remembered that I needed to get something," I told Aaron, just as we made it to the door.

"Yo ass always forgetting something," he stared at me. "Go ahead; I will stay here with Aniya and the basket," he said, and I walked off. When I got on the aisle, where they kept the pads, tampons, and things like that, I grabbed a box of tampons and walked back to the register. After paying for my item, I walked back to where I left Aaron. He was in the middle of a conversation with some guy, but since their backs were to me, I couldn't tell who the guy was. I took my time making my way over, because Aaron could sometimes be a little long-winded. He knew damn near everybody, and whenever we went somewhere, people were always stopping to talk to him. As I got closer to them, I couldn't help but notice that the guy's build looked a little familiar. I didn't know if I was just jumping the gun with my assumptions, but something in my heart was telling me that I wasn't. I guess Aaron must have felt my presence, because he turned around and looked at me. When the guy turned around, we immediately locked eyes on one another. We both stared at each other as recognition set in, and then he told Aaron something and quickly jetted out of the door.

"C'mon, Keya. Why you just standing there staring? You didn't see me trying to get your attention?" Aaron asked, as he walked towards me with Aniya and the basket. "Aye, what's wrong with you?"

I was staring straight ahead, and my eyes had started to tear up.

"Keya, what the hell wrong with you?" Aaron gently grabbed my shoulder.

"Um, who was that you were talking to?" I forced myself to say.

"My nigga Harold that works for me; why?" he asked, but I couldn't open my mouth anymore.

"C'mon, mane. People staring at us; let's go outside," he said and pulled me and the basket outside. Once we were outside, he stopped and forced me to look at him. "Keya, I'm not gonna ask you again. What's wrong with you, and why did you ask me about Harold?" he said.

I swiped away my tears and looked at him. "Because, that was the guy that was with Sam when he kidnapped me," I said, and immediately Aaron eyes scanned the parking lot. I knew that he was looking for the guy, whose name I had just learned was Harold. But by now, he was long gone.

"Fuck, fuck, fuck," he yelled, and his rage caused me to jump and Aniya to whine.

People were looking at us like we were crazy. "Shhh. It's okay baby; calm down," I told Aniya as I gently rubbed her head.

Aaron snatched me by the arm and pulled me, and Aniya along. After strapping Aniya in her seat, and making sure that I was in,

Aaron hopped into the car and skated out of the lot. I had to grip the door handle just to hold on.

"Aaron, please slow down. Aniya is in here," I said, but he looked straight ahead.

"Please, you're scaring me," I said. Aaron slowed the car down a little, but not much as I would have liked him to. I just did my best to hold on, and every couple of minutes, I would check the backseat to make sure that my baby was okay. Her daddy was definitely on one, and I knew that the situation had him like that. We rode in silence, and after fifteen minutes, we finally pulled up to the house. When we got in the driveway, Aaron jumped out and left the car running. I walked to the door and unlocked it, while he grabbed Aniya and brought her into the house. He put her in my hands and walked back out to the car to get the box of pampers and wipes and brought them back in, too. Aaron tried to walk out of the door without saying anything to me, but I ran up behind him and grabbed hold of his arm.

"Where are, you going?" I asked.

"Keya, let me go. You already know where I'm going, and no, it's not up for debate," he said.

"Please, Aaron, don't go out and do anything that will get you back in jail," I pleaded.

"I'mma say it one more time; let my fucking arm go, so I can leave," he said, and I let go of his arm. I couldn't hold Aaron hostage, and I wasn't going to even try to negotiate with him, because his mind was already made up.

"Fine! Do what you gotta do, but just promise me that you will be careful?" I found myself saying, although in my heart, I didn't want him to leave. Aaron stared at me for a minute, and then without warning he leaned in and kissed mine and Aniya's forehead. He didn't say anything to me, as he turned around and jetted out the front door.

With Aniya, still in my arms, I walked over to the couch and took. At this point, I was starting to question everything, and everyone around us. It was like everybody had a motive, and it felt like I couldn't trust no damn body. Something had to give, because I didn't know how many more blows that I could take. I closed my eyes, and did something that I had found myself doing a lot lately. I prayed to God, and asked him to keep Aaron safe. And I also asked that he allow my life to return to how it was, before all this happened...back to the time when things were normal.

28
Laydii

"Bae, what you in here doing?" John asked, as he walked into the room that I was setting up for our baby's nursery.

"I'm just trying to get this nursery together," I told him, as I placed another pastel on the wall. I stepped back and looked over my work. The room was coming together nicely, but I still needed to add a few more things.

"You doing a good job, baby," John said gripping me around the waist and kissing my neck. He knew that was my spot. I turned around and looked at him.

"I know, but it would be nice if you would help me out," I said, and he sighed.

"Laydii, I can't look for this nigga, and do all this other shit that you want me to do, too. Why don't you call Keya over, and y'all get the room together?" He said.

"Excuse me? I didn't make a baby with Keya, and I thought that you would at least want to help me with fixing up your daughter's room," I said.

"Okay, you right, and as soon as I get back, you have my word that I'm going to help you more," he said.

"Whatever," I said waving my hand.

"Come here," John grabbed me around the waist. "My baby be missing, Daddy?" he said, and I laughed.

"Go ahead with that shit, boy. You are making me mad," I said with a playful pout.

"Seriously, I got you, baby," he said. "I know that I been out a lot, but it's so much shit going on that needs my attention right now, and I'm trying my best to handle those situations and give you the time you need too. Just hang in there with me, and we gonna get back on track in a minute," he said.

"I hear ya, but I will believe it when I see it," I said with a smirk. Just then, John's phone rang, and he pulled it out of his pocket and looked at the caller ID. After looking at the screen, he placed it back inside of his pocket without answering it.

"Look, I'mma about to go. Do you need something before I leave?" he asked.

"No, but who was that on the phone?" I said.

"That was Jeremy. He was probably just calling to see where I'm at. I'll just call him when I get in the car," he said, and his phone rang again. This time, he didn't even both look at his phone.

"Just answer the phone, and tell him that you're on the way," I said.

"What for, when I just told you that I will call him back when I get to my car," he snapped.

"John, I know that's not Jeremy on the phone, so who is it?" I asked. He was getting defensive, when all I had said was that he should answer his phone and tell Jeremy that he would be there soon. That was really suspicious to me, and I could almost bet that it wasn't him calling John's phone.

"I'm gone, Laydii, cause I see that you just want to argue, and I ain't got time for that," John said and tried to walk off, but I grabbed his arm and forced him to look at me.

"Why are you getting so defensive if it ain't nobody but Jeremy on the phone?" I asked with a raised brow.

"Because, I don't like how you trying to treat me like I'm a boy. I said that I would call him back, but you just gonna make me answer my damn phone." He snapped.

"Wait! I'm not trying to treat you like you're a boy. It is just a little suspicious to me how you're not answering his calls now, but any other time, you would answer them. Are you hiding something from me John?" I asked with my hands on my hips.

"Whatever, Laydii, I ain't got time for this shit. I'mma get up with you later," he said, as he stormed out of the room. He slammed the door when he left out, and I sat in the rocking chair. A few tears slipped from my eyes, as I tried to figure out what the hell had just happened. We hadn't argued like that in a long time, but his behavior was off to me. I stood up, walked into my bedroom, and grabbed my phone. After going to my contacts, I scrolled down and went to John's name so that I could shoot him a text message.

Me: What was that all about?

After sending the message, I placed the phone down and walked into the kitchen to fix myself something to drink. When I came back into the room, I saw that John still hadn't replied to my text message, so I sent him another one.

Me: Hello! You don't see my text?

Hubby: I'm busy, Laydii, and I ain't got time to go back and forth with you.

Me: I'm not trying to go back and forth with you. I just want to know why you are acting like that all of a sudden?

I waited for ten minutes, and he never replied to my text. With my phone in my hand, I walked out of the nursery because I was no longer in the mood to fix it up. That whole argument was nonsense, and it had ruined my day. Once I was inside my bedroom, I decided to take a quick shower to calm my nerves. I stayed in the shower for about fifteen minutes, before I got out. As soon as I got back into my room, I walked over and picked my phone up. I wanted to see if John had replied to my last message, but he hadn't. I put my phone on the nightstand and put my clothes on. After realizing that he wasn't going to respond, I laid across the bed and decided to take a nap. My mind was wandering, and I couldn't help but think that John was up to his old ways.

29

Aaron

Later that night….

"Find that muthafucka, and bring him to me!" I said pounding my fist onto the table. Harold was now missing, and nobody had been able to find him anywhere. When Keya told me that he was the one that was with Sam when he kidnapped her, I lost my damn mind. I had trusted that nigga, and all along, he had been plotting against me and my crew.

"Detrick, you brought this nigga in; you sure yo ass ain't plotting against me, too nigga?" I asked.

"Mane, you know me better than that, and you know that I wouldn't do no snake shit. I'm just as fucked up about this as you are. And I want to find that muthafucka and dead him damn myself," Detrick said.

"Fuck, I can't trust no muthafuckin body," I said. I picked up my bottle of Hen and took a huge gulp from it. I slammed the bottle down onto the table and it tilted a little.

"So, nobody knows where this nigga rest his head at? Where the baby mama lives or nothing?" I asked everybody.

"Aye, I looked everywhere, but that nigga is ghost," John said. "But to be honest, I sort of felt that it was something up with that nigga when he asked us how much longer we had to look for Keya."

"He asked y'all that shit, and you didn't think to tell me?" I roared. I couldn't understand how I had missed the signs, and now John was telling me that the nigga had basically shown his card, and he had failed to mention that to me.

"At the time, of course, I was looking at the nigga upside his head. I even asked Detrick how he knew him, and when he told me that Harold had looked out for him on a lil situation, I let the shit roll off my back. That was my bad, though, and I'mma make sure that we find him." John said.

"Damn right y'all gonna find that muthafucka and bring him back to me. I don't care how long it takes, or what y'all gotta put on hold, but I need him in my face within the next couple days, or shit is gonna get ugly for everybody," I said. I ain't never been this hard on my team, but they had basically dropped the ball. I knew for a fact that Harold had been setting us up, and I couldn't let this shit go. He had played a part in kidnapping Keya, and for that, his ass had to pay with his life.

"Aaron, I know that you might not trust me right now because of what Harold did, but I promise you man, that I didn't have shit to do with it, and I'm going to make it my business to find this nigga and bring him to you. He making me look bad out here, and I can't have folks thinking I'm on some snake shit." Detrick said.

"Detrick, you always been my lil hitter, and I ain't never doubted your ability to put in that work for me, but right now, your words don't mean shit. I need him found ASAP, and I'm through discussing it until he is. I locked my eyes on Detrick and waited to see if he would fold under pressure, but he held his head high. Detrick had been down with me for a minute, and I had never had any problems with him trying to cross me. For now, I would trust that he didn't have shit to do with this, but I was serious when I said if I found out that he did, he was getting dealt with too.

"Aight, you dismissed," I said, while lifting the bottle of Hen from the table. I took another long gulp of it. Jeremy was quiet, and I could feel his eyes on me as I drank from the bottle. I had a feeling what he was thinking, but right now, I didn't need him saying shit. I had started drinking heavily since I had been released from jail, but it wasn't anything that I couldn't control. Shit was just stressful right now, and I needed this drink to get my mind right.

"Aye, man, don't you think you might need to lay off that for a little minute? I mean, you been going kind of hard." Jeremy said.

"Nigga, don't even do that. I ain't got no problem if that's what you're trying to say." I told him.

"I'm saying, mane, every time I turn around, you hitting the bottle. Maybe you should take a little break. Spend some time with Keya and your daughter, and let me and John handle everything. I know she really needs you right now," Jeremy said, and I frowned.

"Fuck you mean take a break? Nigga, that muthafucka violated my shorty by kidnapping her, left my daughter in a house by herself, and had Keya folks not went over to her house when they did, Aniya might have ended up dead. I ain't about to take no break until I have their blood on my hands." I said.

"Aight, mane. My bad! I just thought that you needed a break, but since you said you good, I guess that's it." Jeremy said.

"I'm good, dawg, and I appreciate your concern, but you know that I can't let this shit go, until I find them niggas."

"I feel ya, man. But do you think that Detrick really got som' to do with this shit?" Jeremy asked.

"Nah, I don't think so. Harold just plotted on his ass, like he did the rest of us." I said.

"That's what I'm thinking, cause Detrick ain't even built like that. He been loyal to us from day one," John added.

"Yeah, I believe he loyal, but if I find out differently, then I'm killing his ass too. I don't give a fuck how long he been with us. Disloyalty will not be tolerated!" I said, and they both nodded their heads in agreement.

We chopped it up for a little while longer until I got ready to head to the crib. When I made it home, Keya was sitting in the living room on the couch watching TV. She had on some little shorts, that exposed her thighs, and a fitted tee. Keya had gained her weight back, and even a little more, but it looked good on her.

"Where is Aniya?" I asked, as I sat down beside her.

"She's asleep," Keya said with her focus on the TV. I stared at her, and I could tell that she knew I was watching her, because she started to fidget. She finally turned and looked at me. "What? Why are you staring at me like that?" she asked.

"Keya, where did we go wrong?" I asked her, but instead of replying she held her head down. I lifted it up with my hand, and forced her to look at me. "Aye, didn't I tell you to stop doing that? You don't have to be afraid of me," I said. "I'm still the same nigga that you Keya."

"I know, but it's like I'm so ashamed of what I did," she said, but I didn't say anything. I couldn't, because I was still dealing with her deceit myself. We became silent, and then out of nowhere Keya asked a question, that made me look at her sideways. "Did you kill him?" she asked, and I frowned.

"Keya, let me make something clear to you. What I do in the streets ain't got nothing to do with you, and I don't ever want to hear you ask me any more questions that involve my business. Just know that I'm handling things like a man should do to keep his family safe. Aight!" I said, and Keya slightly nodded her head. *Damn, why did I have to love this girl so much?* I asked myself. It was like the harder I fought to keep my feelings hidden, the more they came out. I couldn't resist the urge any longer, and I wanted to taste her sweet lips bad. So boldly, I leaned over and pulled Keya into a kiss. Surprisingly, she engaged in it too, but after a few seconds of kissing, she suddenly pushed me back.

"You been drinking again, haven't you?" Keya asked.

"Just a little," I said, pulling her back to me, but she pushed me back again.

"No, Aaron! You're drunk, and I don't like it when you're like that. When did you start drinking anyway, because I could remember a time that you would only take one drink, and that would be it." She said.

"Since all this shit went down," I replied. "Keya I got muthafuckas betraying me, and niggas thinking they can take me out. My life is stressful right now, and sometimes I don't know if I'm coming or going. We ain't together, and right now, the bottle is my best friend," I said, as she stared at me.

"And I understand, but hitting the bottle is not going to make those problems go away. Besides that, I don't like for Aniya to see you when you're drunk," she said. "Please leave that alcohol alone, Aaron." Keya's eyes pleaded with me, and it kind of fucked me up. Especially the part about her mentioning my daughter.

"Aight, I'mma do my best to cool out on the drinking," I said and grabbed her by the rim of the shorts that she had on. Keya was looking so sexy to me, even in her lounge clothes. It had been a long ass time since we took it there, and I missed the way she used to call out my name, when I would dig in her guts.

"What are you doing?" she asked, as I slid my hand inside of her shorts and twirled my fingers around.

"Just let me make you feel good," I said, and Keya slowly nodded her head. I pulled her shorts all the way down, and saw that she wasn't wearing any panties. Her pussy was shaved and smelling good, just how I liked it. Her body trembled a little as I ran my hands along her smooth thighs. When we locked eyes, it was like I couldn't wait to feel her insides, but I didn't want to rush the moment. I slowly lowered my head between her legs and started to tickle her pearl.

"Mmm," Keya moaned.

"You taste so fuckin good," I said as I dipped my tongue in and out her hole. Keya slowly started to rotate her hips around, and I took my hand and grabbed one of her breasts. I used two fingers to squeeze her nipple gently while still feasting on her pearl.

"Oh, my god, Aaron. Yessss," Keya hissed. Her ass was lifting from the couch, and she was trying her best to get away from me. I took my hand, wrapped it around her waist, and pulled her closer to my face. Using my free hand, I spread her legs as wide open as they could go and went to work on her clit. Her legs shook violently as she gripped my shoulders and tried to push me back. "I'm about to cummmmmm," she screamed out, and I continued to rub my face in her hotspot.

A few minutes later, she came on my tongue. Keya was panting heavily as she looked at me with a smile on her face. After standing to my feet, I dropped my pants and boxers and eased back between her legs. With my dick in hand, I slowly stroked up her slit and then slid halfway into her. But as gentle as I was, she still tensed up like it was painful to her.

"Am I hurting you?" I asked, and she shook her head no. I slid the rest of my dick inside of her, and she gripped me even harder. I slowly slid in and out while leaning my head down to suck on Keya's breast. Her breaths were short and heavy, and I had to look at her to make sure that she was okay. When I looked into her face, she had her eyes closed tightly, and it didn't look like she was enjoying the sex much. So, I slid my dick out and stared at her.

"Why'd you stop?" Keya asked, while sitting up on the couch. She pulled her t-shirt down over her legs and stared back at me.

"Cause you ain't ready," I replied.

"What do you mean, I'm not ready?" She asked with her eyebrows furrowed.

"You lied to me, Keya." I said.

"Lied about what?" she asked.

"About that nigga touching you." I stared at her.

"No I didn't, because he didn't touch me?" she said, but I could see in her eyes that she was not telling the truth.

"And you still lying," I said and stood up. I put my boxers and pants back on and headed up to my room. I could hear her calling out to me, but I ignored her. I didn't understand why she felt that she had to lie to me about what had gone down, but until she told me the truth, I was good on her. I hopped into the shower and changed clothes. Once I was out of the shower, I walked out onto my balcony and fired up a blunt. Shit had gone from bad to worse, and I didn't know when it was gonna end.

30

Sam

"Mane, do you think that she remembers who I am? What if she told Aaron? That nigga is gonna kill me!" Harold rambled on.

"Shut the fuck up, nigga! You better hope that I don't kill yo punk ass," I snapped. His ass had been whining like a bitch ever since he ran into Aaron at the store, and Keya was with him. I didn't know why he was so scared when he had planned to take Aaron out anyway.

"I'm saying, mane, I know recognized me; I just know it." his bitch ass said with fear in his voice.

"Fuck out my face with this shit. If she tells him, then what? You plan on working with him to take me out?" I stared at him with my gun in my hand, and he looked back at me with fear in his eyes.

"Naaahhhh, you know that I ain't gonna do that." He stuttered.

I laughed, then placed my gun down beside me. "Just stick with the plan, nigga, and everything should be cool." I said.

"I can't do it, mane. It's too risky for me to go back around them, cause I know that she remembered my face. What if they went to the police?" He said, and I laughed.

"Nigga, listen to what the fuck you just said. His ass ain't going to no damn police," I said. "He a street nigga, and he ain't gonna snitch on no damn body."

Harold stared at me like he wanted to say more, but his bitch ass was too weak to step to me. He wasn't about that life, no matter how hard he tried to make it seem like he was.

"Look, have the police came to you yet?" I asked, and he shook his head no. "Okay, then; let's just find a way to get at them niggas, get that money, and get the fuck out of dodge," I said. Harold picked up a blunt and began to toke on it. I looked at him and tried to figure out what was going through his head. I knew that he was scared that Keya had told Aaron about him, but that was on him. I didn't give a fuck if his cover was blown. I had only been using him anyway to see what information I could get on Aaron and his crew.

Harold was the younger brother of a nigga named Lenny, that had been over at the house that night Aaron and his crew killed June Bug. Lenny didn't hang with us on the regular, and would mostly just come around here and there. He lived on the North side of Memphis, and ran with some different niggas. That's why I didn't know shit about him having a younger brother, until Harold approached me. He told me that he had heard on the streets that Lenny was cool with us, and asked if I knew who was responsible for killing his brother. I told him about Aaron and his crew, and how we had been back and forth with our beef. I even told him that Aaron was responsible for killing my mama, and he believed me.

Suddenly, I thought back to the night I set everything in motion….

"I can't believe this bitch called the police on me," I mumbled to myself as I parked my car down the street from my mama's house. I looked around, and when I didn't see anybody out, I jogged down the block to her house. I was about to kill the bitch that had been behind the problems in my life, and I could already see her blood on my hands. Just as I was going on the side of the house, I saw the lights of a car coming down the street. I ducked behind a bush, and the car came to a stop in front of my mama's house. At first, I thought that it was one of the many John's that she had coming through to get their dicks sucked, or whatever else she did to pay for her crack. But after the person in the car cut the car off, they just sat there.

I waited to see if they were gonna leave, before I decided to get up. But they didn't move, and recognition started to sit in that the car looked familiar to me. Suddenly, the window of the car eased down, and Aaron's face came into view. That's when it came to me, where I had seen the car before. It belonged to Keya's punk ass baby daddy. The crazy thing was, I had heard about Aaron looking for me, after I shot at him. But I didn't know that he knew where my mama rested her head. I was mad, because now he had an advantage on me. But the longer, I sat that crouched down, the more I thought about it. Maybe Aaron didn't have an advantage, and just maybe him coming around was work in my favor. I hurried to take out my phone out of my pocket before he let the window back up.

When I had my phone in hand, I snapped a few pictures of him. Just as I took the last picture, Aaron looked around one more time, then the window went back up. He sat outside of my mama's house for about another five minutes or so, before he finally pulled off the block. I stayed on the ground a little while longer, just in case he had decided to circle back through. After laying there for about ten minutes, I figured that he was gone, so I stood to my feet and dusted myself off.

Instead of killing my mama that night like I had decided to do, I headed back to my car to devise my plan. And the night that Aaron and his crew came looking for me, I had snuck out a back window and hid on the side of the house. I had noticed that some more of his people was posted up out front, but they hadn't seen me. When Aaron and those other two niggas came out and got inside of the car, I snapped some more pictures. I called that crime stoppers number and told them that I knew who had killed my mama. They had asked me to identify myself, but I wasn't going to do that. When I snuck back into the house and saw that my nigga, along with everybody else was dead, I immediately got pissed off. The next day, I sent in those pictures to the police and called the crime stoppers back. I once again gave them Aaron's name, and told them that he was a big drug lord that was going around killing everybody that owed him money.

Shortly after that happened, Keya had texted me to offer her condolences for death of my mama. That's when I lied, and said that Aaron was responsible. I knew that she would believe me, especially since I had those pictures as proof. I also knew that she wasn't going to tell anybody that I had told her, because that would've been like snitching on her own baby daddy. After Aaron went to jail, I slowly eased my way back into her life, and that's how I was able to kidnap her. Me and Harold came up with the idea for him to find a way to get into Aaron's crew. I needed him to keep a watchful eye on them, so that I could always remain one step ahead. When he finally got in, and told me that Aaron had been released from jail, I was just about to hit him up for Keya's ransom. But before, I got the chance to make the call, was when Keya had shot me, and got away. Now I didn't know whether or not I could trust Harold, or if he would do me in to save his own ass.

"Aye, we gotta come up with a plan quick, cause we need to get up out of town before the police come around here looking for you." Tank said walking into the room with a beer in his hand.

"I already know. That's why I need this nigga over here to quit bullshitting and see if he can tell me where one of their stash houses at or something," I said while looking at Harold.

"I told you that they don't have no permanent stash houses. Aaron don't trust nobody, not even me," Harold said.

"Why do I feel like you lying nigga?" I asked.

"I don't know, but that's the truth. He told me from the beginning that he was gonna keep his eyes on me. The only thing that they let me do is serve plays, and that's it. I don't know nothing about his shipments, where his stash houses at, or none that other shit that you talking about." He said.

"That ain't gon' cut it, homey. I need something quick, and if you can't deliver, then it won't be any reason for me to keep you around," I said.

Harold, stood up and without uttering a word, stormed out of the house.

"Say, we need to kill that muthafucka." I turned and told Tank.

"That's exactly what I'm thinking," he agreed.

31
Harold

Later that night....

I was a dead man walking, and I had to get the fuck out of town and quick. There was no way that Keya had forgotten who I was, and I hated that I had been caught slipping. From the time that Sam had told me she had gotten away, I did my best to stay away from the crew. I wanted to see if Sam would come up with another plan to take them out, but that shit hadn't worked in my favor. Aaron now knew that I was an enemy, and there was no way that I could make a sneak attack without them expecting me. On top of that, I had Sam trying to send me back in to the wolves. I couldn't trust his ass for shit, because he wasn't somebody that you trusted. It was his fault that our initial plans had been fucked up in the first place, because he gave Keya the opportunity to escape. He should have just stuck with the plan that we had set up, but nah, he wanted to cuff the bitch. Now look where that had gotten us.

I pulled my car up to my baby's mama, Monique's house and killed the engine. Nobody knew where she lived, and I figured that I was safe until I figured out my next move. Besides, I needed her to handle me quick, because my nerves were shot the fuck out. After walking up to her door, I stuck my key in and turned the knob. The house was completely dark except for the light on the TV that was in her room. I walked straight past the room down the hall to my son's, Mikell's, room. When I opened the door, he was sleeping peacefully in his little bed that was in the shape of a car. The cover was kicked off him, and his leg was dangling from the bed. I walked over and put his leg back on the bed and picked the cover up, and laid it on top of him. I loved this little boy more than I loved myself, and there wasn't anything that I wouldn't do to protect my son. He was my life, and who I lived for. Mikell had also been real close to my brother Lenny, and that's why it fucked me up so bad, that Aaron and his crew had taken the only uncle away that my son had. But I didn't care how long it took me, or even if I had to get an Army behind me, I was going to get revenge.

Easing out of the room as quietly as I could, I made my way back to Monique's room. Stepping inside, I saw that she was laid across the bed with just a tank top on. I smiled to myself, because she was always ready for a nigga even when she was asleep. Monique had dark brown skin, a round face, chinky eyes, and a small mole above her lip. She was average height and had a slim build. We had been fucking with each other ever since we were thirteen years old, and she had my son when she was sixteen. We both had just turned twenty a few months back, but the way we held each other down, was like that of a much older couple. And even though, I occasionally did my thing on the side, I always came back to Monique.

I walked over to the bed and roughly shook her leg to wake her. "Mmm, what's up baby?" Monique rolled over and smiled at me.

"Come take care of this," I told her placing my hand on my dick. Without hesitation, she slid out of the bed, and dropped down to her knees. I lifted some to remove my pants and underwear, and then sat back down. Monique wrapped her small, soft hands around my dick and stroked up and down at a steady pace. The shit was already starting to feel good, but I wanted her to hurry up and wrap those lips around me. "Put it in your mouth," I told her.

She lowered her head and slowly took me into her wet, inviting mouth. "Damn girl! That's the shit right there," I said, pushing her head up and down real fast. I was pushing her head so hard that she started to gag. "Suck that shit up!" I said, while looking into her eyes.

"Damn, boy, you trying to kill my ass," Monique said.

"Shut the fuck up!" I pushed her head back down and leaned my head back. She had slob dripping down to my balls, and I was about to bust, but I wasn't ready to nut yet. So, I forcefully snatched her head up and tossed her onto the bed. While climbing on top of

Monique, I lifted her shirt and gripped her breasts. I raised one of my legs and rammed my dick inside of her.

"Owwwwwww! Got damn it, boy. Take it easy," she cried out.

"Nah, I'm 'bout to murder this pussy," I said, now lifting both of her legs and placing them on my shoulders. I was taking all the frustrations that I had out on Monique. My tongue made its way to her breast, and I sucked a nipple into my mouth. I slowly flickered my tongue back and forth over it. She cooed, as I took my teeth and gently bit down. Monique was a freak, and she always enjoyed a little pain mixed with pleasure. Even when she claimed that I was being too rough. Her pussy became soaking wet, and I could feel her walls starting to contract around me.

"Yessssssss," she hissed.

I flipped her over and rammed my dick into her from the back. "Throw dat ass back," I said spreading her butt cheeks and going as deep as I could. Monique started to rock her big ass back on me, and I had to slow her down. My balls were slapping against her ass, and sweat was profusely seeping from my pores. I reached my hand around the front of her and gently rubbed her clit.

"Oh, my god, Harold," Monique screamed.

"Fuck, this pussy feeling good," I said, then lifted one of my legs and began to hit her with some lethal strokes. A few minutes in that position, and I was nutting all up in her pussy. "Uhhhh," I grunted while falling back onto the bed. My heart was beating fast, and I had to take short, steady breaths to get it to return to normal.

"What you cook?" I asked her.

"I made some pork chops, rice, mixed vegetables, and biscuits," she said, and my stomach instantly started to growl.

"Bet that. Go fix me a plate," I said while smacking her on the ass. She climbed out of bed and walked into the bathroom. I heard the water come on, then a few minutes later, she returned with a towel. She cleaned my dick and took the towel back into the bathroom. I closed my eyes for a brief minute just thinking about what my next move was gonna be. I must have dozed off, because Monique came in and tapped my shoulder.

"Here yo plate go, baby," she said handing me the heaping plate of food. I grabbed the plate from her hand and sat up. Sticking my fork into the rice, I took a bite. Monique came over to me with a Heineken and sat it on the nightstand.

"Preciate that, bae," I said picking it up and taking a sip of it.

"You good! Do you need something else?" she asked.

"Nah, but I do need to holler at you about something."

"Okay, wassup?" she asked, taking a seat on the bed beside me.

"Some shit done popped off, and we might need to leave town for a few."

"Are you crazy? I can't leave town. What about my job? What about Mikell's school?" she said rambling on.

"Aye, chill out. He gone be straight, and I'm sure, wherever we go, it's gone be schools for him," I said and laughed, but Monique didn't crack a smile. "Look, I understand that you hate to be uprooted like this, but what other choice do we have. Ain't I always took care of you?" I asked her.

"Yes, but-"

"Ain't no buts! If I always look out for you and my son, then do this for me," I said leaning over and kissing her neck.

"Stop boy, don't be trying to make me feel good about this shit!"

"Did it work some?" I asked with a sly grin.

"Nope, but I'm in this with you. But just so we're clear, though, whatever issues you got, you need to handle them fast. Cause I'm not about to be dragging my son across the world every time you get your ass into something," she told me with a straight face.

"I got you, baby!" I said and continued to eat my food. I really didn't need Monique's permission to take her or my son anywhere. I just figured that I would at least tell her about it first. Then, if she would have said no, I would've dragged her ass kicking and screaming if I had to.

32

Laydii

One month later....

"So how is the pregnancy going?" my mama asked. She and my niece Laila had come to pay me a surprise visit.

"It's going pretty good, and I'm not having any more morning sickness," I told her. I had just turned six months pregnant, and I was happy because the end was almost near. True, the morning sickness was gone, but all those other symptoms had started to kick in. I couldn't go for more than two hours without having to pee, my back hurt all the time, and my nose had started to spread. I didn't understand how some women had multiple kids. I would probably give John one more, but after that, it was a wrap for me.

"That's good to hear!" she smiled. "And what about Keya? Is she good?"

"As good as she can be considering everything that has happened to her." I said.

"You know, it's a damn shame, that Sam did her like that. I mean, how could you kidnap and rape somebody that you claimed to have loved at one point. Chile, I swear that boy is a maniac, and I hope when they find his crazy ass, they throw him in jail, and let somebody take advantage of him. Then see how he like it. And that's why I had told Toni, that he was missing some marbles, when she falsely accused him of rape," my mama said, and it was like a thought came to her. "You know what Laydii, now that I think about it, I'm going to call that detective, and tell him that they should look into Sam when they open this investigation back up. I don't know why it had never come to me before, but until this very moment all that mess had slipped my mind. And it's like the more I think about it, Sam would have had reason to kill my baby," My mama said, and instantly I felt nauseous.

What kind of person was I, to keep that type of information hidden from my mama? It was her daughter, and she did deserve to know. But I just couldn't tell her what Tim had told me. At least not right now. My mama may have been a little ghetto, but she was not in the streets and she would have taken something like that straight to the police. And as bad as it may have seemed, I wanted John and the crew to handle Sam with street justice. Not just for Toni alone, but for what he had done to all of us. When I looked at Laila as she played, I felt that my decision was justified. She will never be able to see her mother or father, because of what Sam may have done to Toni.

"Baby, I'm going to get out of here. I'm just not feeling good anymore," my mama said, bringing me from my thoughts.

"Okay, I will walk you guys out," I told her. I gathered up my niece, while my mom got her things together and then we all walked over to the door. I placed a kiss on Laila's cheek, and she grabbed my face with her little hands.

"Love you, Laila, and I love you, too, ma. And please don't worry; everything is going to work out," I said as I gave her a hug.

"I know baby, and I will let you know what the detective said. And you make sure that you're taking care of yourself, okay!" she said.

"I will," I said as I closed the door behind them. As soon they were gone, I slid to the floor and cried like a baby. We had come such a long way in our relationship, and something like this could immediately wipe away all that we had been trying to build. I just hoped that John and the crew were able to find Sam, and get rid of him soon.

33

John

"Aye, how many times do I have to tell you to quit calling my phone so fuckin much." I said to Kim as soon as she got inside of my car. We were supposed to be going to pick out some items for the baby, and I had told her that I would be here an hour ago, but I got caught up with Laydii. She hadn't wanted me to leave, so I had to tell her that Aaron put me on a job. And that's when she finally gave in, but made me promise to hurry back home.

Kim put her seatbelt on and smiled at me. "I'm sorry, John. I thought that maybe you had forgotten since you were supposed to be here over an hour ago," she smirked.

"It doesn't matter how long ago I was supposed to be here. I said don't call my phone if it's not important, but you keep doing it anyway. I'm telling you, if you keep playing these games, Kim, I'mma stop coming around," I snapped.

"I said that I was sorry. You don't have to worry about me calling anymore," she said, folding her arms across her chest.

"Yeah, aight! Where you trying to go?" I asked, as I pulled off from her apartments. I didn't know how much longer I would be able to pull this shit off. Laydii was constantly down my back about me not spending time with her, and I was stressing myself out trying to make two women happy all at once. I didn't want Kim trying to find a way to tell Laydii about the baby before I got a chance to tell her. Her ass was sneaky, and that was all that I needed was for her to blast me.

"Let's go to Babies "R" Us," Kim said, and I headed in the direction of the store. Once we finally got there, I hopped out and Kim rushed to keep up with me.

"Wait up, John. You know that I'm carrying a load here," she said, and I sighed. That was another thing with her; she was only seven months pregnant, and her ass acted like she was getting ready to deliver at any minute.

Every time that I talked to her she was complaining about something. "My back hurt, my feet are swollen." Just something to remind me of the fact that she was pregnant.

"Kim, yo ass act like you about to have that baby right now. Damn, I know that you pregnant; you don't have to keep reminding me," I said, as we walked into the store. After that, Kim didn't say anything else. She silently grabbed a basket, and I guess she knew that she was getting on my nerves, because while we were in the store, she tried her best to be nice to me. We ended up getting a baby bed, changing table, a mobile, and a whole lot of other shit that the baby probably wouldn't need but Kim had insisted that he would. An hour and three thousand dollars later, we were finally done shopping.

"So tomorrow, I'mma get one of my homies truck and come back and get the baby bed and stuff for you," I told her as we left the store.

"Okay. And are you going to put it up?" she asked.

"Yeah, who else is going to put it up?" I said with irritation. It was like any little word that she spoke, got on my nerves now.

"Whatever John. You don't always have to be so mean to me. I understand that this isn't the ideal situation, but you have to come to terms with the fact that I'm carrying your son, and I didn't get myself into this alone," she said.

"You right, and I apologize. I'm just so stressed Kim, and it's fuckin with me that I'm even in this situation. Maybe once everything is out on the table with Laydii, I won't have to worry so much," I said.

Kim ran her hand up the back of my neck and started massaging my shoulders. I ain't gon lie; the shit felt good, and I was already starting to relax. When we got back to her place, she asked me if I could help her move something in the room she was setting up for the baby. I told her yes, and we both got out. As we walked up to the door of her apartment, Kim did her best to get my attention by switching her ass extra hard. I pretended like I hadn't noticed shit. She took out her key and opened the door to her apartment, and we both stepped inside.

"So, what you need me to move?" I immediately asked her. I wasn't trying to be here no longer than I needed to.

"It's back here," Kim said, walking towards the back, and I followed behind her. When we got in the room, she told me that she needed me to move a desk that she had been using. I moved it to her bedroom like she asked, and when I was done, I asked her to get me something to drink before I left.

While Kim grabbed me something to drink, I walked back to the living room and took a seat on the couch. A minute or so passed, and she finally emerged from the kitchen with a drink in her hand. "Here you go," she said handing me the can of coke. I took the can from her hand, and after popping the top on it, I took three long gulps, and it was gone.

"Aight, I'mma about to be out," I said and stood up to leave, but Kim immediately jumped in front of me and placed her hand on my chest.

"Do you really have to go?" she asked with her bottom lip poked out.

"C'mon, Kim. Don't start that bullshit," I said. "I did what you wanted me to do, so what other reason is it for me to stick around?"

"I got one good reason," she said, while eyeing my dick through my pants.

"Nah, it ain't finna go down like that," I told her and went to step around Kim, but she grabbed my dick and squeezed it. My mind was telling me to get the fuck up out of there, but it was like my dick had a mind of its own. Before I knew was what happening, I was back on the couch with my pants pulled down around my ankles, and Kim's wet lips around my shit.

"Yeah, girl. Suck it real nice and slow," I said, as I ran my fingers through her hair. She was going hard with it, too, as she gripped my balls and sucked on my dick like she was sucking on a popsicle. "Fucccck," I grunted.

"Does this feel good to you, baby daddy," she said, taking my dick out of her mouth and gliding her fingers on the tip of it. As I looked at Kim, my mind started to ask me what the hell I was doing? She had now put my man's back into her mouth and was sucking on it a rapid pace.

"Hold up, hold up; this shit ain't right, Kim," I said trying to pull her head up, but she kept on sucking me like her life depended on it. *Fuck it,* I thought. The damage was done, so I figured I might as well let her finish. Kim kept sucking me like a vacuum cleaner sucking up dirt, and before long I felt my nut building. She licked me a few more times, and I let loose inside of her mouth. "Aargh," I said, as my dick twitched and I released the last of my cum down the back of her throat.

Kim smiled up at me, and I felt guilty as fuck. I hadn't cheated on Laydii in a long time, and I had just made the mistake of letting Kim dome me up. *Fuck is wrong with me?* I thought to myself. I stuffed my dick back inside of my boxers and pulled my pants up.

I walked over to the door, but before I left out, I turned to Kim. "Yo, this better not be no fuckin setup, or I'mma fuck your ass up if it is. And I'mma tell you one last time, don't call my phone again unless it is important."

34

Jeremy

A week later….

"Go higher, Daddy! Pweassse go higher!" my son said, as I pushed him on the swing. I had decided to bring him to the park so that we could spend a little time together. I had kept my word to Nancy that, once we found Keya, I was gonna spend more time with Lil' Jeremy. I finally understood what she had been trying to tell me. I hadn't spent as much time with him as I should, and from this day forward, I was gonna make sure that I did just that.

"See, Jeremy; he is having a blast! I knew that he would like it," Tina said.

"Yeah, he is. But shit, it doesn't take much for his little ass to have fun anyway," I said, and Tina laughed. I found myself staring at her, and picturing how our life would be if we were to become seriously involved. It was like she was a fresh breath of air for me. Never had I had feelings for any woman like I did for her. It was just so fucked up, because we were both still in dead ass relationships that we weren't happy in. I honestly didn't know why I stuck around with Nancy, because we barely even had sex. Hell, half the time, I wasn't even at home, and the times that I was, I would play with my son and kick back on the couch and watch Sports Center. I didn't pay Nancy's ass any attention, because if I did, all she would want to do is talk about was how I was ignoring her, and that had gotten old. I leaned over and planted a kiss on Tina's lips, and she wrapped her arms around my neck.

"Jeremy, you muthafucka!" I heard Nancy scream.

"Damn," I said, pulling back from Tina. I should have known that I couldn't go a day without some type of drama. How she kept finding me was a damn mystery. I had told her that I was taking Lil' Jeremy to the park, but I hadn't told her which one. I was starting to think that her ass had a tracking system on my car or something.

"Why the fuck is you out at the park with this woman, and you're kissing her while our son is over there playing by himself," she screamed.

Me and Tina were sitting on a bench, and our backs were to Nancy. Once she saw who I had with me, she was gonna cut the fuck up. Nancy and Tina weren't friends, but they had crossed paths a few times, and she knew that Tina was Keya's sister. I didn't care about Nancy finding out about us, but I knew that Tina didn't want anybody to know right now since she hadn't broken things off with her boyfriend.

"Jeremy Davis, do you fuckin hear me talking to you?" she said, as she walked around the bench to where we sat. When Nancy got in front of us, she looked between me and Tina with a shocked expression.

"Tina! What the fuck are you doing with my man? You bitch!" she said and tried to attack Tina, but I snatched her ass up before she could do anything. She was still kicking and screaming inside of my arms, and I fought to keep her restraint.

"Let me go, Jeremy. I want to get at this bitch bad," she said while bucking her body against me.

"Calm the fuck down," I gritted. "You see these kids out here and your damn son. Act like you got some fuckin sense. Tina shook her head, and I hoped that she didn't say anything that would make this situation worse.

"I'm calm, Jeremy. Can you please put me down?" Nancy asked.

"I'mma put you down, but I swear you better not show your fuckin ass again," I said into her ear. She nodded her head, and I placed her on her feet. As soon as she was down on the ground, she sprinted over to Tina and slapped her hard as hell.

Whap!

I sighed, and was just about to intervene again, when Tina stood to her feet and punched Nancy in her face. Nancy's head snapped back, and she grabbed her nose, because blood instantly squirted from it.

It was like, after that, Tina and Nancy locked on each other and was going at it. I walked over to them and tried pulling them apart, but their asses were like Pit Bulls in a dog fight. Tina was throwing vicious blows and Nancy was countering back. If it wasn't for my son being out here witnessing his mama acting a fool, I would have let them have at it. Nancy was always putting her hands on folks, and now it was like she had fucked with the wrong person. Tina was going blow for blow with her, and it was looking like she was getting the best of Nancy.

"Aye, y'all need to chill out for these folks call the police," I said, finally pulling them apart. Nancy was jumping up and down, and Tina stood with a smirk on her face.

"You fuckin bitch. Wait until he is not around, and I'm going to fuck you up," Nancy screamed.

"Bitch, it's whatever! You don't need to be mad at me; your problem is with him," Tina said.

"You knew he was my man, and your slutty ass goes and fuck with him. I should fuckin kill you!" Nancy spewed, still trying to get loose from my hold.

"Calm the fuck down, Nancy! I'm not gonna tell you this shit again. Do you see your son looking at you right now?"

Nancy turned her head to where Lil Jeremy was sitting in the sand watching us. She snatched her arm away from me and walked over to him. After placing him on her hip, she turned and looked at me and Tina one more time before storming off.

When I glanced around, all the parents had their children clutched to them and wore shocked expressions. I was so pissed that she had shown her ass like that, and I just wanted to leave. I grabbed at Tina's hand so that we could go, but she snatched it back.

"Fuck wrong with you?" I asked.

"You put me in this situation, and I ain't fuckin with you right now," she said.

"Look, I ain't make you do shit that you didn't want to do. Yo ass just feeling guilty because of what Nancy said, but if you want to act like that, then cool; I'm out." I said and walked off towards my car. She drove herself here, so she could drive herself back home.

I jumped into my car and immediately pulled out a blunt. I snatched my lighter up and flicked it a few times, but it wouldn't light. When I looked at the lighter, I realized that it didn't have any more lighter fluid. *Fuck,* I thought to myself. When I glanced out the window, I saw Tina walk over to her car and get inside. Not even a minute later, she pulled off. I cranked up my car and went the other way to the store. I needed to get a lighter quick so that I could fire this blunt up.

35

Keya

A week later....

"Girl, I have so much shit to tell you," Tina said with eagerness all in her voice. Me, her, and Laydii had decided to have lunch today at Texas De' Brazil. Tina and I had just made it here a little while ago, but Laydii hadn't made it yet. She did text and say that she was running a little late, and would be here in the next ten minutes, or so.

"So, what's up girl?" I asked while taking a sip of my water.

"Um, don't be mad, but I've kind of been seeing Jeremy." Tina said with a sly grin.

The water that I was drinking shot out of my mouth, and I had to get a napkin to wipe my chin. "Come again! You said that you have been seeing Jeremy?" I asked.

"Actually, we've been talking for quite some time now." She said and took a sip of her drink.

"Tina, have your lost your fuckin mind?" I mad whispered at her.

"Nope," she continued to smile and shrugged her shoulders.

"Girl, what is Kenny gonna do once he finds out that you're out here creeping? I mean, you know that he is a slick stalker, and I'm surprised that he hasn't already found out." I said. Tina's boyfriend Kenny followed her around like he was a little puppy. He was jealous if he saw her talking to any guys, and I didn't see how she had the opportunity to mess with somebody else since he was always up her ass.

"That's just it, baby sis. I don't want to be with him anymore. Kenny has been doing the same thing since we graduated from college. He hasn't tried to find a job in his field, and every time that I bring it up, he gets an attitude. Plus, I'm tired of being the one that handles all the bills in our house. It was time for me to get a boss nigga like you," she said, and I instantly frowned.

"Okay, so do you think that by getting with Jeremy it will solve all of your problems?" I asked. "And another thing, being with someone with money doesn't make you happy, Tina."

"No, but it does leave a bitch satisfied at night. I mean, the multiple orgasms that I received while gripping those dreads." She said trailing off.

"Hello, Earth to Tina. Don't nobody want to hear about that shit," I said, bringing her back from whatever fantasy she had drifted into. "But seriously, Tina, you're only thinking about your sexual gratifications right now, and that's not what makes a relationship work. Have y'all thought about the people that you would be hurting in the process with this thing y'all got going?" I asked. She was too old to be acting this way, and she wondered why I always called her childish. It was for the simple fact that she acted more like a teenager, rather than the twenty-four-year-old that she actually was.

"Nancy already knows." She replied.

"Wait, how do you know that she knows about y'all?" I asked in confusion.

"About a week ago, me and Jeremy was at the park with his son when she popped up out of nowhere. She acted a damn fool, too. The bitch even slapped me in the face, and we ended up fighting," she said.

My mouth hung wide open as I stared at my sister in disbelief. This shit here was crazy, and she knew better than to get herself wrapped into this type of drama. "Tina, y'all are going about this all wrong, and nothing good is going to come of this situation" I said.

"Wassup y'all!" Laydii said walking over to the table. She leaned in and gave me a hug, and then walked around and hugged Tina.

"You look cute today," I told her. She was rocking a tan oversized, off the shoulder, Marilyn Monroe shirt, black leggings, and a pair of black Tom Ford wedge sneakers with tan trimmings. Her now long hair was pulled up into a bun on top of her head with a few pieces left out. She hadn't gained much weight since being pregnant, and her skin was smooth with a nice glow to it.

"Thanks boo," she replied and folded her hands on top of the table. "What did I miss?" she asked while looking between me and Tina.

I looked at Tina out of the corner of my eye and smirked. "Girl, too much to discuss right now. We'll have to fill you in later. But why the sad look? Is everything okay with my niece?" I asked. The doctors had recently told Laydii that her blood pressure was too high and that she needed to stop stressing or it could affect the baby. It was almost impossible for her not to stress, though, considering all the drama that was going on around us.

"No, she's fine, and everything is okay." she said with a fake smile that I could see right through.

"Laydii, please don't start shutting me out again. I apologize for bringing that shit up with you and Aaron, and I hope that you're not still upset about that?" I asked, and Laydii shook her head. "No, it's not that." She replied and looked between me and Tina.

"Let me ask y'all something? If your man was suddenly unavailable whenever you tried to reach him, or always claimed that he was out handling business, would you think something of it, or am I just tripping?"

"Girl, do you think that John is up to his old ways again?" I asked.

"I don't know, but something is not right, Keya. Take, for instance, last week. He told me that he was meeting up with Jeremy and Aaron, but when I called you, I heard Aaron in the background, so when John came home, I asked him did he and the guys get everything handled, and he said that they did." She said.

"Wait, what day was this?" Tina asked.

"Last Wednesday, why?" Laydii said.

"Last Wednesday I was with Jeremy," Tina replied.

"Wait a minute, what! You were with who?" Laydii asked gripping her chest in a pearl-clutching manner.

Tina laughed, and I just shook my head. "Girl, me and Jeremy have been messing with each other for a while now," she said.

"Oh, my goodness, Tina. Bitch give up the dirt," Laydii squealed.

"Un-un, don't encourage this heffa," I said.

Tina stared at me with a screw face. "What? I'm saying; we need to figure out what is going on with John, then we can get back on your homewrecking ass," I laughed.

"Bitch, bye!" Tina said, pushing my shoulder. "Anyways, I will tell you all about it when little Miss Prude over here is not around. But Laydii, if you feel like something is off in your relationship, then nine times out of ten, it is," Tina said.

Laydii nodded her head, and a sad expression suddenly covered her face. "I feel you girl, and I knew that I wasn't crazy. I'm not sure what his ass is up to, but I'm not for this shit. He had better pray that, whatever it is he is doing, I don't find out about it.

Because if I do, I'm cutting his dick off," she said with a serious face. Me and Tina busted out laughing, but Laydii just smirked.

"Girl, I'm sure that it's nothing. John knows that you don't need to be stressed out." I said. I was telling her what I thought was the right thing to say, but in my head, I was thinking that I wasn't so sure.

"Anyways, so what's up with you and Aaron?" Laydii asked.

"Um, nothing really," I said.

"Hi, can I get you something to drink?" the server walked up and asked Laydii.

"Let me get a water with lemon?" she replied.

"Sure, and can I get you ladies anything else to drink while I'm grabbing her water." Me and Tina both shook our heads no. The waitress walked off to retrieve Laydii's water. Once she was out of earshot, I jumped back to the conversation.

"Oh yeah, and I forgot to tell y'all that I think Aaron knows about what Sam did to me," I said.

"Wait, how do you know?" Laydii asked me.

"Because we started to have sex one night, and I couldn't really get into it. Aaron stopped, and when I asked him why, he told me that I wasn't ready. He said that he knew I was lying about what Sam had done to me, and then he stormed out of the room. I mean, I wanted to do it y'all, but it was like all I kept thinking about was how Sam kept forcing himself on me, and my body just wouldn't allow me to enjoy it," I said.

"Well, that's understandable, Keya. You went through something tragic, and it may take a while before you are able to enjoy sex like you used to," Tina said.

"I agree. And I also think that you should go ahead and tell Aaron," Laydii said.

"I don't know y'all. I want to tell him, but what if he looks at me differently?" I asked, but before they could say anything, the waitress walked over and sat Laydii's water down on the table.

"Is it anything else I can get for you all?" she asked.

"No, that will be all!" I smiled.

"Alright! Well, as long as you keep your card flipped to green then we will continue to bring more meat selections out. Also, feel free to take advantage of our salad bar, because it's delicious," she said and walked off.

We resumed our conversation again after the waitress left. Laydii and Tina told me that I should probably seek counseling for what Sam had done to me, but I wasn't so sure. I didn't know if I wanted to sit and tell someone that I didn't know all my personal business. Hell, I didn't even want to tell the person that I shared a child with. I was gonna think about it, though, because I kept having these bad nightmares, and they wouldn't go away.

After awhile, Me, Tina, and Laydii finally got up to visit the salad bar. After we had our plates piled high with the salad of our choice, we returned to our seats. We ate for a few minutes, and then resumed our conversation. We ended up discussing everything under the sun. It felt good to be out with my sisters, but my mind kept wandering back to Aaron. I loved that man so much, but if he couldn't forgive me for what I had done and allow us to move past it, then I was just gonna have to focus on me and my daughter.

36

Jeremy

Two days later….

"So, this is it, huh?" Nancy asked, as I grabbed the last of my things. I had found me a three-bedroom condo, and I was letting her and little Jeremy keep the house. It was about time that I stopped messing around and ended this dead ass relationship. I would still be there for my son, and even Nancy if she needed me. I just couldn't pretend like everything was good between us when I knew that I wasn't happy.

"That's it," I replied.

She put her head down, and I saw her trying to discreetly wipe away the tears that were falling down her cheeks.

"Come here, Nancy," I said holding out my arms to her. She slowly walked over into my embrace, and wrapped her arms around me. I leaned down and kissed the top of her head. "Look, me and you both know that this relationship has been over for a long time. And it wouldn't be fair to you, if I stayed in the relationship when I don't really want to be here. You a good girl, and I'm sure it's somebody out there that will love you like you deserve to be loved," I said.

"Jeremy, whatever I did I can make it better. I won't even stop you if you want to be with Tina every now and then. Just say that you will stay with me and your son." Nancy cried.

"Nah, it ain't nothing that you can do to make this better. I'm not in love with you, Nancy, and if I was being honest with myself, I never was. Do I have love for you? Yes. But that's about it. From the very beginning, our whole connection was forced. I appreciate you for giving me a son, and for that, you will always be taken care of, but us trying to make this relationship work just ain't happening." I said.

"Why would you bring me here if you knew that you didn't love me? You dragged me away from my family and friends and brought me to this hood ass place just to abandon me and your son for another woman," she screamed.

"That was never my intention, and if I can recall, you were the one begging to come here when I really just wanted you to stay back in Atlanta. So, don't try to act like the fuckin victim Nancy when you knew what shit was from the jump." I said stepping away from her.

"You are a fuckin coward, and I wish I would have never met your ass," she said.

"You wish you never met me, yet you were willing to accept me fuckin with Tina if I stayed with you. Huh?" I asked. She put her head down, and pretended to stare at the floor. "Don't hide from the truth now." I taunted.

The shit was pitiful, because she had just admitted that she would allow me to fuck with Tina if I promised that I wouldn't leave her, and as tempting as it had sounded, I just couldn't deal. I'm sure every guy I knew would call me crazy for turning down such a proposition, but if they had to put up with Nancy's crazy ass, then they would understand where I was coming from. No man wanted a woman whose self-esteem was so low that they would allow their man to fuck with other bitches as long as he came home to them. And if it was women out here that were saying that they would tolerate that type of behavior, then I felt sorry for the dudes that fell for the shit. It was only so much that a woman would deal with before she snapped out and killed a nigga for playing with her feelings. I would rather just let Nancy's ass go now and deal with her being mad about that, rather than having her trying to kill me over some bullshit.

"You can you just walk away from your son like it's nothing?" she asked.

"I will never walk away from my son. What I'm walking away from is you!" I stated and grabbed up my stuff. I was over the back and forth, melodramatic shit. That's why I wanted to leave when I knew that she wouldn't be home, but I felt I owed her a little more respect to tell her that we were done for good this time. When I left out, I could hear Nancy breaking up shit, but that was on her. She had to live there, and her craziness was no longer my problem.

After I left the house, I went to my condo. I didn't have any furniture in it yet, but I had plans of furnishing it soon. I really wanted Tina to be the one to do it, but she was still playing games. I wasn't about to be walking around here being no side nigga to her, so if she didn't decide what she wanted to do, and soon, it would be deuces to her ass, too. Just as I put my bag down on the counter, my phone vibrated inside of my pocket. I grabbed it out and saw that it was Detrick.

"What it do, boy?" I said, answering the phone.

"Aye, I got some info on our little friend," he said.

"Aight, where you want me to meet you at?" I asked.

"The spot!" Detrick replied and hung up.

That was all that needed to be said. We didn't discuss no business over the phone, and when we did, it was kept it to a minimal.

After snatching my keys from off the counter, I walked back out of the door, hopped in my car, headed to the spot where Detrick was waiting for me. It took me about ten minutes to make it there, and when I pulled up, I saw Detrick's whip. He had finally upgraded from that raggedy ass Crown Vic to an Audi. I eased out of my car and went inside to see what news Detrick had for me.

~~~~~~~~~~~~~~~~~~ **Later that night**

"There go Harold's truck right there," Detrick said to me.

I looked up and got a glimpse of his green Tahoe. "Yeah, it is," I said while eyeing the truck.

Me and Detrick were at the hotel that Harold had been hiding out at. The nigga must not have done his homework on us if he thought that he could try to betray us and we not find him. Since him and his baby mama had cut their phones off, I couldn't get my pops' guy to do a track on them, so we ended up putting a twenty thousand dollar hit on his head. Cats out here didn't care who you were and would give you up in a minute if the price was right. We had eyes and ears all around, and once some of our peoples down in Alabama got wind that he was in the area, they hit Detrick up and told him exactly where we could find him.

"So, what you want to do, J-Dawg?" Detrick asked.

I sighed, because I wanted to murk his ass right now, but I knew that Aaron would want me to wait until he talked to him. We still hadn't caught up with Sam and figured that Harold knew where we could look for him. Unfortunately, we hadn't been as successful with finding him as we had been with Harold. That nigga must have been tucked away good, cause nobody had seen him nowhere. I guess that's how it was when you had the police and everybody else after you.

"This the plan. Let's wait right here, and if he come out, we gone snatch him up and take his ass back to Memphis." I said.

"What if his baby mama and son with him? Then, what?" Detrick asked.

"Then, we wait. I don't want to bust no move if his son is around. I don't care about his bitch, but I got a son, and I ain't about hurting no kids." I said.

"I feel you, and I'm the same way," Detrick said handing me the blunt that he had. I took it from him and took a couple of pulls. I called John's phone for the fifth time since we had been there. He was supposed to be have rode with us, but he hadn't answered his phone when we left out. Come to think of it, he had been MIA a lot lately, and I was gonna have to see what the deal was with that. We waited for three hours to see if Harold's bitch ass would emerge.

"Mane, do you think this nigga gon' come out?" Detrick asked.

"I'on know, dawg. It's going on five in the morning, and if we don't get him before the sun comes up, then we just gone have to wait until tomorrow and see if we can catch his ass then." I said.

"Damn, I shole wanted to get at his ass, too," Detrick said, but I wasn't paying much attention. I had just gotten another text message from Nancy talking about how she didn't want me to leave her. Detrick yelled out that Harold was walking outside, so I put my phone down to peep out the scene. Sure enough, that was his ass outside in a pair of pajamas and a wife beater. Harold lifted the trunk to his truck and started digging around for something that was inside of it.

"Aye, Detrick you stay in the car, while I run up and holler at him," I said.

"Aight, I got you." Detrick replied.

I climbed out of the Impala that we had borrowed from one of the crack heads in the hood and crept over towards Harold. He was still digging around inside the trunk and didn't even hear me coming.

Dumb ass nigga out here living reckless, and don't even know to keep watch of his surroundings, I thought to myself just as I crept up on him.

"Wassup, Harold. I been looking all over for you," I said to him with a twisted smile. He dropped the clothing that he had in his hand and turned around to look at me.

"Aye, mane. You can take me, but don't touch my family. They ain't got shit to do with this," he said. I hit him in the head with the butt of my gun. "Fuck," he said while rubbing the spot where I hit him at. He pulled his hand down and looked at the blood on his fingers."

"Nigga, shut the fuck up! You don't tell me what the fuck to do. I don't take orders from your bitch ass," I said, grabbing him by the back of his neck and pushing him in front of me. "Walk muthafucka," I gritted.

Harold walked ahead, and I scanned the lot to make sure that nobody was out watching us. When I didn't see anybody, I walked over to the car and popped the trunk. Right before I tossed him into the trunk, Detrick came around the back of the car and hit ass with a haymaker so hard that I swear I heard a few bones crack.

"Fuuuck," Harold grunted while gripping his jaw. He looked at Detrick like he wanted to do something, but thought better of it. Seeing as though I still had my gun on his ass, he knew not to test us.

"Look, mane, we ain't got time for all that right now. When we get back to Memphis, you can do whatever you want to do to his ass, but for now, let's toss him in the trunk and be out before somebody comes out here and sees us." I said.

Detrick nodded and pushed Harold into the trunk. Once he was inside, I saw that he was still gripping his jaw, but I didn't give a fuck. I slammed the trunk down on his ass and hopped into the car. Me and Detrick pulled off, just as the sun was coming up.

37
John

The next morning....

"John, John" Laydii stood above me loudly yelling my name.

"What?" I groaned as I rolled over at looked up at her. Laydii was standing above me with her arms folded over her breast, and I knew that she was mad because I had stayed out most of the night.

"What time did you finally come in last night?" she asked.

"About three-thirty. Why?" I said with my eyes half-closed.

"Wrong answer. I stayed up to five, and you still weren't here, and then I finally went to sleep because I was tired of waiting. So, what time did you come in?" she asked.

"Aight, I must didn't pay attention to the time. It was probably a little after you went to sleep." I said.

"You want to keep lying to me I see. And another thing why didn't you answer your phone all the times that I called, and where were you?" she asked.

"Damn, can I brush my teeth first before you start hitting me with all these damn questions." I said. I was trying to throw her off, because I couldn't tell Laydii why I hadn't answered her calls.

"John, I'm not fucking playing with you. I'm asking you where you been, and you talking about brushing your teeth. Are you serious right now?" she snapped.

I sat up on the couch, and rubbed the sleep from my eyes. I was so tired, and didn't want to deal with this shit but I knew in order to get her off my back, that I would have to give her some answers. "Okay, I was with Jeremy and Aaron and we were out handling business. I couldn't answer my phone, because we were in the middle of something and then my phone died. I apologize about coming in late, and it will never happen again." I said.

Laydii laughed this maniacal laugh, while shaking her head. "You must think I'm stupid, don't you?"

"What the hell are you talking about now? I just told you what happened." I said.

"First off, you were not with Jeremy and Aaron so don't even sit there and lie." She pointed her finger in my face.

"So, you calling me a liar?"

"If you ain't telling the truth, then what do you call it?" she asked.

I jumped up from the couch, and looked down at her. "I don't have to deal with this shit. I told you what was up, and you still trying to argue," I said, and walked off towards the bathroom, but Laydii followed behind me.

"I don't understand how you just sat there, and lied to my face like it was nothing. After all the stuff that we have been through, I figured that things had changed. But no, you are still the same lying nigga that you have always been." She spat.

"Laydii, watch your fucking mouth. Don't keep coming at me with all this bullshit, and expect me to sympathize with you just cause you carrying my seed. For the last time, I was with Jeremy and Aaron, and I'm not going to keep saying that." I said.

"Okay. So, if you were with them, then why did Jeremy call my phone twice last night looking for you?" She folded her arms across her chest, and tapped her foot.

I was stuck. She had called me out on my lie, but I kept my game face on. "That don't mean shit," I said. "I didn't say that I was with them the whole night."

"You are so full of shit. The last time that he called me it was about three, and he said that it was real important that he spoke to you, and for me to let you know that he had called. So, that lets me know that you hadn't even seem them," She said.

Fuck, I knew that I should have answered when they called me. Now, I was caught up and didn't have anybody to blame but myself, I thought.

"Aight, I wasn't with them. I didn't want to say this, but you been stressing a nigga out so much with all this talk of finding Sam. Then it's like when I do go out to help look for him, you complain about us not spending time with each other. I didn't want to deal with none of that yesterday, so I went and chilled over my brother's house." I said lying through my teeth. I couldn't let her know that I was really at the hospital all night with Kim because she had been in pain, and thought that she was going into premature labor. Nah, that would-be suicide if I told her that.

"Wow! I can't believe that you just said that to me. You of all people should know how I feel about Toni's death, and how I need to find out if Sam did it or not. I trusted you, and hadn't even told my mama because you said that you were going to handle it. Do you know how guilty I have been feeling to keep that away from her? So, for you to throw that in my face, is just flat out wrong," she said, and tears started to well in her eyes.

"I apologize baby. I didn't mean to say it like that, and I know that you want us to hurry up and find Sam so that you can learn the truth. But just because we find him, it doesn't mean that he will confess to killing her." I said staring in her eyes. She tried to pull away again, but I wrapped my arms around her waist and pulled her close to me. "We will find him, but I need you to understand that you might not ever learn the truth, and stressing yourself along with everybody else out, will not give you the answers that you need to heal. I promise that I won't disappear on you like that again. I just needed to take some time to myself away from everybody." I half told the truth. I pulled Laydii into my arms, and rubbed her back.

I could hear her sniffling, as she cried her eyes out in my chest. It made me feel like shit, because I shouldn't have ever said that to her, even if it was how I felt. I was putting the blame on her for my fuck up. "Please stop that crying," I said, gently lifting her head, and forcing her to look at me. I used my thumb to wipe away the tears that was sliding down her cheeks.

"John, I don't want to be hurt anymore, and I will not tolerate you lying to me. If I find out that you're up to something, then we will be over for good this time, and I put that on everything that I love," she said. The way that Laydii looked at me made me realize just how serious she was. Of course, she had said that in the past, and then she would turn around and forgive me. But It was something about the way that she had said it this time, that made me really believe that she would leave my ass for good. Laydii walked into our bedroom and slammed the door behind her. I headed for the bathroom so that I could relieve my bladder, and handle my hygiene. I didn't' want to hurt Laydii, but if this baby that Kim was carrying was really mine, then I would just have to let her know. If she left me behind it, I would be hurt, but I wouldn't turn my back on a child that I had created, not even for the person that I loved almost more than I loved myself.

38
Aaron

Later that night….

Whap, Whap, Wham! Were the only sounds that could be heard through the room as Harold got his ass beat by John and Detrick.

I stood back like a proud papa, with a satisfied grin on my face. We had him hauled up at the warehouse where we handled our business, and he had been getting his ass beat for the better part of an hour. Once Jeremy and Detrick had him, they brought him back here and waited until I came. They both knew how much I wanted to talk to him first and see what his reasons were for helping Sam kidnap Keya. I also had needed to see if I could get Sam's whereabouts before we killed Harold's bitch ass.

"That's enough," I said, but Detrick hit him one more time in the gut.

"Uhhhh," Harold grunted.

"Aye, nigga. I said that's enough. I need this muthafucka alive long enough to tell me why he thought he could kidnap my bitch and plot to kill me," I said to him.

"My bad, Aaron. This snake ass muthafucka just pissed me off. I brought him in this, and he got me out here looking like I ain't to be trusted." Detrick said, while glaring at Harold.

"I know, and for that, he will be dealt with, but I need to get some answers first." I said while looking at him. Detrick nodded and walked over to where John and Jeremy was. They all waited to see what I was gonna do next. Of course, I was gonna kill his ass, but like I had said, I needed to see if he knew where Sam was, and if he was the reason he came after me.

"Aye," wake up nigga. Ain't no sleeping right now," I said lifting Harold's head up with my hand.
"Tell me where that nigga at, and we can go ahead and get this shit over with. I thought I wanted to know why you betrayed me, but now I'm thinking that don't even matter. In the end, I'm just gonna kill you anyway. So, let's not waste each other's time," I said.

"Y'all killed my brother," I heard Harold mumble through a mouth filled with blood.

"Fuck you just say, nigga?" I asked stepping a little closer to him. He was tied to the chair and could barely hold his head up as he spoke. The nigga's eyes were swelling by the second, and he looked as if he was half dead. Harold spat a glob of spit mixed with blood out of his mouth and slowly lifted his head to look at me.

"I said y'all killed my brother," he spoke more clearly this time.

I looked around the room at everybody, and they all stared back at me with puzzled looks.

"Who the fuck is your brother?" Jeremy asked walking closer to us.

"Lenny," he said, and his head dropped back down to his chest.

"Aye, wake up nigga. I grabbed his head again and forced him to look at me. Nigga, I don't know
who the fuck Lenny is." I said to him.

"He was in the house that night y'all went in looking for Sam. He didn't have nothing to do with that shit, but y'all shot him anyway." He said just above a whisper.

I let his head drop again and looked around at my crew. "Y'all hear this nigga?" I asked everybody.

"Yeah, we hear that shit," Jeremy said and smirked. Detrick and John just laughed.

"How the fuck was I supposed to know that was your brother? Nigga, if you wanted revenge, then you didn't have to sneak into my crew to try and get at me. You could have just come to me on some street shit, and we would've handled it like that. What was you able to gain anyway, besides this death sentence. Nothing," I said answering my own question. Harold had gone about shit all wrong. The only thing that he could have done was tell Sam of our moves. Other than that, he hadn't gained shit from trying to plot against me.

"That would have been too easy," he said, while lifting his head.

I laughed. "Pussy ass coward. You like to go after muthafuckas when they ain't looking, I see. You would have never lasted in my crew, because we only have thorough breeds running for us." I snarled.

Harold said something else, but it was hard to hear him because of how low he talked. His head was dangling around on his shoulder, and he was starting to slip in and out of consciousness.

"Fuck you say?" I asked.

"I said go ahead and kill me muthafucka! But just so you know, Sam is still coming for you, and when he finds you, he's gonna kill you, and fuck your bitch again, and then kill her ass, too," Harold said with a chuckle.

"Is that right? I asked and he smirked. "Well, I guess I will deal with him when the time comes. Just like I'mma deal with you right now. And just like I did to your punk ass brother," I taunted." Harold struggled to hold his head back up. When he finally had it lifted, he looked me in the eyes with a snarl on his face.

"Suck my dick muthafucka," he spat.

"Nah, I'mma do you one better. Since you said that I killed your brother, I'mma about to send your ass to reconnect with him," I said and fired a shot off into his head.

"Aye, clean this shit up," I told my crew as I walked out of the warehouse.

******

"So, you finally came back to see me, huh," Ohani asked, as I sat on her bed watching her strut around in her lingerie. I had been staying away from her, because I knew what being in her presence would mean. We had fucked a few times, and each time that we did, I would go home feeling guilty. I had a feeling that Keya knew that I was still messing around with Ohani, but since me and her wasn't together, I wouldn't consider it cheating.

"I figured that I would stop through here for a little minute. You know, see what you were up to," I said with a smirk.

"I don't think that's the real reason you came over. Just like me, you enjoy our lovemaking sessions, and you couldn't wait another minute to get some more of this good stuff," she said. Ohani slid down to her knees, and I looked into her eyes. She had a huge grin on her face, while she stared back at me.

"What you think you doing?" I asked, as she reached for my belt buckle.

"I'm reminding you why you love to mess with a real woman." She replied.

"Fuck is that supposed to mean?" I frowned.

"I'm saying, your young baby mama couldn't possibly be handling you right, because you're always creeping over here to me. We stay talking on the phone all the time; even when she's at home you are still talking to me," she said, finally getting my belt buckle loose.

"Look, you cool and all, but let that be the last time you say something about my baby mama. She ain't did nothing to you, but you always got something to say regarding her. Please don't make me have to cut your ass off, Ohani. Do we got that understood?" I asked.

"Yes, sir!" she said, reaching inside of my pants and freeing my dick. I slightly lifted so that she could get a better grip on me. After she had my dick in her hands, she stroked up and down my shaft at a fast pace.

"Damn girl. Work that dick!" I said. Her hands were nice and soft, and when I looked into her face, she had the sexiest grin on it. When I saw her lick those pretty lips, I knew that it was about to go down. She leaned her head down and wrapped those lips around my dick and went to work. She was sucking me like she was damn vacuum, and the shit had me almost seeing stars. Her lip action was quite alright.

"Fuck," I grunted.

"Ooh, Aaron, your dick taste so good," she said, licking up and down my dick while letting the slob from her mouth coat it. Ohani took the tip of her tongue and twirled it around my nut sack.

"Aww shit. Damn girl." Her mouth was feeling so good that it was like I was experiencing an outer body moment. And just when I thought it couldn't get any better, she started to deep throat me. I mean, she was taking all nine inches into the back of her mouth, without gagging. I had to wrap my hands in her braids to slow her down. "Aargh," I said, as she hummed on my dick.

Ohani knew exactly what she was doing. This was her first time giving me head since we had been messing off, and I guess she thought that she was gonna try to hook me with her head game. It was good and all, but she still didn't have anything on Keya.

"Why you stop?" I asked, when she stopped sucking me off.

"It's my turn," she said with a wink.

I stared at her like she had sprouted a second head. "Your turn for what?" I asked.

"Your turn to do me," she said with a big smile like I would agree to that shit.

"Look Ohani, I'mma keep it one hunnid with you. I don't go around eating everybody pussy. The only person I have ever put my mouth on is my baby mama," I said, and she instantly dropped her smile. I didn't give a damn how that made her feel, because I had only known her for about three months, and she wasn't about to make me put my mouth on her when I wasn't feeling her in that way.

"Well, that's okay. We will get around to you doing me later. *Like hell,* I thought.

"For now, I just want to get me some of this beast," she said grabbing my dick and stroking it in her hands.

By now, my shit had gone down, and I was contemplating if I even wanted to fuck her or not. I had come over here after killing that nigga Harold, because I didn't want to go home. My mind had been so fucked up, that I ended up hitting another bottle of Hen. I didn't need Keya or my daughter seeing me in the state, so instead of going home, I had come to Ohani's house. Ohani wrapped her lips around my dick and snapped me out of my thoughts.

"You sure you want to do that, because I ain't forcing you to?" I asked looking into her eyes.

"Yes, I want to. I need to get you back hard, so that you can fill me up," she said, and my dick started coming back to life inside her mouth.

"See, there he is. And I think he really likes me," Ohani smiled and stood to her feet. When she lifted the negligee that she was wearing over her head, I admired her body. That sexy ass tattoo of a vine that ran from underneath her breast and wrapped around her stomach to her back still had me in awe. Her breasts were full and plump, and that ass… it sat up just right. I stood up with my dick sticking straight ahead and pulled Ohani close to me. When I looked down at her, she smiled.

"Make love to me Aaron," she said.

"I don't know about making love, Ohani, but we can definitely fuck." I said, because I was tired of her saying that shit.

Ohani walked around me and climbed onto her bed. After rolling the cover down, she removed her panties and tossed them to the floor. I took my shirt off and removed my jeans that were already halfway down. I reached inside of my pocket and grabbed a rubber. Peeling the wrapper from around it, I pulled it out and slid it onto my dick. I climbed onto the bed and pulled Ohani over to me by her ankles. She giggled as I lifted her legs into the air and plunged deep inside of her.

"Oh, my goodness! Aaron, you are so big, and I can never get used to your size," Ohani moaned.

"You like it, when I ram this dick into you?" I asked, as I poked at her walls. Her pussy was nice and warm, and her walls gripped me tightly.

"Damn, girl, fuck me back," I said gripping her butt and pulling her closer to me. She was a little stiff with it at first, but she started to fuck me back, and it started to feel better once she loosened up. Ohani was clamping her muscles around me, and I bit her nipple gently while never stopping my strokes.

"Mmm, Aaron, this feels so good," she cooed.

I flipped her over and slid into her from the back. Her ass was bouncing back on me, and I smacked her on it.

"Oh, my god," she screamed out.

We fucked for about another twenty minutes before I finally busted inside of the condom. After we were done, I told her that I needed to go home. Even with me and Keya not being together, I never stayed out all night. Of course, Ohani was a little upset, but I didn't give a fuck. I wasn't feeling her as much as I did in the beginning. It was just something about our connection that didn't feel right. Because as she had said, the sexual chemistry was there, but that was about it. I left out of her house with my mind made up that I wasn't coming back again.

39

John

"Do you think you're going to be good here by yourself?" I asked Kim, as we walked inside of her apartment. She had just gotten discharged from the hospital, and the doctors had told her to take it easy. She was now eight months pregnant, and the time was getting close for her to have the baby. With each day that passed, I became nervous as hell about her having this baby. The good thing was that I hadn't been back to her house unless it was something that pertained to the baby. She would try to grab my dick, but I always pushed her hand back. She knew that I wasn't going to do much to her since she was pregnant. That's what she always pushed my buttons.

"You're not staying?" She asked with a sad look on her face.

"I can't stay over here with you. Laydii was already mad when I went in late the other night," I said.

Kim rolled her eyes. "I am so tired of hearing about Laydii. You do have a baby on the way with me, too, John, or have you forgotten?" she asked.

"Aye, that's still to be determined. Besides, you knew that I had a girlfriend when you first came to me with this shit. And from day one, I told you that we either do the shit my way or no way at all." I said.

"I know, but it's like every time that I need you, all you ever say is that you can't do something because of Laydii. Maybe you should just go ahead and tell her since I know for a fact that this is your baby that I'm carrying." She said.

"Like I said, we'll know for sure when the baby gets here. Until then, I will tell my girl when I'm ready."

"Whatever!" I don't even know why you are around if you doubt my son so much. I mean, one minute you're buying stuff for the baby and giving me money like you know that he is yours, and the next, you're screaming DNA. I don't get it," Kim said.

"I didn't say it wasn't a possibility Kim. All I said was that, when the time was right, I will tell my girl. And as far as me giving you money, how else you gonna pay the bills around here? Especially since you ain't got a job no more," I said.

"That's because it was a struggle getting up every morning and going to work. It was hard on me," she said and I laughed.

"Kim, you worked in customer service where you sat on your ass all day. How hard was it for you to do that, huh?" I asked staring at her with an intent gaze, but Kim avoided eye contact with me. Kim thought that I was stupid, but she wasn't running game on me like she thought she was. Kim had quit her job about a month ago and had been depending on me to pay her bills. I kicked out enough money for her to pay her rent, but her utilities and shit like that, she had to pay that on her own. I didn't know how she was paying them, but I hoped for her sake that she was smart enough to have a savings.

"Well, I'm not asking you to pay my bills, John" she said.

"Look, I don't give a damn about that little money that I give you to pay your rent. That's chump change to me. But what I need you to understand is that I still have a girlfriend, and all that extra stuff you be wanting me to do, it ain't happening. Now, if you gotta problem with that, then I don't know what to tell you. I love my girl, and I'm not about to make any apologies for being with her," I said.

Kim stood with a frown on her face, but I didn't care about her being mad. I meant every word that I had just said to her.

"Aye, I got to go. Just call me if you have any more problems," I said before walking over towards the door.

"Maybe I will, maybe I won't," she mumbled.

"If you don't, then that's on you. Either way, I'll be good," I said and opened the door. I looked back at Kim one last time, shook my head, then shut the door, and left. I hopped into my car, and just as I was getting ready to pull off, my phone rang. I looked at the caller ID and saw that it was Jeremy, so I answered the call.

"What's going on?" I asked.

"Not a whole lot. But aye, I been meaning to ask what's going on with you? Yo ass was supposed to make that trip with us the other day, but you went missing. I even called Laydii's phone, and she told me that she hadn't talked to your ass either. Everything aight?" he asked.

"Not really, but ion really want to discuss it over the phone," I said.

"Well, I'm at the crib right now, and Aaron is supposed to be on his way over if you want to slide through and rap about it," Jeremy said, and I agreed. We ended the call, and I headed over to his house. When I pulled up, I grabbed my blunt out of the ashtray and got out of my car. It was the beginning of fall, and the wind was blowing hard. I walked over to the door and knocked. Jeremy opened the door, and I walked inside.

"When you get some furniture?" I asked, looking around at the new couch and loveseat set.

"I had this shit delivered yesterday. A nigga couldn't be up in this bitch another night without furniture," he told me laughing. "You want a beer?" he asked.

"Yeah, let me get one." I replied and laid back against the couch pillow.

Jeremy walked into his kitchen, and a few seconds later, he returned with a Heineken in his hand and passed it to me. I popped the top on it and took a couple of sips. I placed it on the table and sighed.

"So wassup, mane. Life that bad for you?" Jeremy asked.

"You don't know the half of it," I said, and there was a knock at the door.

"That's probably Aaron right there," Jeremy said and walked over to answer it. When he opened the door, Aaron walked in and threw me a head nod. "What's going on. Laydii let you out today?" he laughed and took a seat on the other end of the couch.

"Not really. Laydii ass ain't feeling me at the minute," I said.

"Ah, shit…what you do this time?" Aaron asked.

"Aight, so y'all niggas ready for this?"

"Mane, just hurry up and tell the story. Ain't nobody got time for the theatrics," Jeremy said, and we all laughed. That nigga always thought everything was a joke.

"Fuck you, nigga," I said. "Anyway, it was this bitch name Kim that I was fuckin with when me and Laydii were broken up last year. It wasn't anything serious, just us hanging out here and there, and she would dome me up sometimes. Well, one night, I went over to her house, and we fucked. Now, she done showed up talking about that she pregnant," I said, and they both looked at me in shock.

"This nigga dead," Jeremy said, laughing, but I didn't see shit funny.

"Aye, mane, that shit ain't funny. Do you know how Laydii gonna fuck my ass up once she hears about this shit?" I said.

"Exactly. And that's why you need to wait until that bitch haves the baby before you tell Laydii anything." Jeremy said. "Don't you agree, Aaron?"

"Nah, I don't agree. I say tell her now, dawg. You said that it happened while y'all was broken up, and I know that she may be mad, but she can't be too mad, because y'all weren't together, and you just found out yourself. What she can be mad about is that you now know, and you chose to keep it away from her. I'm telling you yo, tell her as now, mane. That way, if the baby is yours, she will have time to digest the shit, and if it comes out that's it not yours, y'all can go on with your lives. Don't listen to this nigga over here," Aaron said.

"I don't know, man. It's like Laydii knows that I'm hiding something from her, too, because she been questioning me a lot lately," I said.

"Why would she be questioning you? Have you been doing shit out of the normal?" Jeremy asked.

"I mean, besides taking Kim to her doctor's appointment, I ain't been doing shit. Oh, but she do be calling my phone with just random shit, no matter how many times I done told her to only call me when it's important. Laydii be tripping and stuff about my phone going off, and I have to pretend like it's one of y'all nigga's calling. Then, one day I'm at Kim's moving some furniture for her, and she damn near forced my dick down her throat." I said.

"Aye, mane, it sounds like she gonna be a problem already. But see that's where you messing up at. You're giving her the upper hand because she probably knows that you haven't told Laydii, and she thinks that she can pull these little stunts by calling when she wants to and shit like that. You need to get that bitch in check. And another thing, nigga, what was you thinking running up in her raw anyway? These broads out here scandalous as hell, and you taking chances like that," Aaron said.

"Mane, I was full of that damn liquor. Plus, when I went over to her house, I didn't have any intentions to fuck her, but she just kept trying to throw the pussy on me, and like a fool, I took it." I said.

"Yeah, yo ass definitely fucked up on that one. Now you got Laydii and possibly this other broad pregnant at the same time. How far along is she anyway?" Aaron asked.

"Eight months, mane," I replied running my hand down my face.

"Well, Jeremy was right about one thing. Laydii is gonna fuck your ass up," he said, and he and Jeremy laughed.

I stood up to leave, because I wasn't in the mood for their jokes. This wasn't their life that was about to be turned upside down. I had to get up out there before I ended up going off on my niggas. "Aye, I'mma holler at y'all later," I said.

"Aye mane, you know we just fucking with you," Jeremy said.

"Yeah, sit back down, dawg, and we gone figure out a way for you to break this shit to Laydii," Aaron said.

"I'm good. I'll fuck with y'all on the rebound," I told them just before walking out of the door. Once I was outside in my car, I pulled out the blunt that I had taken inside of Jeremy's house with me and fired it up. I backed out of the yard and headed home with a ton of things going through my mind.

40

Keya

One month later….

"Happy Birthday, baby," I said to Aniya, as I held her in my hands. She was squirming around trying to stop me from kissing her, but I gripped her tight and pulled her close to me and planted wet kisses on her fat cheeks. She laughed, then I laughed too.

"So, what you want to do for her birthday?" Aaron asked, as he walked into the kitchen where me and Aniya were having our moment. He reached for her, and I placed her in his hands. "Happy Birthday, Daddy's baby," he said.

She put her short arms around his neck, and I just stared at them. She was such a daddy's girl, and it made me so happy to see the bond that they had was unbreakable.

"I wanted to have her a party, but since it's so much shit going on, I'm thinking maybe I'll just take her to Incredible Pizza and let her play," I said.

"That's cool, I'mma come with y'all."

"Okay, what time do you want to go?" I asked.

"Let me make a few phone calls, and then we can be out." Aaron said.

"Alright, well let us go get dressed," I told him and stood up from the table. I reached for Aniya, who was still in his arms, and she tucked her head into his chest. "Ain't this some shit. I'm the one that spends all day with her, but all she wants is you," I said placing my hands on my hips. Aaron laughed while looking down at Aniya.

"Come on, baby. Go to your mama so that she can get y'all ready. Daddy going to make a few phone calls and then we can go have fun," he said handing her over to me. I took her from his hands and put her on my hip. I was getting ready to head for the room I was staying in when Aaron called out to me.

"Don't take all day getting dressed," he said, and I smirked. Aaron's phone rang, and he looked down at it. "I'm serious," he said just before leaving the kitchen. I could hear him talking, but I couldn't make out what he was saying.

"Come on, baby; let's go get you ready to have some fun." I told Aniya and walked to my room.

Aaron's door was closed when I walked by, and that made me feel some type of way. I knew that he was seeing somebody, and I was almost certain it was the same girl from Laydii's house, but what could I really do about it? Nothing, because I was the reason that we weren't together now.

I walked into the room and placed Aniya down in her walker. I had already taken a shower before I went down to breakfast, so I put my clothes on. A few weeks ago, I had gotten me and Aniya matching t-shirts made that had a Minnie Mouse on the front with the number one above it, for the age she was turning. I paired my T-shirt with a pair of skinny jeans. I had gained a little weight over the last few months from sitting in the house and not really doing anything, so I now had a little pudge in my stomach, but not enough to where it was too noticeable. I put my black and white Nike Shox on and looked in the mirror to make sure my bob was intact. Because of the state my hair was in, when Sam kidnapped me, I had to have a few inches chopped off. Although I loved having long hair, the bob was very becoming of me, and I planned to keep it cut like that for a while.

Once I was done getting myself together, I went to get my baby girl dressed. She was wearing a pair of denim leggings, with her T-shirt, and she had the same Nike Shox as me in her size. After I had finished getting her dressed, I got the hair box out to do her hair. I parted her long, curly hair down the middle and gave her two puffs that made it look like she had Minnie Mouse ears. She looked so cute, and I couldn't wait to take pictures of her.

About ten minutes later, Aaron knocked on my door and let himself in. Although casual, he still looked good. He wore a plain Black Tee, with a pair of jeans, and some black and red Jordan's. He had just gotten a fresh haircut the day before, and his facial lineup looked good on his smooth, chocolate skin.

"Y'all look good," he said, and I blushed.

"Thanks!" I replied. "Give me like ten minutes, and I should be ready. I need to put my makeup on."

"Keya, you don't need makeup. I really don't know why you wear that shit anyway," he said as he walked over to my bed and took a seat on the edge of it. Aaron was right about me not needing makeup, and the only reason I wore it was to enhance my natural beauty.

"Thanks, but I like to keep myself dolled up. You never know, I might meet Aniya a new stepdaddy," I said with a sly grin.

"Aye, don't get fucked up. Aniya only got one daddy, and you ain't about to have her around no other niggas," he said.

"Okay!" I said, while walking into the bathroom to put my makeup on.

"Okay, my ass. You can try me if you want to," I heard him say.

After I was done with my makeup, we drove to Incredible Pizza. Once we were inside, me, Aaron, and Aniya went over to where the kiddie rides were. Aaron put Aniya in this airplane that lifted from the ground and took her halfway into the air. Aniya giggled the whole time that she was on the ride, and after it was over, we had to damn near pry her from it, Then, she had a fit once we had her off. We found her another kiddie ride, and when she got off that one, it was the same thing. We let her ride about three more rides, and then Aaron asked me if I wanted to grab something to eat. I told him that I did, and we walked over to the buffet. Since it was a Saturday, it was pretty crowded and the line was long as hell. I was scanning over the selections of food that they had, when suddenly I had to use the bathroom to the point where I couldn't hold it.

"Hey, I'mma run to the restroom really quick," I said to Aaron.

"You want me to get you something?" he asked. I scanned the bar once again, and when I saw that they had brought out some more pepperoni pizza, I told him to get me that. I gave Aaron my plate and rushed off to the bathroom. After I was done using it, I washed my hands and walked out. I was so busy looking around for Aaron and Aniya that I bumped into somebody.

"Oh, I'm sorry," I said to the guy.

"You good shorty," he said eyeing me from head to toe. "Aye, I ain't trying to run no game on you or anything, but you are so fuckin sexy to me," he said with a smile.

"Thanks," I said, blushing. I got a good look at him, and he was looking good, too. He stood a little over six feet in height. His frame was medium built, and he had that same chocolate skin like Aaron. I don't know what it was, but I was addicted to chocolate men.

"Well, I guess it was good talking to you," I said and got ready to walk off.

"Excuse me, do you mind if I have your name?" he asked.

"It's Keya." I replied.

"Nice to meet you, Keya. I'm Daniel," he said.

"It's nice to meet you, Daniel, but I need to go," I told him.

"Aight, well before you go, do you mind if I ask you for your number?"

"Umm," I started to say.

"Nah, it ain't happening playboy." Aaron said coming out of nowhere. He had Aniya in his hands and a frown on his face. The guy Daniel looked between me and Aaron.

"Oh, my bad, I didn't mean to step on no toes," he said and walked off. After he was gone, I stared at Aaron.

"Wow, Aaron that was rude," I said, and Aaron frowned.

"This what you over here doing? Talking to niggas while me and your daughter sitting and waiting for you?" Aaron asked.

"I was just coming out of the bathroom, and I accidently bumped into him. He asked me if he could have my number, and just when I was getting ready to tell him no, you came out of nowhere. What's the big deal anyway?" I asked.

"I'm saying; it's rude as fuck to be entertaining some nigga, and your baby daddy is not too far from you," he said.

"Look, Aaron, let's go sit down and talk. I don't need everybody all in our business," I said.

"Aight, but we gone finish this as soon as we get to the table," he said and walked off. I followed behind him with a frown on my face. *He is blowing this way out of proportion*, I thought.

When we got to the table, Aaron put Aniya back in the booster chair. I sat down, and pretended to play with her. "So, you want to talk about how you just disrespected me?" he asked.

"How did I disrespect you, Aaron?" I asked with confusion written all over my face.

"You out there talking to niggas, while me and Aniya waiting for you. This is her birthday, and you out there grinning in the next nigga's face." He spewed.

"Damn, you making a big deal out of this. I told you what happened, and to be honest with you, Aaron, I didn't have to tell you that. We are not together anymore, or have you forgotten?" I asked.

"Yeah, I remember, but I really ain't trying to hear that we ain't together shit. Keep playing with me, Keya." He said, and I rolled my eyes.

"Whatever!" I said nixing him off, but then I thought about it; I wasn't going to leave it alone. Aaron wanted to call me out on my stuff when I hadn't even done anything, so I was about to call him out. "You know what? It's not whatever. Since you want to say something to me about what I was doing. What about you?" I asked.

"What about me?"

"Just the other week, you came in super late, and as soon as you came into the house, you went straight for the shower. Now lie and say that you weren't out fuckin a bitch." I said.

"I wasn't," he lied with a straight face.

"You are such a liar, Aaron, and I'm over this conversation."

"Nah, if you got some shit on your chest, then now is the time to get it off," he said leaning back in his seat with a smirk on his face. He pissed me off so bad, and if it wasn't for us being in a room full of people, I probably would have smacked that damn smirk off his face.

"I'm done talking, Aaron," I said and picked up one of the pizza slices that was on my plate. It was cold, so I sat it down and looked out at everybody. Aniya's birthday was ruined, and I wish that I would have just brought her here by myself.

"You ain't eating?" he asked.

"No, I lost my appetite," I said.

"Keya, I don't want to argue with you anymore," Aaron said like he hadn't started the whole thing.

"You don't want to argue, but you started it. You know what, never mind. Look, can we just go," I asked.

He stared at me before he finally stood up. He grabbed Aniya, and we all left out. On the ride home, the car was extremely quiet, and I knew that my accusations about him were right. He had slept with somebody else, and maybe it was high time that I moved on since, clearly, he was out here doing him.

~~~~~~~~~~~~~~~~~~~**Later that night**

"So, you still mad?" Aaron asked me, as I sat on the couch reading a book. I had just laid Aniya down for the night, and all I wanted to do was relax, but of course he wasn't going to let me do that.

"No, I'm not mad. I just don't feel like talking," I said as I continued to read my book.

"Look, Keya, I apologize for blowing up on you like I did. And maybe I did overreact. I guess you can say that I was still thinking about that comment that you had made earlier." He said.

"What comment?" I said lifting my head from my book.

"About you trying to find a step daddy for Aniya." He said.

Hmm, picture that, he's in his feelings, I thought to myself.

"Oh, my god, I was just joking. But let's be real here, Aaron. All we are doing is co-parenting, right? You made it perfectly clear that you weren't trying to be with me, and I've accepted that, so if some guy tries to holler at me, and I want to give him a shot, then I will."

"Aye, yo ass is really testing me right now," Aaron said.

"How am I testing you?" I asked.

"Keya quit playing stupid." He said staring me down.

I shook my head. "You are really giving me a headache, Aaron. I don't understand why you're getting so upset about me dating somebody else?"

"Cause, I don't want no other nigga having what's mine," he said.

"What?" I said with a slight chuckle.

"You heard what I said." Aaron said looking into my eyes.

I was so confused. Since I had been living back in the house, Aaron hadn't shown any signs of him wanting us to reconcile, and now since I had mentioned dating somebody else, he suddenly wanted to claim me as his girl again.

"Aaron I'm not yours, and the only reason you're probably saying something about us now, is because I mentioned me possibly dating somebody else."

"Keya, I've been thinking about us for a little minute, and just because I haven't said anything, doesn't mean that it hasn't been on my mind." He said.

"But how can you think about us getting back together when you haven't even forgiven me?" I asked.

"What you mean? I forgave you." He said.

"No, you haven't, and you want to know how I know that you haven't? It's because you have been calling me Keya ever since you got out of jail. I was always your lil mama, and you not calling me that only means that you have not forgiven me, and that we are just not there anymore." I told him, and tears started to come to my eyes. I was so tired of crying, but that was the only emotion that I got nowadays.

Aaron was quiet, and it looked like he was thinking about what I had just said to him. It was true, though, and he knew it. He was still mad at me about the Sam situation, and I didn't know if he would ever forgive me.

"I guess you right, and I want to forgive you, but it's like, every time I think about everything, I get pissed about it all over again. It also doesn't help that I know you ain't being honest about what happened with you and Sam," he said, and I almost died.

"Whatttt are you talking about?" I asked stammering over my words.

"Aye, you know what I'm talking about," he said while looking into my eyes. The crazy thing was, his stare wasn't menacing; it was more like he was pleading with me to be honest about the situation. I didn't know if I was ready to reveal to him what Sam had done. I put my head down, and Aaron walked over and sat down beside me. He took his hand and gently lifted my chin.

"Please, lil mama, tell what me what happened?" He asked.

At those words, another tear slipped down my cheek, and I broke down and told Aaron everything. Once I was done, I thought that he would be disgusted and look at me in a different way, but instead of turning his back on me, Aaron took me into his arms and held me tight. By now, I was completely in tears, almost to the point of being inconsolable. Aaron was gentle with me, though, as he wiped away my tears and told me that everything was gonna be okay. For a long time, we didn't say anything. He allowed me to cry on his shoulder, and I found comfort in doing so.

"I love you, Keya. You and my daughter mean the world to me, and I don't know what I would do if I didn't have y'all in my life. I know that we can't get back to where we were right away, but I think that we should both work on building our trust again, and maybe we can find a way to make this shit work out," he said wiping the last of my tears away with his thumb.

I looked at Aaron, and I could see it in his eyes that he did still love me. It was funny how tragic situations could bring you back together. I knew that me and Aaron were from two different worlds, but that no longer mattered to me. I loved him, and he loved me, and that was what was most important. "Aaron, I love you, too, and I'm willing to work at rebuilding your trust if you will allow me to." I said.

"It's time we got our shit together, Keya, but I need to know that you're all the way in this with me this time. That means, if shit gets a little rough, you can't go running like you always have. You know the type of lifestyle I live, so you know the risk that comes along with it. If you can't handle that, then tell me now, and we can go our separate ways," he said.

I didn't rush to give him an answer, because I wanted to let his words sink in before responding. He stared at me, while I thought about it. In the end, he was who I wanted to be with, and I didn't think I could live my life without him. "Aaron, I want to be with you, and I'm willing to accept what you do, if you make me one promise." I said.

"What's that?" he asked.

"Don't make this shit a lifetime. Find something to invest your money in, and when the time is right, get out. We have a daughter now, and I don't ever want to tell her that you can't come home because you're locked up, or worst, you're dead," I forced myself to say.

"I got you, Lil Mama, and actually, I've been thinking about that, too. I'm working on a plan, and if you hang in there with me, I promise I'mma get out," he said. I nodded while looking into his eyes. We stared at each other, and then he leaned in and kissed me. I opened my mouth to allow his tongue entry, and we kissed with so much passion that it made my toes curl. "Mmm," I said, as we took the kiss deeper.

"Damn, I love yo ass," he said.

"I love you, too," I told him. Aaron kissed me again, and I could feel the love behind that kiss. I climbed onto his lap, and he stared at me.

"What are you doing?" he asked.

"Make love to me, Aaron." I said, while gazing down at him.

"Are you sure that you ready to do that?" he asked.

"I'm positive. I need to feel you inside of me," I told him, and then lifted the shirt that he had on and tossed it to the floor. I kissed on his neck, as he ran his hands up and down my back. We continued our passionate kiss while undressing each other. I climbed back onto his lap, and he guided me down onto his penis. As it went in, it hurt a little, but I took the pain, because I knew that the pleasure would soon follow. I worked my hips around in a circular motion.

"Damn, I missed this pussy," Aaron said, while gripping my butt and slamming me down onto his dick. He wrapped both arms around my waist and guided me up and down. Our skin slapped with each pump, and I could already feel myself on the verge of cumin. Tears started to leak from my eyes as I laid my head on his shoulder.

"I love you, Keya," he whispered into my ear.

"I love you, too," I said. "Oh, my god, I love you, baby," I cried out, as a gut-wrenching orgasm took over my body.

"Argh shit! I'm about to come, Lil Mama," Aaron said. A few minutes later, he was cumin inside of me. I still had my head on his chest, as I listened to the rapid beat of his heart. It was like music to my ears to hear that.

"Keya, yo ass better not ever leave me again." Aaron said breaking our silence.

"I promise I won't," I told him.

Aaron turned my head to face him and placed a kiss on my lips. As I ground on him, I could feel his dick come back to life inside of me. We made love one more time, before finally going to bed wrapped in each other's arms.

41

Aaron

My phone buzzed around on the nightstand waking me out of my sleep. I glanced down at Keya's beautiful face while she still laid in my arms from the night before. I didn't want to move her, but I knew that I needed to answer the phone before it stopped ringing. Keya must have felt me moving, because she woke up and looked at me.

"I need to get that, Lil Mama," I said to her.

"Okay," she said rolling out of my arms. She turned on her side and faced me. I picked my phone up, and when I did, it stopped ringing, but then it started back again. When I looked at the caller ID, I saw that it was Ohani. I didn't want to give Keya any suspicions by not answering, but I didn't want to answer and she figure out that it was a woman calling. I decided to just call Ohani later, so I hit the ignore button.

"You could have answered," Keya said.

"I thought that it was important, but it wasn't," I said to her.

"Aaron, we weren't together, so if you were talking to somebody, then it's nothing that I can be mad about. I finally realized that I'm the reason we weren't together in the first place, so I have no other choice but to deal with whatever comes my way," Keya said.

"Let's not talk about any of that. We said that we were both going to start fresh from here on out, and that's what we're going to do," I said. I leaned in and gave Keya a quick peck on her lips. "Now, I'mma go jump in the shower. You want to join me?" I asked, while pinching her exposed nipple. She giggled, and we both got up to take a shower before Aniya woke up. After our shower, we got dressed in some lounge clothes and decided to just hang around the house and enjoy each other's company.

With everything that had been going on, we both needed a small escape from everything and everybody around us. We played with Aniya, watched movies, and just kicked back like we used to do in the earlier stages of our relationship. After a while, Aniya got sleepy, and Keya said that she would lay her down for a nap. I used that opportunity to smoke a blunt and call Ohani back. I stepped onto my balcony and slid the door close behind me. I kept my chair facing the door, just in case Keya came while I was on the phone.

When I dialed Ohani's number, the phone rang a few times before she finally picked up.

"Well, hello stranger," Ohani said into the phone.

"Wassup, girl? I see that you called me earlier," I said.

"I was just calling because when I spoke to you yesterday you said that you were going to call me back later, but you never did," she said.

"That's my bad. I took my daughter out for her birthday, and some shit popped off that needed my attention." I told her.

"Well, I can understand that. Did you have a good time with your daughter?" she asked.

"Look, Ohani, I think that we need to take a step back. I got a lot on my plate right now, and it wouldn't be fair if I strung you along," I said skipping all the small talk. It wasn't any sense in trying to prolong the situation.

"Um, I thought we were really feeling each other, Aaron? I mean, what has changed since the last time that we talked?" she asked.

"Me and Keya gonna try and work things out, and I want to make sure that I go in giving her my full attention. I hope you can understand that," I said.

"Yes, I understand," she said.

"Good!" I started to say, but she cut me off.

"I understand that you are a selfish ass nigga that used me to get some ass. You stayed up all night talking to me on the phone while your bitch was right there in the house with you. You've been to my house to fuck me several times, and now you are trying to tell me that y'all are going to work shit out. Wow, I showed you how it was to be treated by a real woman, and you just shitted on me Aaron?" she spat.

"Aye, you got the game twisted, shawty. You think sucking my dick and spreading your legs anytime that I come through is showing me what a real woman is? Fuck outta here with that shit. I love my girl for reasons that your ass would never know. You or no other bitch can say what she has done for me, because I don't pillow talk and tell you what's going on with us. All you knew was that we weren't together, so stop talking about what the next bitch is doing, and worry about finding a nigga that you don't have to entice with sex just to get them to like your ass. Try stimulating a nigga's mind, instead of trying to get his dick hard," I said.

"Fuck you, Aaron. You are just like every other guy. Too stupid to realize when a real woman is in your face. No, you would rather wife some ratchet bitch, than to appreciate what I had to offer you" she said, and that shit pissed me off.

"Bitch, you basic, and ain't shit special about you. Tell me, what makes you stand out above every other woman?" I asked. Ohani thought that, because she was older, she could look down on Keya, but the truth is, all she really had to offer me was sex, and that wasn't even better than Keya's. I mean, she could suck a dick and all, but even that could use some improvements.

"I don't have to prove anything to your ass," Ohani said.

"Yeah, just like I thought. Lose my fucking number," I said and hung up. Her ass had me firecracker hot. I didn't hit women, but if Ohani had been in front of me, I probably would have choked her ass out for saying some shit like that. My phone beeped with a text, and it was from Ohani. I sighed while opening the message.

Ohani: Nigga you will pay for playing with my feelings. MARK MY WORDS!

Me: I'll wait for it!

I figured that would make her reply, but after a few minutes of waiting, no other messages came through. I finished the rest of my blunt, and when I was done, I went into the house and spent the rest of the day with the two of my favorite ladies.

42

Laydii

One week later....

"Get up, bae," John said popping me on my butt for the second time. I grudgingly rolled over and glared at him. My ass had been in a good sleep, and here he was disturbing me with his games.

"What am I getting up for?" I asked with a yawn.

"Cause, I got a surprise for you," he replied.

"Oh, really?" I asked, while flipping the cover back. I scooted to the edge of the bed, and smiled at him. "So, what's the surprise?"

"C'mon now, girl. It wouldn't be a surprise if I told you, now would it? Now get your ass up, cause we got things to do," he said.

"Okay, I'm getting up now," I said. Once I slid off the bed, I stretched and rubbed my stomach. My baby girl was really moving around. I walked into the bathroom to handle my hygiene, and once done, I grabbed the clothes that I was wearing for the day. John was already dressed, and he watched me intently as I put my clothes on. He had this silly grin on his face, and it looked like it was killing him to keep whatever he had planned to himself. Hell, he was making me more anxious than before to know what he was up to.

After I was done getting dressed, John and I walked out to the car hand and hand. When we made it to the car, he kissed my hand, and opened the door for me. After I was inside, John closed the door and ran around to his side.

"Baby, please tell me what the surprise is," I pleaded with him, as we pulled away from our condo.

"Nope, you will see it soon enough," he said, and I pouted. I figured I would just wait to see what the surprise was, because I knew that he wasn't going to tell me. My eyes were glued to my phone as I watched some of the funny videos that were on Facebook when John came to a sudden stop. When I looked up, I saw that we were parked in front of a building where they did massages at.

"Are you getting me a massage, John?" I asked with the biggest smile on my face. I had never had a massage before, so I was too geeked if this was what he had planned.

"C'mon, let's go see," he said and opened his door. John walked around to my side and opened my door, and I climbed out. When we got inside of the building, I looked around, and it had a nice ambiance. The ceilings were high, there was white furniture with gold trimming, and it smelt great. They had soft music playing over the speakers, and I was really impressed.

"Hi, how can I help you?" the receptionist asked.

"I have an appointment for ten-thirty," John replied.

"For Jackson?" the receptionist asked while looking at us.

"That's us," he said grabbing my hand.

"Perfect, right this way," she said leading us down a long hall. There were several rooms with the doors closed, and I figured that they were occupied with people that were getting massages. We finally stopped at a room, and when we walked inside, there were two tables set up with all the things needed for a massage. I turned and looked at John, and he had a smile on his face. "Is this a couple's massage?" I asked.

"Yeah, why? You don't want me getting a massage with you?" he asked with a slight chuckle.

"Yes, I would love for you to do this with me," I said. I was so surprised that John had not only set up a massage for me, but for both of us to do it together. We had never done anything like this before, and the gesture had definitely earned him some brownie points.

"You guys are so cute together," the receptionist said while smiling at us.

"Thank you," I smiled.

"Alright, well go ahead and get undressed and put these white sheets over you guys. Since you are pregnant Mrs. Jackson, you will be receiving the maternity massage. It's safe, and we have one of the best masseuses to get the job done for you," the receptionist said.

Mrs. Jackson, hmm, I like the sound of that, I thought. "Thank you," I said again.

"No problem, and they should be right in with you shortly. You guys enjoy," she said just before leaving the room.

I stared at John the minute she was gone. "What?" he asked with a sly grin.

"Thank you, baby. This really means a lot to me," I said.

"You know I got you. A nigga been hearing you loud and clear. I know that we hadn't spent a lot of time together, and I promise, from this day forward I'mma make sure that I do everything in my power to get in that quality time with my baby," he said and kissed my lips. We got undressed, and a few minutes later, two women massage therapists came into the room. They asked us if we preferred music or silence, and me and John both agreed to have the music played during our massages. John had paid for one-hour massages, and when they were over, my body felt good and relaxed. The lady that I had, had done an amazing job, and I was going to request her the next time that I came back.

When we got back into the car, John reached over and grabbed my hand. I smiled and relaxed in my seat. He drove off to the next destination, and about fifteen minutes later, we were pulling up to this salon called Tamara's. I had heard of it before, but I hadn't had the chance to visit it. One of things that I had heard about the place was that the stylist was known for whipping some hair, and making it look like you had gone to a salon that only some of the celebrities visited. Supposedly they were just that good in there. Me and John got out of the car and walked inside of the salon. I looked around the place, and saw that it was a really nice shop. When the receptionist noticed us, she asked if we had an appointment, and John told her that we did. After getting my name, the receptionist walked me over to one of the styling chairs, while John waited in the lobby. I waited for a few minutes, and then I noticed a pretty lady about my height with a slim build walking my way. Her skin was dark and smooth looking, and she had these big piercing eyes. The natural hair that she rocked looked healthy, and she had it done up in a mohawk.

"Hey, how are you? I'm Tamara the owner of the shop and you're Laydii, right?" she asked.

"Yes, I am. And it's nice to meet you Tamara," I smiled.

"Likewise," she replied, and placed a towel and cape around my neck. "So how do you want your hair?"

"Um, a simple wash and blow out will be fine," I replied while looking at her through the mirror. Tamara slowly ran her hands through my hair, and I figured that she was doing an assessment to check the state of it.

"Okay, I'm going to have my shampoo girl wash your hair, and when she's done I will take care of you from there," she said.

"Okay. That sounds good," I told her.

Tamara called a shampoo lady over, and she took me to the wash bowl. As she washed my hair, I drifted in and out of sleep, because her hands felt so good.

"You're done," the girl tapped my shoulder, and wrapped a towel around my head. She led me back over to the styling chair, and told me to take a seat. After that Tamara immediately went to work on my hair. It took her no more than thirty minutes to have my hair looking on point.

"So, you like it?" Tamara asked.

"Yes, I love it," I said twisting my head from side to side. My hair had so much bounce to it, and it looked real healthy.

John had already paid for my hair service, so I asked Tamara for her number so that I could come back to see her. When we left Tamara's, John hit me with another surprise. He took me to a nail shop, where I got my feet and hands done, and I also had my eyebrows waxed. I left that place feeling a little exhausted. I appreciated all that he had done for me, but after being pampered all day, I needed a nap. I yawned and laid my head against the headrest, and before I knew it, I had drifted off to sleep.

****

It felt like I had been asleep for an eternity, when I felt John shake me from my sleep.

"Wassup, baby?" I asked with my eyes still half closed.

"I got one more surprise for you," he said, and I opened my eyes to look at him.

"Another one?" I asked in shock. It was like he was just pulling out all stops, and I didn't know where this sudden change of attitude had come from.

"Yeah, another one. And you definitely gone like this one," he said. Shortly after he was pulling into the lot of a big white building, and I stared out at it. The sign read showroom, but I had never heard of it or seen it before. When I looked around the lot, I noticed that John's car was the only car there.

"What is this place?" I asked John, but all he did was smile.

"C'mon and get out, so you can see this surprise," He said. I followed his lead and got out of the car, but I was still a little skeptical. We slowly walked to the big red double doors of the building, and John held one of them open so that I could walk inside. I hesitated a little, because I didn't know what I was about to face.

"Go ahead," he ushered me in. I shook my head, and walked through the door. When we got inside, I looked around the lobby, but there wasn't much detail that gave me a clue as to what kind of place it was. The only thing that stood out, was the different pictures of people lined along the wall having some type of event or another. John placed his hand on the small of my back, and we walked further down the hall.

What in the world is he up to? I thought to myself as we came upon another set of double doors. "Okay, John, you are really making me nervous now. What is this place?" I asked for the third time, but he was still being tight-lipped about it. I was starting to get upset, because I had no clue where we were, and he didn't want to tell me anything. When hc opened one of the doors, I noticed the lights were out. He slightly stepped inside, and I could see him running his hand along the wall. Out of nowhere, "surprise!" everyone screamed just as John hit the light switch.

"Oh, my god," I said with my hand over my mouth.

I did a quick scan of the room, and saw my closes family and friends all gathered together. The surprise was that John had gathered everyone together to throw me a baby shower. As I continued to look around the room, I noticed how well decorated it was. There were a dozen balloons floating around with streamers that hung from the walls. From the ceiling, there was a huge sign hanging that said baby shower on it with pink and white letterings. A long table sat in the middle of the floor, with all types of food piled high. The room had eight more tables, that I assumed, the guests would sit at. They were also decorated beautifully, and each one held a picture of me that John had taken when I was just three months pregnant. On a table, off to the side, sat a huge three-tier, strawberry cake with a baby, and blocks adorned the top. Then, there were the gifts that were piled so high that had the ceiling been any lower, they would have probably touched it.

My mouth hung wide open as I turned to John. "Surprise, baby," he said, while staring down at me.

I smiled, and a few tears slipped from my eyes. Although I was tired of crying, I didn't mind those tears, because they were happy tears. I finally got a good look at everyone that was there, after I wiped the last of my tears away. Keya, my mom, Laila, Jeremy, Aaron, Aniya, Tina, even Keya's parents were there. John's mom, and brother, who I hadn't seen in a long time was also there. When I looked to the right of me, I saw my dad standing off by himself with a smile on his face. I hadn't seen him in a few years and had only spoken to him a few times over the phone. We didn't have that great of a relationship, but I was still happy to see him. John had really shown out, but in a good way this time, and I couldn't have been happier.

"Thank you, baby," I mouthed to John.

He bent down and gave me a quick peck on the lips, just before Keya approached us. I pulled away and looked at her with both eyebrows raised.

"Hey, girl," she said hugging me tightly.

"Did you know about this?" I asked, and Keya gave me a mischievous grin.

"Tsk. Tsk. I can't believe my girl kept this away from me," I said waving my finger at her playfully.

"Sorry boo, but I promised John that I wouldn't tell you anything. But girl, it almost ate me ass alive, and I was so happy when the day finally came so that I wouldn't have to walk around with this secret anymore." She said, and I laughed.

Suddenly a thought came to me. "Wait, where is everyone's cars parked at? When me and John pulled up I didn't see anyone parked out front, but y'all were already here," I said looking between Keya and John.

"That's because it's a parking lot in the back, and I had everyone to park back there," John said.

"Damn, y'all got me good," I said.

"Yeah, we did, but do you really like it?" Keya asked.
"No, I love it," I said while looking around the room once again.

"Good, because I worked my ass off to make sure this day went perfect. Oh, and as soon as I get everyone situated, we're going to get everything started," she said, and sauntered off. I smiled as I watched her make her way around the room.

Shortly after, everyone came up one by one, and started to shower me with hugs, and tell me congratulations on my baby girl. When it was my dad's turn to hug me, he held me in his arms, and I felt like a little girl all over again. The little girl that always needed their father's love, and approval. And with me wrapped inside his arms, I could feel some of the love that I had always longed for.

"You look beautiful, baby girl," He said as I stood back and stared up at him.

"Thank you, Daddy. I'm so glad that you're here," I smiled.

"I wouldn't have missed it for the world. And when you and this young man get ready to walk down the aisle, I won't miss that either," he said, and I looked over at John.

"Trust me, it won't be too much longer before we cross that path," John said, and my dad nodded.

"But hey, maybe one day next week we can have lunch together, because I know that you really won't have the time to talk to your old man right now. Will that be okay?" My dad asked me.

"Yes, I would love that," I smiled.

"Good! I will call you next week, and we can go from there," He said, and I told him that will be fine. "Alright, well I guess I will see you in a minute baby girl," he told me and gently rubbed my stomach.

My dad walked off and headed back towards the tables. Surprisingly, he took a seat at the same table that my mom was occupying, and almost immediately they started talking. My mom whispered something into his ear and he let out a hearty laugh. After my dad finally stopped laughing at whatever my mom had just told him, he looked at her in a way that I couldn't quite describe. *Hmm,* I thought to myself. I would have to ask my mom later what that was all about. But for the time being, I just wanted to enjoy the beautiful day that had been planned for me, and focus on those that had come together to make sure it was one that I would never forget. As I sat down in the chair that had been decorated for me, I thought about how much I missed Toni and how I wished that she was there with us. Although, she was gone in body, I knew that her spirit lived on and that she was smiling that pretty smile of hers down on us from heaven.

Suddenly, John walked to the middle of the floor and asked for everybody's attention. I stared at him, and when he realized that I was looking, he gave me a wink and smile that made my heart melt.

"Alright, everybody, I would like to start off by saying thank you all for sharing in this day with me and the lady of the hour. Also, I would like to especially thank Keya for helping me set everything up, and for making sure that all our family and friends were here to celebrate this day. You did a good job, girl, and Laydii should be thankful to have such a good friend like you in her corner. Lastly, I would like to thank Laydii, the woman who I love with all my heart for giving me one of the best gifts in the world. I know that everybody might think that we're young, and that we probably can't handle a baby. But with the love that we have for each other, I know that we'll be able to give that same love to our daughter. This day is for you baby, and I can't wait to meet the precious little girl that we created. Thank you all again for coming out, and now we can celebrate," he said and walked back over to me. Everyone was rooting and clapping, and I couldn't do anything but just stare at John. He was showing me a side of him that I had never seen before, and I had to admit I loved it.

"That's right, John" I heard my mama say, and I turned my head and looked at her. I was glad that she had finally accepted the fact that I was with him, because there was a time when I could remember that she hated his guts.

After John's little speech, the baby shower got started. Keya did the hosting, along with my mom and John's mom. I smiled the whole time, as I played silly games, ate until I felt like I was gonna burst, and opened all the gifts that everybody had brought for us. Once it was over, John loaded all the gifts that he could inside of his car, and Aaron had to follow us in Keya's truck with the rest of the gifts. I was so tired from all the day's activities that I ended up falling asleep in the car just as John pulled away from the building.

43
Sam

"Aye man, you need to lay off that shit. That's the second time yo ass done spaced out on me," Tank said, as I nodded in and out of sleep. I had just hit like six lines of blow, and my ass was through. My head bopped some as I looked at Tank. "Do you hear me, muthafucka," he yelled. Yo ass needs to be helping me come up with a plan to get at them niggas, instead of getting high every five minutes" he spat.

"Muthafucka, you get high just as much as me. Fuck you talking about?" I said, now coming off of my high. He didn't need to be coming at me about how high I got, when most of the times, his ass was right there snorting that powder right along with me. Just then, Tank's older sister walked into the room. She had been over his house for the last couple of days moping around. I didn't know what was up with her ass, and I really didn't care either. The bitch was stuck up, and thought she was too good for me. I had tried to holler at her, but she had turned my ass down. She said that she didn't mess with guys like me. Whatever the fuck that meant.

"Would both of you niggas shut the fuck up. I am trying to get some sleep, and y'all are disturbing me," she yelled.

"Ohani, ain't nobody got time for your bullshit right now. A nigga pockets hurting, and I'm stressed the fuck out. Care your ass home, if you want some peace," Tank said to her.

"I can't go home," she yelled back.

"Why the fuck not," he asked.

"Because I don't want to be alone," she whispered and broke down crying. I shook my head, because I was starting to see how much she manipulated Tank. In the little time that I had known Ohani, I saw how full of drama she was. Let her tell it, everybody was always out to get her.

"Aye, what's up with this crying shit?" Tank stood up and wrapped her in his arms. I smirked, while picking up the blunt that I had laying on the table. I wasn't much of a weed smoker, because I mainly preferred that white girl, but every so often, I would smoke a Kush blunt to intensify my high.

"That guy that I was talking to, he broke up with me last week," Ohani said, and I laughed to myself.

That's what yo stuck-up ass gets, I thought.

"Fuck that nigga; if he can't see that he missing out on a good woman, then that's his fuckin loss. Don't be sitting around here moping around over him. That's why I'm always telling you to take they ass for what they got, and move on to the next. Quit trying to fuckin fall in love," Tank said while staring at her.

"I guess you right. I just hate that I let that nigga in my world, only for him to turn around and play me for the next bitch," Ohani said, while wiping the tears away from her eyes. Tank wrapped his arms around her again.

I chuckled to myself, because it was funny as hell to see the side of Tank where he was comforting somebody. The nigga was hood as shit, but when it came to sister, he was soft as cotton. I guess them growing up in different homes hadn't affected their bond at all. He always going to visit her in Florida, and I guess that's how they remained close.

"You good?" he asked her, and she nodded. A few seconds later, she walked out of the room.

"Aye, this nigga Aaron gotta go. I'm tired of this fuckin cat and mouse game shit that we keep playing. I say we just run up on the nigga and tell him to take us to his stash," I told Tank. Every day, I had been thinking of a way that we could get at him, cause I no longer had Harold as an option. Not too longer ago, he had stopped answering my calls, and I suspected that he had probably left town. That was probably best for him, because he not only had Aaron to worry about, but me if I ever caught up to him.

"I feel ya," Tank replied, and we both looked up as Ohani came storming into the room. She stood by the door, and folded her hands over her breast.

"Tank, what are y'all in here talking about?" she asked.

"Nothing! I thought you had went back to bed?" he asked.

"I was going back to bed, but then I had to use the bathroom, and I overheard y'all talking," she replied. "Did y'all say something about a person named Aaron?"

"Quit being so fuckin nosey," Tank snapped.

"C'mon, Tank. Answer the question." she told him with her hands now on her hips.

"Yeah, why? You know him or something?" he asked.

"I mean, I'm not for sure it's him, but the guy that I just broke up with, his name is Aaron," Ohani said, and my ears perked up.

"Oh, really," Tank said with a sly grin.

"Yeah. I mean I could be wrong, but how many Aarons is it around here?" she asked.

"Shit, it ain't but one that I know of. Do you know any other ones Sam?"

"Nah, I just know one" I said with a half-smile. If Ohani had been fuckin with Aaron, then it was about to be on. We would could just use her ass to led us to him.

"Aye, Ohani, what this nigga look like?" I asked her.

"He's tall, dark brown skin, deep dimples. Why? Are you trying to holler at him or something?" she cracked up with laugher.

"Get your fuckin sister, Tank, before I murder her ass up in here," I warned. Ohani's comment briefly took me back to the night that I killed Toni, and was reconnected with the muthafucka that had ruined my life. I didn't play that gay shit, and she needed to chill out before she ended up like they did.

"Aye, fuck all that," he said waving me off. "So why didn't you tell me before that you were fuckin with Aaron?"

"Because that was my business." Ohani replied.

"Smart mouth ass!" he said, and she pursed her lips. "But anyway, why did y'all break up?" Tank asked.

"He said something about him getting back with his baby mama," she said.

"Damn, that's fucked up," I put on like I actually carcd, but in reality, I could give two fucks about how Aaron had done her. I just needed to stay cool, and hopefully she could give us what we needed to finally take this nigga out. And depending on how I felt afterwards, I might just let her make it for that bullshit she said.

"Aye, why don't you tell us where this nigga live, and we'll go handle him. We gone make sure that we teach his ass a lesson for fuckin you over," I said.

"I don't know where he lives," Ohani said.

"Damn, in the time that y'all were messing off, he never took you to his crib?" Tank asked.

"No, because his baby mama was living with him before they even got back together," She said, and me and Tank just looked at her. Now I see how Aaron was able to run game on her ass. It was because she was dumb as fuck.

"Aye, you making me look bad out here, mane. How you gon' lay up with a nigga, and he got the next bitch living with him?" Tank asked.

"Whatever! It wasn't even like that. She was only living there because they were co-parenting," she said.

"Yeah, that's what is was," I said, and Ohani shot me a death glare.

"Look, do you know anything about this nigga, besides what his dick looks like?" Tank asked, and I could see that he was getting just as frustrated as I was with her ass.

"I know where his peoples stay at," she said with a smirk.

"You do?" me and Tank asked simultaneously.

"Yup. He took me over there the first night that we went on a date," She said.

"Aight, so tell me where they live." Tank said, and Ohani shook her head no.

"C'mon sis, tell us what's up. We need to get at this nigga ASAP. Plus, you know that I'mma look out for you" he said. Ohani gave a look like she really had to think about the shit, but I knew that her ass was just putting on a front. She wanted us to get at that nigga for the way that he had played her.

"Okay, I will tell y'all. But I'm only doing it because I want him to pay for fuckin with my feelings," she finally said.

44
Laydii

Two days later….

"John, where are you going now?" I asked him. He wasn't here the night before, and by the time he did come in, I had fallen asleep. Now he was already up at dawn getting ready to leave out again.

"I gotta link up with Aaron," he said going into the closet to grab his clothes. He had just gotten out of the shower and had a towel wrapped around his waist. His light brown skin glistened from the water that was left from his shower, and his curly hair was waved up from him washing it. I eyed his package through the towel he was wearing, and I started to become wet. We hadn't had sex in a few weeks, and my body needed it.

When he looked up, he saw me watching him, and he smirked. "What? You see something you like?" he asked. I bit my bottom lip when he took his hand and gripped his dick through the towel. My pussy started to pulsate, and I wanted him inside of me.

"Maybe," I said in a seductive voice. John walked out of the closet and placed the clothes that he had in his hand on the chair that was on the side of our bed. I watched him the whole time as he walked closer to me, and when he got to the foot of the bed, he gently pushed me back onto it. My breasts slightly rocked, and I giggled. He stared at me with those piercing brown eyes, then slowly leaned his head down and kissed me. Our tongues danced around, as he ran his strong, muscular hands up my gown to my breasts. He gripped them and then took his other hand and stuck his finger into my honey pot. My mouth fell wide open. "Mmm," I moaned, as he continued to work his fingers in and out of me.

"Turn on your side," He said, and I laughed because my stomach was so big that, that was the only way that we could have sex. That, or from the back, but I preferred the side better. It felt good doing it that way. After I had turned onto my side, John lifted my leg and slid his dick into me. I gasped as he slowly started to rock in and out of me. I was so wet that each time he stroked inside of me that my pussy made a gushing noise.

"Fuck, girl, this pregnant pussy is so good." he grunted. He gently wrapped his hand around my stomach, and started to pump in and out of me at a more rapid pace.

"Oh, my goodness, this feels so good," I screamed out.

As best as I could, I threw it back and met him stroke for stroke. After about ten minutes of him assaulting my kitty, he came inside of me, and I came shortly after. We laid in the spoon position for a minute, both catching our breaths, then he pulled out of me and walked to the bathroom. The shower came on, and John called for me to join him. reword. I pulled my gown completely over my head, and tossed it to the floor. I stepped inside of the shower, and got in front of John. The water hit my body, and it felt great.

"Aye, so Keya's gonna come stay over here with you while me and Aaron out handling business," John said as we washed up.

"Okay, that's fine," I said. John stared at me, and it was like he wanted to tell me something else. "What?" I asked with my brows furrowed. "Why are you looking at me like that?"

"I love you, Laydii, and one day I want to make you my wife. I know that I haven't always done right by you, but just know that, even in my bad times, I never stopped loving you," he said and smiled. I half-smiled and wondered where this was coming from. I knew that he loved me, but it was the way that he had said it that made me feel like something was bothering him.

"I love you, too, John, but is everything okay?" I asked.

"Everything is good. Just promise me that you won't leave me, Laydii," he said staring into my eyes.

"Okay, wassup John. You acting real strange. You know that my ass not going anywhere," I said to him with pursed lips.

"Nah, I need for you to promise that you won't leave me," he said, and I stopped washing up.

"John, I promise that I won't leave as long as you continue to do right by me," I said, and his facial expression changed. I knew he wanted me to say that I would be with him no matter what, but the truth is, I wasn't taking anything less than what I deserved this go round. I hoped for his sake that he was being on his best behavior, because if I found out anything differently, then this relationship would be over for good this time. I was so serious. And I hoped that he didn't think that me having this baby would make me stay if he was doing something to hurt me again.

"I guess that I can respect that," he said, but I knew that he didn't mean it. John probably wouldn't ever let me go. Especially with me being pregnant.

"You really don't have a choice," I said.

We both became silent as we continued to shower. After we were done taking our shower, we got out and dried off. I put on a pair of stretch maternity pants, with a maternity baby doll top and a pair of comfortable socks.

"I'm getting ready to head out," John said, the moment he was done putting on his clothes.

"Okay, be careful," I told him.

"You know I'm always careful," he said, and I smacked my lips.

"Oh, I left some money on the coffee table for you and Keya to grab some dinner. We'll probably be out for most of the day and night. Just call my phone, if you need anything," He said. "And another thing. Don't leave the house. Y'all order some pizza or something like that, but just don't leave."

"And how long will I have to stay cooped inside of the house?" I asked.

"Just let us handle this business, and I will let you know," he said.

I trusted John, so if he said not to go anywhere, then I was going to listen. Him and Aaron obviously had good reason for having me in Keya stay in the house.

"Alright I won't, and I love you," I said.

"I love your pregnant ass, too," he said and rubbed my stomach. My daughter kicked, and me and John both laughed.

"You know she will be here soon making her appearance," I told him, and he nodded.

"I know, and I can't wait to meet my baby girl," he said. "But I got to go. Fucking around with you, I'm late. I laughed, and he kissed my lips before he left out of the door.

After he was gone, I grabbed my phone and called Keya to see what time she was coming over. She picked up after the fourth ring.

"Hello," she said.

"Hey, what time are you coming over," I asked.

"I should be that way in the next hour," Keya said.

"Okay, well if I don't answer the door, just call my phone. I think I'm going to take a quick nap. John just wore me out," I said laughing.

"Ewe, too much information," she said.

"Whatever, heffa, I will see you in a minute," I told her, and we ended the call. I laid my phone down beside me and closed my eyes to take a quick nap.

~~~~~~~~~~~~~~~~~~~~~

"So, what's been up, girlie?" Keya asked. She had just arrived at my house about thirty minutes ago, and we were sitting in my bed having girl talk.

"Nothing really. I'm so ready to have this baby," I told her.

"I know you are. I remember being pregnant with Aniya and feeling the same way," she said.

"How is my goddaughter?" I hadn't seen Aniya since the baby shower, and Keya's parents had gotten her earlier in the day to take her to the zoo. Between Keya's parent, her sister, and Aaron's auntie, my goddaughter stayed on the go more than a grown person, and I hardly ever got the chance to see her.

"Girl, spoiled as hell. She is such a daddy's girl that it doesn't make any sense," she said, and I laughed.

"I know that Aaron be over there spoiling her, and I'm sure that John will be the same way when our baby gets here," I said.

"So, I take it everything been good with you and John?" she asked.

"For the most part. I mean, we haven't been arguing lately and he's been answering his phone like he should. But I can't help but to feel like he is hiding something from me, or it could just be that I'm being paranoid again." I said.

"Maybe he's not hiding anything, and maybe you are just being paranoid. He seems to be real excited about the baby coming, and girl you should have seen the way that he acted when he asked me to help him plan the baby shower. I could tell then that he had grown a lot from the old John. So just try your best to keep an open mind, and maybe you'll see that he has really changed." Keya said.

"I hope so, because I don't think I can handle it if I find out he is messing around again," I said. Keya gave a knowing look, and we both became quiet.

"Oh, I meant to tell you that the police contacted me with their monthly check-in. They told me that they were still looking for Sam. Supposedly no one has seen him, and since there are no addresses listed, other than his mom's, the police said they don't know where else to look for him. But they did say that they were going to keep looking, and once they find something out, that they will contact me immediately," Keya explained.

"Girl, his pathetic ass is somewhere out there hiding, and that's what makes this shit so scary. It's like nobody knows where he is, and he can just pop up out of nowhere at any minute. I keep telling John that they need to hurry up and find him, because I know it in my heart Keya that he was the one that killed Toni. I'm not exactly sure why, but something tells me that it had nothing to do with her accusing him of rape. If that were the case, he would have been tried to kill her long before that night. It just still doesn't make any sense to me, and I don't ever think I'll be able to let it go until I get some answers," I said.

"I feel the same way that you do, and it still messes with me that he turned out to be that way. I mean, who would have ever thought that he would have kidnapped me, and held me hostage." She said.

"Exactly. It's like he done snapped and turned into this crazed maniac." I said.

"I told Aaron about the rape," Keya said out of nowhere.

"Wow, Keya. What did he say?" I asked.

"He was sympathetic and told me that it was gonna be okay" she said, and I smiled.

"See, I told you that you should have been told him. I knew that you were afraid of what he was going to say, but Aaron loves yo dirty panties girl, and he is not afraid to let it be known," I said.

"I know, and that's why I'm glad it's finally out. Even if he did have to force me to tell him. But look enough of this sad talk. Let's talk about happy shit," Keya said, and we both laughed.

"I agree," I said. I then asked her how school was going, and she admitted that it was a little hard, but that she wasn't going to give up. I told her that I understood, and that once I returned, I would probably feel the same pressures that she was experiencing. Because it was definitely going be hard trying to balance a family, school, and everyday life all at the same time. I didn't mind any of that though, because I was ready to get back to working towards my goals.

Keya and I continued to talk about everything, and after a few hours had passed, we ordered a pizza. That was the only thing that would could think to order, since the guys didn't want us to go out. Shortly after, we went into baby's nursery and started to sort through some of the items that I had gotten from the baby shower.

Knock. Knock. Knock. Someone knocked at the front door.

"I'll be right back. It's probably just the pizza guy," I told Keya as I walked out of the room. "Who is it?" I called out.

"Pizza delivery," the male's voice said.

"Alright, just a minute," I told him as I snatched the money from the table that John had left for me. "Keya, the pizza is here."

"Hello," I said to the pizza guy when I had the door open. Suddenly, he came barreling into me, and the pizza bag that he was holding flew from his hand. Right after, two masked people walked in, and one pulled a gun out and fired a shot into the pizza man's chest.

45
Aaron

Later that day….

I looked down at my phone as it rang for the fifth time. Ohani had been calling me back to back, but I didn't have any words for her.

"Damn, mane, you blowing up over there," John said.

"Dawg, it's that broad Ohani that I brought over to your house a while back," I said.

"Oh yeah, what happened with you and her?" John asked.

"Shit wasn't working out. She was getting too attached, and when I told her that me and Keya were getting back together, she flipped out on my ass." I said.

"That's fucked up. I don't know what be up with these hoes," he said, and I agreed.

"Speaking of which, did you ever tell Laydii about the broad that claim she got a baby on the way by you?" I asked.

"I couldn't do it, mane. She been under so much stress that I just couldn't bring myself to tell her," John replied.

"You should have told her anyway, mane. Now when she finds outs, she gonna feel like you betrayed her by keeping it a secret," I said, and he sighed. "That's your life, though, and you the only one that has to live." I said putting an end to the conversation. I wasn't going to drill it in his head about doing the right thing. I just knew that, by holding secrets, you made shit worse than what it actually was. I had learned that the hard way when Keya left me over that shit with me and Laydii. And after it all went down, and I had time to think about it, I realized that I should have just kept it real with her from the beginning.

*****

"Aye, I think that's the place right there," John said pointing to a house.

I looked down at the address that was in my phone, and saw that it was the same one of the house we were at. We had finally gotten word of where Sam was hiding out at. Detrick was talking to some broad named Kasha, and she had told him that, a little while back, her and her friend had gone over to some nigga named Tank's house, and Sam was there. Detrick threw the broad a few dollars, and she came up off the location of the house quick. I pulled the car that I had gotten from one of the crackheads up to the curb, and cut it off. I wasn't about to be caught out here in my own whip ever again. That's what had gotten me caught up with them other charges, and I wasn't taking any more chances.

After checking out the scene, me and John eased out of the car and jogged over to the house. It was an old house, and both houses on the side of it were boarded up. As we got closer, we noticed that the front of the house had bars on the windows, and the front door was one of those security type doors with bars on it too.

"Fuck," I said.

"What you want to do, dawg," John asked while looking around.
"Let's go around the back and see what it looks like back there," I said.

"Aight bet," John replied as we crept around the side of the house, and made our way into the backyard.

"Damn, it's bars on those windows too," John said as we stared at the back of the house. It wasn't no way for us to gain entry into the house.

"Do you think that they in there?" John whispered.

"I'on know, mane. I don't see any lights on," I said, and stared at the house a little while longer.

"Aight, so we just gone come back later. That way, it gives us time to peep shit out more, and maybe we can try to catch them niggas coming in or going out," I said.

"Yeah, that's sounds better, cause ain't no way we getting in there with those bars all over the place," John said.
"Exactly. Aye, let's get the fuck out of here though," I whispered.

We both looked around, and when we didn't see anybody, we jogged back over to the car. As soon as we were inside, I immediately crank up and pulled off. I felt my phone vibrate inside my pocket, so I reached inside, and pulled it out. When I looked at the screen, I saw that it was Ohani calling yet again. *Fuck it, I need to gone answer, and let her know what's up,* I thought as I hit the answer button.

"What Ohani?" I snapped into the phone.

"Aaron, please don't hang up. I need to tell you something," she said, and I could hear the desperation in her voice.

"Well make it quick before I hang up," I said.

"Alright, but please don't be mad when I tell you this," she said, and it felt like Déjà vu all over again. The last person that told me not to be mad when they told me something was Jeremy, and at the time, he was telling me that Keya was missing.

"Look Ohani, say what the fuck you gotta say."

"Okay. I'm sorry, but I told my brother where your friend lives," she blurted out.

"You told your brother where who lives?" I asked.

"The guy whose house you took me to," she said, and I had to pull the car over and park.

"Fuck you mean you told your brother where my nigga lives?" I fumed.

"I'm sorry, Aaron. I was upset that you had played with my feelings, and I was just being spiteful. But then I had time to think about everything, and I realized how wrong that was. Especially since I know that my brother wants to rob you." she said. I could hear her crying through the phone, but I didn't give a fuck about all that.

"What's your brother's name?" I calmly asked. I needed her to give me some answers, and yelling at her wasn't gonna do any good.

"His name is Tank," she said, and I banged my hand on the steering wheel. When I glanced over at John, he had a questioning look on his face, but I held my finger up to him.

"Bitch, do you realize what the fuck you did? Your brother runs with the nigga that kidnapped Keya, and had me locked up" I said.

"Oh, my god! I am so sorry, Aaron. Please don't be mad at me. I knew that Sam was wanted for kidnapping, but I had no idea it was for your baby's mama. Besides, him and my brother both said it was some type of mixup. I didn't think that they had a reason to lie, so I didn't think too much of it." she said.

"This shit was not good. Ain't no telling what these niggas have planned to do. "Ohani, how long ago did you tell them this? And have you talked to them lately?" I asked.

"It was like a couple of days ago, and I've been calling Tank's phone since yesterday. I felt guilty about what I had done, and I wanted to stop him before he did something to hurt you, or get himself into trouble. I even went by his house earlier today, but he wasn't there. I don't know Sam's number, so I don't know how to reach him. That's when I figured I would call and tell you what I had done. I'm sorry Aaron. I really am," she said.

I was quiet as I digested Ohani's words. This bitch had put my family in danger because she was in her fuckin feelings. I needed to get back to John's house and make sure that everything was straight.

"Hello, please Aaron. I am so sorry," she cried into the phone.

"Ohani, I want you to listen to me good. If something happens to my family, I'm coming for your ass. And don't take that as a threat, because I don't make threats." I said and hung up.

I pulled the car back into traffic, and as I drove, I filled John in. He was just as furious as me, and he was talking about going to Ohani's house and killing her after we checked in on the girls. I pulled my phone back out and called Keya's phone, but she didn't answer. John called Laydii's phone, and he got the same results. I even dialed up Detrick, and he didn't answer. When I called Jeremy's phone, it just went straight to voicemail.

"Where the fuck is everybody at?" I said speeding down the expressway.

"Mane, I'on know, but this bitch got me seeing red," John spewed.

"I know, and trust we gon handle her," I said. I felt fucked up about this shit, because I was the one that had brought Ohani around. I had no idea that she was connected to the same muthafucka that I was beefing with. *Small fucking world,* I thought. A few minutes later, we pulled up to John's house, and the first thing that caught our attention, was that it was a pizza delivery car parked out front.

"Damn, they must be alright if they ordered a pizza," John said and breathed a sigh of relief.

"Nah, something ain't right. The door is completely shut and the car still running. And if they just ordered a pizza, why the fuck they ain't answering their phones?" I asked.

"Shit, I ain't think about it like that. Go around the block and pull up on the back side," John said, and I immediately pulled off. When I drove around the corner, I parked, and me and John got out. The way that John's condo was set up, the garage was on the back of it, and if you didn't park in the front, you could pull onto the next street and go in through the garage that way. We crept up to the back, and when we got to the back door, John pulled out his key and stuck it in the door. We eased inside, and as soon as we did, we heard screaming.

"You got your gun, right?" I whispered to John, and he nodded.

We both pulled out our pieces, and slowly crept down the long hall. I could hear Laydii talking, as we got closer to the front.

"Sam, you are crazy," I heard her scream.

"You know what? That's the same thing your sister said when I killed her ass." Sam said.

"Oh, my god. I knew that you killed her you psycho muthafucka," Laydii yelled. Suddenly, we heard movement, and heavy footsteps.

"Aye, sit your ass back down before I put a bullet in your stomach," Sam said, and I damn near had to yank John's arm off to stop him from running in there.

"Come on mane, I need to get in there quick. This nigga in my crib threatening my girl and my baby," John whispered.

"I know, but we got to think before we just run up in there firing off shots. We don't want to give that nigga an opportunity to shoot one of the girls," I whispered back.

John breathed heavily. I knew that he was ready to go in there guns blazing, but we needed to think rationally about this. What if we accidently shot one of the girls, and then what? Nah, we needed to get them out of there, before we handled Sam.

"Sam, you have the money, so please just leave," I heard Keya say.

"Fuck that; I want y'all to call them niggas. Tell em to get here right now, before I put a bullet in one of y'all heads. And they better come alone," he said.

"Okay, whatever you want me to do, I will do it. Just stop waiving that gun at us," Keya said.

That was it, I couldn't listen anymore. He had a gun pointed at Keya, and he was probably gonna try to kill her and Laydii. I couldn't let shit go down like that, and It was time to put an end to his ass.

"Here I am muthafucka," I said stepping into the room with my gun drawn. John came in on the other side of me, and he had his gun on Sam, too. It was another nigga standing over by the front door, and I noticed that he didn't have a gun. When I looked down on the floor, I saw that they had shot the pizza man.

"I'm glad you finally here," Sam said.

"Yeah, so why don't you take the gun off them and put it on me," I said.

"You don't make the demands, nigga. I got the gun on your bitch, so it looks like I got the upper hand. If you shoot me, I still have time to fire off a shot into one of them." Sam said pointing to

Laydii and Keya. They both had fear in their eyes, and it fucked me up to see they were in danger because of my carelessness.

"Aye, don't move muthafucka," John said while pointing his gun at the nigga by the door.

This caused a small distraction, as we all glanced over at the guy. He had a scowl on his face, and I figured that he was Ohani's punk ass brother. I heard the click of a gun, and when I looked back, Keya had the gun that I had given her pointed at Sam. Sam looked down at Keya, and then back at me.

"C'mon now, Keya, what the fuck you gonna do with that?" he asked her.

"Don't you remember what happened last time," Keya said, and Sam chuckled.

"Aye, Keya, you done turned into a lil killer, haven't you?" he asked her.

"You did this to me," she said becoming enraged. "You set all this shit up from the very beginning. Sending Aaron to jail, the kidnapping, even Toni's death. Didn't you? What about your mama Sam? I know now that Aaron wasn't the one that killed her. So, did you kill your own mama just to make it look like Aaron, did it?" Keya asked.

"Yeah, I did that shit, but I had my own reasons for taking that bitch out. Yo nigga over there, was just my escape," Sam smiled sinisterly.

"Oh, my god," Keya shook her head. "You are fucking crazy nigga."

"Lil mama, fuck with this nigga is talking about. He just trying to mind fuck you," I told her.

"We need answers, Aaron," she said with tears streaming down her cheeks. I looked over at Laydii and she was also crying. I was trying to assess the situation, and see the best way to handle it. John still had his gun pointed at the nigga by the door. Damn, I had to get my girl and her friend up out of here. But like Sam had said, if I bust on him, he still had an opportunity to shoot one of them. I wouldn't be able to handle it if one of them got shot, so I needed him to focus on me.

"Look, nigga. I'm tired of this back and forth shit. Let the girls go, and me and you can go ahead and shoot it out. How about it? The better man walks away," I said.

I glanced at Keya, and could see that her hands were trembling bad. "Come on nigga. I'm who you fucking want, right? I took your bitch and had a baby by her. I run a million-dollar operation, while you still running around jacking muthafuckas just to eat. Ain't that's why you so mad? Because you ain't me," I smiled, and I saw Sam grit his teeth.

"Nah, I don't think so muthafucka. You may have fucked Keya and had a baby with her, but the way that pussy got wet for me not too long ago let me know just how easily I could get her back. And let's not forget, how quick she ran back to daddy when they locked your bitch ass up," Sam said, and I lost it. I charged at him full speed, and he swung his gun around and aimed it at me.

"Aaron Noooooooooo," Keya screamed, and gunshots rang out from every direction.

46
Jeremy

Two hours later....

"Mmm, baby this feels so good," Tina said, as I stroked deep inside of her from the back.

"I know. And you like it when I be putting this good dick inside of you," I said and popped her on the ass.

"Yes, baby, I love it," she moaned.

Tina had lied to her nigga and told him that she was going out of town for work. It wasn't hard to believe, since she was a Support Specialist Training Manager, and the job required her to travel often. But instead of her going to work, she had come over to my house, and we had been laid up ever since the night before. I enjoyed being around her, and I was starting to feel something for her that I had never felt for any other woman. And although we had gotten together on some creep shit, I could still see the good in her. I was thinking that maybe we could take this thing to the next level.

I hit Tina's ass with a few more deep strokes, and she gripped the sheets tightly while throwing her ass back on me. "Damn girl, this pussy is getting wetter and wetter," I said. Her shit was feeling so good and tight that I couldn't hold it in any longer. I pulled my dick out and let my nut shoot onto her plump, round ass.

"Shit," that was a good one right there," I told her. I hopped out of bed and ran to the bathroom for a towel. After I had one, I walked back into the room and cleaned Tina up. She giggled, as I ran the towel over her ass. When I was done, I climbed back into the bed and pulled her close to me. She giggled and stared into my eyes. "Why you staring at a nigga like that? I got a booger in my nose or som'?" I said.

"Boy, you are so fuckin silly." She laughed.

"Oh, I get it, you think you in love with me?" I said pecking her lips.

"Well, what if I am?" Tina said while fiddling with her hands. She bit her bottom lip, and looked at me.

"Then that will just make two crazy muthafuckas in love," I told her.

She stared at me, and I knew what was going through her head. "What, you don't think that I love you?" I asked.

"I mean, I, you…Hell, I don't know what to say," she said with a laugh.

"Well, I do, and I'm ready for you to leave that nigga and finally be with me. It's cool spending time together here and there, but I'm ready to take this shit to the next level. Being a side nigga just ain't my shit, and I ain't ever wanted to be with a broad as much as I want your crazy ass," I said.

Tina was quiet, and I figured that she was about ready to tell me that she couldn't be with me, but when her lips pressed against mine, I knew what was up. She pulled back from the kiss and gazed into my eyes again.

"I want to be with you, Jeremy, and I'm going to tell Kenny when I get home that it's over between me and him." She said.

"Dig that! It's about time, cause I ain't trying to share your ass no more," I said. "Now, let's go get in the shower so yo ass can go serve this nigga his walking papers," I said, slapping her on the butt.

Tina poked out her bottom lip. "Are you kicking me out?" she asked.

"Nah, I just want you to hurry up and get this shit over with."

"You are so mean," she said.

"Fuck you mean? If you finna be with me, then I don't need you staying another night in the crib with that nigga." I said dead ass.

She smirked, while standing up. I walked into the bathroom and cut on the shower. Once the temperature was warm enough, I climbed inside, and shortly after, Tina joined me.

"Kenny just called and asked what time I was coming home," she said.

I didn't say anything as I continued to wash up. She was staring at me, like she was waiting for me to say something but I didn't. What was I supposed to say to that?

"Why are you so quiet?" she asked me.

"I'm just wondering if you gonna go through with this shit for real," I said.

"I told you that I was. I love you, Jeremy Davis, and you are who I want to be with. Kenny has never made me feel like you do," she said and stood on her tip toes to give me a kiss. I picked her up by her butt, and she grabbed a hold of my dreads.

"Aight, if you say that's it with you and him, then I'mma take your word for it. And another thing, I might as well go ahead and warn you now. If yo pops come to me with that shit like he did, Aaron, I'm knocking his big ass out," I said, and Tina laughed. I placed her back on her feet, and she stared up at me.

"Boy, you are not going to do nothing to my daddy, because he will fuck you up," she said while snaking her neck.

"Yeah, aight!" I said.

"Seriously though, he finally accepted Aaron, so I'm sure he will have no problem with accepting you, too. Just don't piss him off, Jeremy, because I know how you are with your mouth" she said.

I smirked and continued to wash up. I had meant what I said about not taking any shit from her pops. Aaron tolerated the bullshit, but I ain't no way that I was going for that disrespect. Especially with Tina being a grown ass woman, that was fully capable of making her own decisions. After we were done showering, I looked around the condo for my phone. I finally found it in the living room, and when I picked it up, I realized that it was dead.

Damn, I'll just put it on the charger in the car, I thought to myself.

My clothes were already laid out for the night, so I walked back into my bedroom and started to put them on. By the time I was done getting dressed, Tina had her clothes on, and she was ready to go. We both walked outside, and when we got in front of my car, I pulled her into my arms.

"Don't make me come looking for you, Tina," I told her with my arms around her waist.

"I won't. I'm going home now, and as soon as I tell him that we are over, I'm going to pack up my clothes and go to a hotel room," she said, and I frowned.

"Fuck is you going to a hotel room for, and I got a place right here? Nah, that ain't gone fly with me, and I'm about to give you the key right now. That way, if I'm still out, you can just let yourself in." I said, pulling my key from my key ring. I had a spare key that I kept inside of my car, and I would just replace that with the key that I was giving Tina.

"Okay. I'll come back," she said with a big smile.

"Aight, gone get up out of here so that you can hurry back," I said and bent down to place another kiss on her lips.

She wrapped her arms around my neck and kissed me back. If I didn't have to hit the streets, I would have taken her ass back into the house and dug into them guts once again. When we finally broke the kiss, we stared at one another.

"I love yo ass girl," I finally said.

"I love-" Tina started to say, but her words trailed off. Her eyes darted behind me, and I followed her line of vision. Some nigga in a hooded jacket, stood behind us. The hoodie was draped over his head, so I couldn't get a good look at his face.

Fuck, I thought to myself. I know this muthafucka ain't finna try to rob us? But then he removed his hood, and I heard Tina gasp.

"Kenny?" she asked.

"Yeah, I bet you thought that I didn't know about you out here creeping with this nigga. But I knew all along, and I was just waiting for the right time to catch yo ass." He said.

"I'm sorry Kenny. I didn't want you to find out this way." Tina said.

"Shut the fuck up," he yelled at her.

"Aye, watch how the fuck you talk to her nigga." I said.

"You stay out of this. This shit between me and girl. And you Tina...you really played yourself for a nigga that is still messing around with his baby mama. Did he tell you that? Better yet, answer me this. Did he tell you that she is pregnant with their second child?" Kenny asked.

"What?" Tina said, and looked at me with a confused look on her face.

"Is it true? Are you still messing with Nancy, and is she pregnant by you again?" she asked.

"Fuck nah it ain't true. Aye, nigga I suggest you get the fuck from around here with that bullshit, cause you don't know what the fuck you talking about," I spat.

"Baby, who do you believe, me or him?" he asked. Tina gazed up at me with tears in her eyes.

"Tell me it's not true," she whispered.

"Listen to what I'm saying. I would never get back with Nancy, and I haven't had sex with her in a long ass time. Even if me and you weren't getting together, I still wouldn't want to be with her. This nigga is lying, and I don't know where he got that shit from," I said while staring into her eyes.

Suddenly I heard a car pull up behind us. When I glanced over at the car, I had to do a double take. It was Nancy, and she had this big ass grin on her face. I knew then that it was her that had told Kenny about me and Tina.

"Tina honey, you might want to go on home with Kenny, because Jeremy and I will never be finished. Ain't that right Jeremy? Tell her about the other night when you came to get Little Jeremy, and we had sex. Tell her how we made love for two hours straight, and how you said that you wanted to be with me and your son. Tell her how I'm pregnant with your baby right now. Go ahead and tell her," Nancy said, and I could have choked that bitch. She was lying through her teeth, and the killer part about it all, was that Tina looked like she believed what the fuck they were telling her.

"I'mma kill your ass Nancy," I pointed my finger at her.

"Wow, so I guess that you were going to try and keep both of us around? And here I was ready to choose you over him. That was my fault though, for believing that you were going to do right by me, and that we were going to have this happily ever after love." Tina said.

"See, I told you that I wasn't lying. Nancy came to me, and told me all about how you and Jeremy had been fucking around behind both of our backs. I was going to just say fuck it and let you be with him, since you embarrassed me so bad. But then I thought about how much time I invested into this relationship, and I ain't about to just let you walk away. I'm even willing to forgive you this one time, and forget it ever happened." Kenny said to Tina.

"Don't listen to this bullshit. They just don't want to see us together," I said while forcing Tina to look at me.

"Just stop it, because I know that you're lying. Admit it, you played me Jeremy," she said.

"I'm telling you the fucking truth. I didn't sleep with that girl, and I didn't get her pregnant" I snapped.

"You know what, fuck you," Tina said to me.

"Yeah fuck him baby. Now come on over here to me, so we can go home and work this out" Kenny told her. Tina looked at me one last time, and just like that she walked over to him. They started to walk off, but then Kenny stopped and turned back around.

"Take this as a warning. Stay away from my woman, or be ready to deal with the consequences," he said.
"What?" I said and tried to rush his ass, but Tina jumped in between us.

"Jeremy, please just let it go. I'm going to go with Kenny now, and you and Nancy can have your lives back" she said with her hands pressed against my chest.

I pushed them away, and stared at Kenny. He had a smug look on his face, and I wanted to knock that shit off, but I wasn't about to fight over no broad. After a while, they walked away, and I watched as they got into their cars and drove off. I turned to Nancy, and she smiled at me.

"See Jeremy. No matter what you do to get away from me, it won't work, because I will never let you go. If I can't have you, then nobody will." She laughed.

"Bitch!" I said running towards her truck. But just as I got to the window, Nancy sped off. "Fuck," I yelled out, as I watched the taillights of the truck disappear down the street.
To be continued...

Thank you all for reading. Please feel free to leave a review. Your thoughts and comments are greatly appreciated!

Love in The Deep South 3: A Memphis Hood Tale-The Finale –
Coming Soon

Ways to stay connected with the author:

amazon.com/author/ nlhudson

Instagram- n.l.hudson

Natavia Presents.com

Twitter- @NLHudson3

Email: Latricehudson2270@gmail.com

Please check back soon for updates on future releases from this author!

Made in the USA
Columbia, SC
05 October 2017